A Dish Full of Stars

by

Lynna Banning

Cover Art by *Teddi Black*

The Wild Rose Press, Inc.
PO Box 708
Adams Basin, NY 14410-0708
Visit us at www.thewildrosepress.com

Publishing History
First Edition, 2025
Trade Paperback Print ISBN 978-1-5092-6339-4
Digital ISBN 978-1-5092-6340-0

Published in the United States of America

Chapter One

It was so hot inside the teepee he could scarcely breathe. The air smelled of leather and something sour—maybe his own sweat and the rawhide cord cutting into his bound wrists. He tried to lie still.

"Jack?" His sergeant's raspy voice.

"Yeah?"

"Whaddya think they're gonna do?"

Jack rolled toward the motionless form beside him. "Do? You mean do *to us*?"

"Well, yeah. What do the Sioux usually do to captured soldiers?"

Jack opened his mouth to answer, then closed it. The Sioux usually killed their captives or tortured them to death, but he wasn't about to tell that to his sergeant. "Sometimes they escape, Matt. Sometimes they let 'em go free."

"What do you have to do to go free?"

"Bribe 'em."

"With what? Hell, we don't have anything except some dried jerky, and they've probably got plenty of that. Money, maybe? I don't have any on me. Do you?"

"They don't want money, Matt. What they want is guns." *Or scalps.* He wasn't going to tell his sergeant that, either.

"Guns, huh? I sure hated to part with my revolver, Jack. My father gave it to me. It was real valuable."

1

Jack gritted his teeth. "More valuable than your life?"

That shut him up, but it only lasted a quarter of an hour.

"Jack?"

"Yeah?" He was running out of explanations for the man lying beside him. Maybe it didn't matter. With no water for two days, they'd be dead pretty soon.

"How come you're so quiet, Jack? Aren't you scared?"

"Hell yes, I'm scared. I'm quiet because I've always been quiet."

That shut Matt up for another quarter of an hour, which gave him time to think. They'd stumbled onto the Sioux on their way back to Fort Kearney. They weren't even scouting for Indians, but when they rode over the crest of a hill, there was a war party, complete with fancy feather bonnets and war paint. They chased Jack and his sergeant until their horses played out, then they lassoed them and tied their hands to the saddle horns. They weren't interested in trinkets or expensive watches, only the horses. That figured. The Sioux always had a good eye for horseflesh.

His hands were getting numb, so he rolled onto his side. Didn't help, so he tried to loosen the rawhide thongs around his wrists. The braves had wet them so they'd get tighter as they dried; any tighter and they'd cut off his circulation. Might be preferable to what he figured was coming.

The Sioux had no use for soldiers. Hated them, in fact. Maybe they had good reason, seeing as how white settlers had invaded their land and kicked them aside. He'd be plenty mad, too, if some marauding bunch of trigger-happy men ran him off his land. He closed his eyes and tried not to think about it.

"Jack?"

"Yeah?"

"You figure they're gonna feed us or let us starve?"

"Hell, Matt, who cares if we starve? Dying of thirst is a lot quicker." He tried to think. It was hard to do, trussed up on the floor of a Sioux teepee.

A footstep outside brought him wide awake, and the next thing he knew he was jerked to his feet. His sergeant was yanked up next to him and stood jigging from one foot to the other.

"Matt, stop moving," he ordered. "The Sioux value bravery, not shaky nerves."

"Okay, Major." The jigging stopped as another brave slipped noiselessly through the teepee opening. He wore deerskin trousers that laced up the side.

"Come," the brave said. Iron fingers closed around Jack's shoulder and shoved him outside. After a moment, Matt joined him. He drew in a lungful of fresh air. Well, air that was scented with smoke and roasting meat. His belly tightened. He didn't care about his empty stomach. Right now, the only thing he cared about was water. He rolled his dry tongue around the inside of his mouth. Just one swallow.

Twenty or thirty painted braves were lined up in front of the biggest teepee in the camp, and he and Matt were half-marched, half-dragged toward it.

"Looks like that's where the chief lives," his sergeant said.

"Shut up, Matt."

They were shoved to a halt, and a tall, imposing Indian stepped through the opening. He wore a full

3

feather headdress, and in his right hand, he carried a baton-like thing made of leather. He pointed it at his two captives, and shouts erupted from the assembled tribesmen.

"What are they sayin', Major?"

"Shut up, Matt," he muttered again. He wasn't going to tell his sergeant what the Indians were shouting about. Not yet, anyway. He watched the braves form two parallel lines. Some gripped spears or wide leather straps; one or two brandished knives or even sabers, of all things. Probably captured from the Army.

The shouting rose to a scream. "Major?" Matt's voice sounded hesitant.

"Yeah?"

"What's happening? Why are they lined up like that?"

"They're lined up because they're going to strip us and make us run a gauntlet."

"What's that mean? What's a gauntlet?"

"It means we're going to run between those two lines of Indians and try to stay on our feet while they beat the living hell out of us."

"Jesus," his sergeant breathed.

"You go first, Matt. They'll save the worst for the second man."

"Jesus," Matt said again. "What happens after that?"

Jack gritted his teeth. "You pray to God they have bad aim or weak arms."

Matt sent him a stricken look. "Oh, God. How do I—?"

A brave seized his arms, ripped off his remaining

clothing, and shoved him forward along the corridor of weapons.

"Move fast!" Jack shouted at his back. "Stay on your feet!" He forced himself to watch his sergeant stumble along the gauntlet, enduring blows and cuts at every step. *Keep moving, Matt. For God's sake, keep moving.*

Toward the end, his blood-spattered sergeant began to totter, and when he reached the finish, his legs gave way. Jack studied the motionless man for a long moment, then drew in a deep breath of the sour-smelling air and took a single step forward.

Chapter Two

He tried to open his eyes. *Where am I? Am I dead?* He gulped in a shaky breath, and the sour scent of his surroundings told him where he was. Another Sioux teepee, but why? He remembered the blows from dozens of spears, the slap of leather straps against his skin, and the sting as the blows drew blood. Blades had sliced into his flesh, his shoulders, his back, even the backs of his legs.

Matt. Where was Matt? He reached out his hand and felt something rough. His sergeant's back, sticky with blood. "Matt?"

No answer. "Matt, are you okay?" He touched his sergeant's shoulder, then gently jostled it. Still no response. Then he felt something else, something solid. Something cold. Oh, Jesus, that was Matt's arm!

He rose up on one shaky elbow and opened his eyes. Matt's eyes were open, staring up at something. But he wasn't breathing. Jack lay back down and tried to suck in a steady breath. How was it that his sergeant was dead, but he was still alive? Just barely, he acknowledged, but alive. There were bloody patches all over his body; any one of them could become infected, and then there'd be a slow, painful death from infection and later gangrene.

He didn't know how long he lay on the floor of the teepee, trying to ignore his aching flesh. Trying not to think. This wasn't a nightmare. This was real. The stifling air he was trying to breathe was real. His sergeant's body crumpled next to him was real. The sharp sting of a dozen sword cuts and the ache in his shoulders and his ribcage and his back—those were real, too.

But he was alive.

He had survived a Sioux warrior gauntlet. Now what? He couldn't lie here and wait for them to finish him off. He tried to lift his right leg. Nothing doing. His left leg didn't hurt so much when he moved it, so he tried to sit up. He twisted his head until he could see the teepee opening. It was laced shut.

He was too weak to go out through the front anyway, so he studied the back of the teepee. A chink of daylight between the bottom of the deerskin wall and the ground caught his eye. Did he still have his knife?

His boots and trousers lay in a heap near his elbow. He patted the khaki and felt the familiar bulge in his front pocket. He worked the knife free, then sat up and unfolded the blade. Then he crawled over and tried to slice an opening in the teepee, but he got so dizzy he had to lie down again.

If he rested a few minutes, he might be able to do it. He could tell it was getting dark outside because the light inside was so dim he could barely see. It had to be now. He tried sitting up again, then crawled over to the tent wall, slashed a long slit in the deerskin, and looked out.

He could see nothing but the back side of another teepee, and…God be praised, a stand of trees! Willows. So maybe there was water nearby, a creek, even a river. He would head straight for those trees and melt into the woods.

He rolled up his trousers, stuffed his boots inside, and edged through the opening. He had just reached the first of the willow trees when a hand closed around his wrist. His heart almost stopped. Whoever it was stayed well hidden in the deepening gloom but kept pulling him forward into the trees.

What the...? Quiet as a shadow, the figure gripped his wrist tighter and crept silently forward, deeper into the woods. He had to work to avoid stumbling over exposed roots and fallen logs, but his abductor, silent as a cat, kept moving forward. They covered maybe fifteen yards, their steps muffled in the soft forest floor when suddenly the grip on his wrist slackened. When he looked ahead, he realized why.

Before him loomed a shadowy thicket of vines and some kind of trees, pine, he guessed from the pungent scent, and through the branches, he spied a horse. *A horse?* Not his own horse; Rambler would whinny at the sight of him. And it wasn't his sergeant's gray mare. The Indians had claimed both animals when he and Matt were captured.

His silent guide tugged him forward into the trees and laid his hand on the horse's neck. His companion mounted, and a tug on his arm told him to mount as well.

The figure in front of him felt small, maybe a young boy. He smelled interesting, like sage and something else. He held onto his rolled-up trousers with one hand and wrapped his other arm around the kid's waist. The horse began to move deeper into the trees. Jack never knew a horse could move so quietly. Any moment he expected to hear a horde of shouting Sioux warriors behind them, but minute after minute passed in complete silence.

After an hour, they left the woods, and the horse began to move faster. Afraid to speak or even breathe for fear his guide would shove him off the animal and leave him behind, Jack stayed quiet and tried not to move too much.

The moon was just rising. For another hour or so the horse moved forward at a walk, and Jack felt the first glimmer of hope. Maybe he wouldn't be caught and shot on sight or tortured to death. Maybe...

They were coming into some hills, not the ones he and Matt had ridden over when they were captured; these were more brushy and studded with pine trees. More hills, and then the horse reached a clearing and halted. Guess this was as far as his rescuer was going to take him.

He slid off the horse's hind end. The boy was also on the ground, moving away from him on foot. *What the hell?*

"We wait," a low voice said.

Jack nodded, then realized the kid couldn't see him in the dark. "We wait," he murmured.

Then the voice gave another order. "Get dressed."

He sure didn't need a second invitation. His behind was already chafing, and barefoot, he couldn't run even if he wanted to. He pulled on his heavy twill trousers, stuffed his feet into his boots, and wished he had something to cover his bare chest. The next minute, the boy shoved a buckskin shirt into his hand, and he shook his head in astonishment. Whoever this was had obviously planned their escape.

"You have a name?"

"No."

His eyebrows went up. "No name? What do the Sioux call you?"

There was a long pause. "Strange One," came the answer.

Ah. Maybe the kid was some sort of outcast, maybe a boy captured from another tribe.

He ran his tongue over his cracked lips. "Got any water?"

A rusty canteen was thrust into his hand. Army issue, he noted. He hated to think about how it turned up in a Sioux camp. The water was followed by a hunk of dried jerky, and Jack gnawed off a bite and handed it back. When the jerky was again passed to him, he wrestled the pocketknife out of his hip pocket and cut off two neat slices.

The kid laughed. *Laughed!* He sounded really young. Kinda made him smile.

"Ride now," the boy said. Man, this kid sure as hell liked giving orders. Kinda rankled him, but he figured right now he didn't have a choice. Jack heard him mount, so he climbed up behind him and felt the horse step forward.

They began to climb into the hills. By now, the moon was sending a pale light into the trees, and Jack could see an indistinct path ahead of them. He figured they'd keep moving until dawn when they'd be high enough on whatever mountain they were climbing that he could see where they were. Maybe.

The trail wound up and up, snaking back and forth on switchbacks as they climbed. After some hours, the sky began to turn peach, and then the sun rose, flooding the hills with hot, coppery light. Jack looked back to see where they were. Jehoshaphat! They were halfway to the top of a mountain. By the time the horse clambered up the last few yards to the summit, the air was so hot it was like trying to breathe inside an oven.

The horse came to a stop and stood panting, its head down. Jack frowned. Indians valued horses, but he'd always thought they treated them better than this.

"Good lookout," the kid said. "We sleep now."

The only shade on top of this mountain was under a scraggly pine tree, but it would do. He lost no time sliding off the back end of the horse and made a beeline for the tree, dropped onto his knees, and stretched out on his belly under the sparse branches. He heard the kid walk the animal into a patch of shade and rolled over to watch.

The boy kept his back turned, gathered a handful of dry grass, and rubbed the horse down. Then he dribbled some water from the canteen into a shallow wooden bowl and held it under the animal's nose.

Jack frowned. "You gonna feed it anything?"

"No. Have water for horse, not food."

"What about some of that jerky?"

"No. Save for us."

He opened his mouth to object when the kid turned around, and he got a good look at him. *God almighty and my sainted mother!*

Chapter Three

This kid didn't look like any boy he'd ever seen!
This kid looked like…like a girl! *A girl?*

His rescuer propped both hands on his—her—hips.
"You not see girl before?"

"Uh…" Well, not like *her,* he hadn't. No girl he'd
ever seen looked like this one. She couldn't be any
more than thirteen. Maybe fourteen. Slim. The deerskin
dress she wore molded itself over a decidedly female
torso. Not only that, her face…Lord almighty, her face
was downright beautiful.

"Close mouth," she quipped. "Bugs get in."

He choked on a laugh, then settled back and folded
his arms under his head. *What the hell am I doing on
top of this mountain with a fourteen-year-old Indian
girl?* If the Sioux caught him with her…. He couldn't
finish the thought.

When he got his breath back, he blurted the first
thing on his mind. "Why are you helping me?"

"Want something," she answered.

"Yeah? What?"

"Want to leave Sioux."

He stared at her. "Huh?"

"Want to leave Sioux," she repeated. "You help."

"Why?" he shot.

She looked straight at him. "I do not belong."

Very slowly he sat up. "Yeah? That why they call

you Strange One?"

"Yes," she said, taking a step toward him. "I am not Sioux."

"Captive, huh?"

She nodded and kept moving toward him. "Captive, yes. But not Indian."

He got to his feet and stared at her. *Jesus, she has blue eyes. Blue! Indians don't have blue eyes.*

She turned away. "Now," she said, her voice matter-of-fact, "I look at wounds." She lifted a small pouch of embroidered deerskin from the leather bag tied around the horse's neck and gestured at the pine tree. "Lie down," she ordered. "Take off shirt." She tossed back the thick braid she wore, then knelt beside him, scrabbled in the bag, and withdrew a tin of something.

"Shirt!" she reminded. She might be a girl, but she sure had a streak of Army sergeant in her.

He stripped off the deerskin shirt. She bent to study the wounds on his chest, then smeared them with some kind of sticky paste that smelled of sage. It stung plenty on his open cuts, and he sucked in his breath, but without a word, she went on methodically smearing the salve over his wounds and prodding at the bruises. He winced every time she touched him, and when she finally sat back on her knees, he heaved a sigh of relief.

Finally, his curiosity bubbled over. "How did you—?"

"Turn over," she ordered. "Talk later."

This doctoring session hurt even more. He guessed his back had taken the brunt of the blows, and he gritted his teeth as she poked and prodded and smeared on her ointment. This sure was a painful way to avoid gangrene, but he guessed he should be grateful. He clamped his teeth together and closed his eyes.

Eventually the smearing stopped, and he heard her voice again. "Take off trousers."

"What?"

"Trousers," she repeated.

That was too much. "Can't," he snapped. "Under these trousers, I'm bare-assed. You understand? No small clothes."

She had the audacity to laugh. "You think I not see before?"

Well, no, now that he thought about it. She was probably some brave's wife. Still, she was awful young to be someone's wife. "You married?" he asked.

"No."

"Oh. Okay." Maybe she was some warrior's whore, or whatever they called them.

"I live with chief," she volunteered.

He suppressed a groan. That was even worse.

"Adopted daughter," she added.

Oh, hell. The minute the chief realized she was gone, the whole tribe would be on their trail.

"Trousers," she said again.

He felt like saluting at her no-nonsense tone, but he wriggled out of them, and she set to work, starting with his backside. Whatever she was doing stung like hell, so he figured those cuts were really deep. After what seemed like hours, the stinging stopped.

"Over," she commanded.

He started to roll over, then suddenly realized what "over" would mean. His entire body would be exposed, privates and all. He bit his lip.

"Over," she repeated.

Oh, hell, she asked for it. Jack sucked in his breath, shut his eyes, and rolled over onto his back.

"Ah, I see," she said.

I see? What did that mean? Then he felt her hands on his chest, felt her fingers move down to his belly, and then...

He blew out a breath. At least there were no wounds on his privates. "Uh..."

"I see nothing new," she said. Her fingers smoothed the sticky stuff over his thighs, then moved down to his shins. Everywhere she touched, it hurt. A lot. He clenched his teeth.

Finally she sat back and snapped the tin of salve shut.

"Are you done?" he ventured.

She made some kind of murmur. "Do more tomorrow. Now I bring water."

Jack rolled his swollen tongue against the roof of his mouth. *Water. Oh, thank you, God.*

She moved to the horse and returned with the canteen. He could hear it sloshing when she lifted it. Sounded almost empty.

"That's all there is?"

She nodded. He reached for it, but she lifted it out of his grasp and produced instead a scrap of muslin. "Not drink," she admonished. "Suck only." She dipped the bit of cloth in the canteen, angled it into her mouth, and closed her lips. Her cheeks dipped inward. Then she soaked another bit of muslin and handed it to him.

"Suck," she ordered. He bit the inside of his cheek to keep from swearing at her. Damn, she made him mad! She was worse than any army sergeant he'd ever known.

15

On the other hand, water, even warm, metallic-tasting, slightly salty water, had never tasted so good. He closed his eyes and sucked. When he opened his lids, she was gone. He heard the horse snort and realized she was packing the salve tin and the canteen back into the leather pouch around the animal's neck.

He tried not to think about that canteen of water because it was all they had, and he knew it wouldn't be enough to keep them alive for very long. *Well, hell, Major Corder, did you survive running the gauntlet only to die of thirst on top of some damn mountain?* Maybe. But here he was—correction, here he and this captive Indian girl were—stuck on this mountain with the sun like an angry fireball above and Indians on the warpath below.

They had to get down off this mountain and find water. From the position of the sun, he figured it was high noon or thereabouts, and that meant they had about eight hours before darkness would cover their tracks. Eight *thirsty* hours.

It was cooler with no trousers, but he pulled them on anyway, then shrugged into the deerskin shirt just as the girl walked toward him, heading for the only patch of shade he could see. It was scarcely big enough for one person, let alone two, and it kept shifting as the sun moved across the sky.

She stopped and studied the shadow where he lay, then dropped silently to the ground, curled up a few feet from him, and closed her eyes. "We wait," she said. "Sleep now."

Jack clamped his jaw shut. He wasn't used to taking orders from anyone, let alone a girl. He was used to *giving* orders. On the other hand, he was at the mercy of someone who was risking her life to help him escape.

How come she wasn't worried about the Sioux braves who must be following them? A single horse carrying two people would leave prints any idiot could see. They had to move. And they had to do it now.

"We can't stay here," he said. "They'll track us right up this mountain."

"They will not track," she said without opening her eyes. "Look at horse."

Jack rose on one elbow, took one look at the horse, and shook his head half in disbelief, half in admiration. Each hoof was cleverly sheathed in deerskin. No wonder it made no noise traveling through the woods.

"While you run past spears," she said, "I make false trail in other direction. They will follow that one."

"You sure about that? Indians are smart."

"Jonna smart, too."

"Jonna? I thought your name was Strange One."

"True. Name also Jonna. From before," she added.

He blinked. "You remember your name from before you were captured?"

"I remember."

"What else do you remember?"

She said nothing for a long time. Finally she sat up, and her eyes met his. "I was eight years. Now I am sixteen. The Indians killed—" She stopped. "Then they took me with them."

"They killed your family?"

"My mother, yes. And father. Brother hide in creek."

He blew out a long breath. "You must hate them."

She looked off into the trees. "Not hate. I am

treated well. Chief make me his daughter, and I learn much."

"But—"

"I leave because I do not want to be Sioux."

He stared at her so long she turned away and again curled up in the patch of shade.

"Sleep now," she advised. "Tomorrow more difficult."

He almost laughed. *More* difficult? What could be harder than getting up this mountain with only one hunk of jerky and a dribble of water?"

Count your blessings, Major. You're not tied up in a Sioux teepee, and you're alive.

He settled back under the tree, breathed in the sharp, piney scent, and felt an inexplicable sense of well-being steal over him.

It didn't last.

Chapter Four

He woke with a jerk. Someone was shaking him, and when he opened his eyes, the Indian girl, Jonna, was leaning over him. "We go now. First I look at wounds."

Oh, God, not again. He was hungry. And thirsty. Mostly thirsty. Dusk was falling, and shadows among the trees were lengthening. He knew they had to get off this mountain and farther away before daylight, but this Jonna was sure determined. She motioned for him to remove his shirt, then his trousers.

He clenched his teeth as she spread more sage-scented salve over his cuts. It stung worse than before. When she finished, she motioned for him to pull on his trousers, and he walked to the edge of the cliff. The air smelled dusty and green, and birds that had been silent all day now began warbling their evening songs. The trail snaked down the mountainside, and far below him, a flat area that could be a meadow beckoned.

God only knew what stretched ahead of them. Nothing looked familiar, and he tried to recall the map he'd carried on his last patrol. Maybe Jonna would know where they were. She might also know of a spring or a creek nearby. It was too much to hope she would know where to find something to eat. That scrap of jerky she carried would only last so long.

They sucked moisture from another bit of muslin,

and when it was full dark, they climbed on the horse and started down the mountain. Jack puzzled over how she could see in the dark, but the horse was sure-footed, and the deerskin booties made their progress almost completely silent. Halfway down, Jonna reined up and sat without moving.

"You hear horses?" he murmured.

"No. I listen for birds."

"Birds! What for?"

She made a gesture he interpreted as impatience. "Birds make noise, no horses. Horses come, birds quiet. Birds noisy now." She kicked the horse into motion.

It grew darker, and the wind began to rustle the trees. An hour passed. Then another hour, and another. Finally the trail leveled out, and the horse picked up speed. From the position of the rising moon, Jack figured they were heading west.

He wondered if she knew their destination. Or maybe there *was* no destination, and she was traveling on nothing but blind instinct and dumb luck. Every so often, she reined the horse to a stop and sat listening. Moonlight made the surroundings more visible, so she stopped more often.

Suddenly the horse's ears flicked. "He hears something," Jack breathed.

"She. Horse is mare."

He gritted his teeth. The sex of the animal wasn't important. What was important was why its ears had twitched. She stopped to listen, then shrugged and again kicked the horse into motion. For the life of him, he couldn't understand why she seemed unconcerned.

He felt naked without his revolver, which was no doubt in the possession of some Indian who was now tracking them. All he had to fight with were his pocketknife and his fists.

"You got a knife in that bag of yours?" he asked.

"No. Carry knife with me."

Oh, yeah? Where was it, then? Not tied around the waist of that deerskin dress she was wearing. Maybe in a pocket? Nah. There weren't any pockets that he could see on that garment. Underneath, somewhere? Tucked in the waistband of her—Was she wearing underclothes? Probably not. Indian braves didn't. He didn't know about Indian women. On the other hand, she wasn't exactly an Indian woman, was she?

Jesus, his mind was wandering.

"Where?" he heard himself say. "Where is your knife?"

She laughed. "Around neck." She tugged at a leather thong, and he caught the glint of a blade.

"Well, at least we're both armed!"

She laughed again. "*I* am armed. *You* have only small—" She broke off and brought the horse to a stop.

Jack peered into the dark, then listened hard. Birds again. Not hoofbeats or someone breathing in the dark, just birds.

"Look!" she murmured. She pointed off to one side.

He peered into the shadows. "I don't see anything," he whispered.

Before his next breath, she was off the horse and moving into the dark. "Wait!" he muttered. Before he could slide off the horse, she was back, carrying a leather pouch like the one hanging around the horse's neck. She handed it up to him, then remounted.

This bag was heavy and bulky with something that

clanked. "Open," she said.

He loosened the drawstring and fished inside with one hand. A lump, and something hard that felt like a...a canteen? He pulled it out and heard the slosh of liquid. "Water!" He looked closer, and the hair on the back of his neck rose. Another Army-issue canteen, rusty with age and badly dented, but full of water.

"You know what this is?" he said.

"Yes. I know."

"What the—? You *know?* How could you know?"

"I know because someone leave it for me."

"Someone? Who?"

"Friend who wants to help."

A chill ran up his spine. "You mean someone knows we're out here?"

"Yes. He does kind thing. I will not marry, but he does kind thing anyway."

Jack's heart dropped into his belly. "That means they know where we are. Hell, they're probably watching us this very minute!"

"No. Only him."

She lifted her head and kicked the horse forward. "We ride, then drink."

He had a thousand questions, but she didn't utter another word until the sky began to lighten, and she turned her head and spoke over her shoulder. "Hills or plains? What you think?"

Well, damn! Apparently she didn't know everything, or she wouldn't bother to ask his opinion. He saw nothing ahead but an endless flat expanse of earth covered with long, waving grass. Hills could provide places to hide, maybe a cave. Plains would be easier riding, but out in the open, they would be

22

exposed. Anyone following them could spot a horse with two riders from way off, and that would be that. Knives and fists were only good up close.

"Hills," he said.

She nodded and turned the horse away from the rising sun.

"What about this man who wants to marry you? Won't he follow us?"

She shook her head. "He will not."

"Why not?"

"Because my answer was leaving the Sioux. He will not follow."

Jack wasn't so sure. The thought of some rejected brave just giving up didn't make sense. In fact, it made his skin crawl. "Do you know these hills?" he asked.

"Some."

She didn't speak again until the parched ground rose in lumpy hillocks and they were well into some scrubby pine trees. By the time she drew the horse to a stop, Jack's throat was so dry he could scarcely speak. Hers apparently wasn't, but the first words out of her mouth raised his eyebrows and dropped a big red warning flag in front of his nose.

She gestured at the leather bag he held. "We drink. And then…" She twisted around to face him and smiled. "Then we steal good horse."

He almost choked. "Are you crazy? Stealing a horse is guaranteed to get us strung up from the nearest tree."

Calmly she pulled the canteen from the leather bag, unscrewed the cap, dribbled some into her mouth, and handed it to him. He glugged down four big mouthfuls of the sweetest water he'd ever tasted in his life. "Did you hear what I said? Stealing a horse is a hanging offense!"

Without speaking, she lifted the canteen out of his hand. Before she could take a single swallow, he snatched it back. "Listen, Jonna, we're not gonna steal any damn horse!"

"Yes, we steal horse," she said quietly. She tipped the canteen to her mouth and swallowed, keeping her eyes on him. "Look around," she said.

He wrenched his eyes from hers and studied the surrounding hills. "Look at *what*?" he demanded.

She pointed at the ground. "Tracks."

Reluctantly he dropped his gaze to the ground and sucked in his breath. Horse tracks. Lots of them. "I see the tracks. I'm praying they're not Indians."

"Look closer. Horses close together."

"So what?"

She studied the tracks, then lifted a hunk of something out of the bag, gnawed on it, and pointed at the ground. "Many horses."

"Okay, it's probably a herd of wild horses. We haven't got time to catch a wild horse, much less get it green-broke and ride away on it."

"No need," she said. "Tracks will lead to horses already broken."

"Oh, sure." He snorted. "Saddled and waiting for us."

She handed over the chunk of jerky. "No saddle. We steal anyway."

Jehoshaphat, this was one stubborn woman. Probably never gave an inch in her life and never thought she could be wrong about anything. But Jesus, Joseph, and Mary, she had one big surprise coming when they found those horses. *If* they found them. Wild horses could run like the wind. All they had was one tired mare with two people on her back.

"We're wasting time arguing about this." He pulled out his jackknife and sliced off a lump of the jerky. Tasted like dirty socks, but it was better than nothing.

"We go now." She kicked the horse into motion, following the tracks on the ground. *She's so damn cocksure she's right about everything she's really starting to get under my skin.* Then again, maybe she knew something he didn't. Maybe she was smarter than the average human. Maybe she was nuts. Maybe....

To hell with the maybes. She might be maddeningly single-minded and bossy, but they were in this together, doing what they had to do to stay alive. He swallowed hard and shut his mouth.

They reached a grove of pine trees. She rode straight for the center, dismounted in the cool shade, and poured some canteen water into the shallow pan she pulled out of her leather pouch. She held it under the horse's nose, and when the animal had snuffled the pan dry, she peeled off some jerky and held it out.

Jack watched, torn between admiration for her care of the animal and fury at her crazy idea about stealing a horse. A horse that likely belonged to somebody, probably a Sioux brave. Or a Cheyenne. One didn't *steal* an Indian horse. If you were lucky, you cornered one long enough to throw a rope around its neck and prayed it didn't snort or whinny when you led it away. *How come she doesn't know that?*

A more worrisome question was what else they would find if they *did* locate a band of wild horses. Were they just wandering around? Or was someone, an

Indian, herding them? Thinking about it made his palms sweaty.

He got the answer late that afternoon, and it was worse than he could have imagined. They came to the crest of a hill, and the sight that met his eyes made him wish he'd died back when he was captured. Below them, dozens of wild horses milled around in a lopsided muddle, and a small band of Indians was herding them into a makeshift rope corral. Not Sioux, he noted. Cheyenne maybe.

Jonna had not said a single word since they spotted the herd. Now she leaned forward and pointed. "That one," she said.

Jack felt like he'd swallowed a rock. She wanted to steal the best-looking piece of horseflesh he'd seen since he joined the army. "No," he said. "Not possible."

"Yes," she countered. "Is possible. Tonight."

"You kidding? That's gonna get us both killed. Those are Indians down there, Jonna. Cheyenne."

She just smiled. "*Is* possible."

This was unbelievable. A headstrong woman was a menace to a man, and he'd had just about enough of her wrong-headed idea. "Prove it," he challenged.

She didn't answer, just nudged the horse forward, keeping to the trees and making no noise. Below them, a dozen Cheyenne warriors were gathered around a central firepit. They got to within thirty yards of the Indian camp, so close Jack could hear the soft murmur of their talk. They slid off the horse and sat watching them, shielded by an outcropping of boulders. The scent of roasting meat made his stomach rumble.

"We wait," she breathed beside him.

So they waited. Hours crept by, and gradually, the

Indians sprawled around the firepit in twos and threes and settled down for the night. Jack leaned his head back against a lumpy rock and closed his eyes.

A long while later, something jostled his shoulder, and when he opened his eyes, Jonna was on her feet, moving away from him. She pointed at something below them, and he crawled forward to look. The entire band of horses was confined inside the crude rope corral. He knew Indian tribes stole horses from each other, but only one or two at a time. Below them was an entire herd.

She motioned for him to stay where he was and then inched forward, making no noise. He grabbed her arm, but she shook him off, and he watched in horror as she slipped closer and closer to the sleeping Indians. At last, she reached the far corner of the rope corral, near that black horse she wanted. When he realized her plan, he clamped his jaw shut so hard his teeth hurt.

No! Don't do it!

Chapter Five

He held his breath and watched Jonna glide silently past the sleeping Indians and slip under the corral rope. While the horses shuffled uneasily, she worked her way forward until she reached the handsome black mare she wanted, and then he lost sight of her. He blinked hard and peered into the gloom, then saw her dark shadow crawl—*crawl!*—close to the horse, reach up one hand, and feed it…what?

That was smart. Dangerous, but smart. He let out his breath but instantly sucked it in again when he saw her next move. Damned if she didn't drop to her knees and—*ohmigod*—crawl underneath the animal! Yeah, this girl was crazy. Stark raving nuts. Unable to look away, he kept his eyes glued to the small figure moving below him.

He almost didn't believe what he was seeing, but for the life of him, he couldn't stop watching. *What the hell is she doing now?* Very slowly she pulled something out of her dress, bent almost to the ground, and lifted one of the horse's hooves. *Jonna, stop! You're going to get yourself killed. You're going to get us* both *killed.* He closed his eyes. When he opened them, she was doing something to another hoof, but he couldn't tell what it was. He clenched his fists. Any minute now, she was going to get kicked to a pulp.

Afraid to breathe, he couldn't stop watching. The

horse didn't seem to mind what she was doing. Maybe she wasn't crazy. Maybe she was a horse-whisperer.

Still crouched on the ground, she now moved silently from hoof to hoof, then stood up and slipped a braided rawhide rope around the animal's neck. *Rope? Where'd that rope come from?* He watched her lead the black horse up to the edge of the corral, slice through the confining rope with the knife she carried, and ease the animal through the opening.

Suddenly one of the sleeping Indians sat up and peered into the dark, and Jack's heart almost stopped. Jonna froze. But the Indian didn't notice her and the black mare standing motionless a few yards away, and he lay back down. Now the rest of the herd was edging out of the corral, following Jonna and the black mare. Jack rubbed his eyes in disbelief. *I never thought wild horses were that intelligent. And the same goes for...*

He found he was shaking like an aspen leaf in a breeze. Straining his eyes, he followed Jonna's slow progress with her prize mare through the shadowy dark and up the hill toward where he stood, and now he could see what she'd been doing underneath the animal—tying deerskin booties on each hoof.

Even from here, he could see her triumphant grin. When she moved toward him, he was torn between slapping her silly for being stupid and brave and kissing her. "My God," he said when she got closer. "I almost had a heart attack watching you!"

She pointed a finger at him. "Not have imagination."

He stared at her. "No imag—You call that 'imagination'? I call it idiocy!"

"No. Is imagination."

"And dumb luck," Jack said. "And a giant helping of foolhardiness," he added.

She gave him an odd look, then turned away. "We go now," she said over her shoulder.

"Hold on, Jonna. You can't just climb on the back of that horse. It's not broke yet. You'll have to lead him. Her," he amended.

"I ride," she said.

Oh, for Pete's sake. She was either really dumb about horses or so determined she wouldn't listen to reason.

He could scarcely believe what happened next. She stood facing the horse she'd stolen, then bent forward and puffed her breath into its nostrils. The horse stood quietly, and after a moment, she began running her hands over its hide—all over, including its hind quarters. It was a damn miracle she didn't get kicked.

"I ride," she repeated. She jumped up and lay on her belly across the animal's back, then twisted into a sitting position, leaned forward, and whispered into the animal's ear. Jack stepped back out of the way, expecting an explosion of squeals and kicks and frenzied bucking.

Nothing happened. *I don't believe this.* He waited, and still the horse stood quietly with Jonna on its back, calmly looking down at him. "Why you not mount?" she asked.

Because I'm still sound asleep and dreaming all this.

She walked the black mare past him and headed down the hill. "Come," she called over her shoulder. "Daylight soon."

He jerked to attention. Daylight was only a few

hours away, and here they were in the middle of nowhere with a stolen horse. He climbed on his mount, lifted the rope around its neck, and gave it a kick.

For the next hour, he sweated bullets, expecting at any moment to feel an arrow slice into his back. Halfway down the hill, she turned toward a thicket of tumbleweeds and willow trees. Beyond lay the safety of the woods, and she tipped her head in that direction.

He found himself listening for bird sounds, and when he heard twittering instead of hoofbeats or the whoops of angry Indians, he let himself breathe again. Now he had time to think. First, for the twentieth time since darkness had fallen, he wondered where they were. Second, he wondered how long the single canteen of water would last them. Third, why hadn't they stumbled across at least a few army soldiers on patrol? Fourth, his whiskers were starting to itch, and he smelled like a sweaty barkeep, but how come *she* didn't smell like a sweaty barkeep?

Fifth...but he couldn't think beyond the sweaty barkeep.

They rode until it began to get light, then rode some more. The horse's hooves were quiet. The birds were noisy. When the rising sun turned the sky pale apricot, Jack started to look for someplace they could hole up until dark.

Suddenly Jonna gave a cry and pointed ahead.

Oh, God, what now?

Chapter Six

He heard water gurgling over rocks, and around the next bend, they came to a creek. The bank was thick with vine maples and alders, and Jack lost no time sliding off the horse and wading in up to his thighs. Jonna dismounted to let the black horse drink its fill, then looped the rawhide rope over an alder branch and headed for the creek. She didn't splash in, as he had, but paced up and down the bank, paying no attention to him. Finally she stopped and in one smooth motion pulled the deerskin dress over her head.

My God, she was beautiful! He couldn't take his eyes off her. She had long legs and…. He swallowed hard. Small, firm breasts and gently rounded hips. The hair covering her sex was dark and soft-looking. He swallowed again.

She perched on a rock beside a deep pool and began to unbraid her hair, shook it out, and slipped into the water. Then she breast-stroked noiselessly over to where he stood.

"Get clean," she said.

"Yeah." He didn't know whether that was an invitation or an order. Didn't matter. He stripped and splashed in up to his chest. The cold water was as big a shock as the sight of her naked figure poised on a rock where she now sat finger-combing her hair. He closed his eyes and let the water close over his head.

Think, Corder. You have to get back to the post. You have to let somebody know you're alive and Sergeant Matt Sullivan isn't. Reason returned when he realized he was still underwater and had to breathe.

"Clean?" she asked when he surfaced.

"Yeah." And cold sober. She had re-braided her hair and pulled on her deerskin dress. He tried not to think about what lay underneath.

"Jonna, we have to figure out where we are. Sooner or later, we're going to run into a Cheyenne brave or a Sioux warrior, and I'd sure like to be close to a military outpost when we do."

She nodded. "Tomorrow."

"Tomorrow, what?"

"Tomorrow we ride in straight lines, make big square."

"Wait a minute. Why don't we…?" But he figured she'd already made up her mind, and when Jonna decided on something, he'd learned she was as immovable as a boulder. He snapped his jaw shut. Maybe they'd be okay as long as they didn't run into any Indians.

That thought kept him awake most of the night. They spent it in a thick copse of cottonwoods, and by morning, he was tired, cranky, and hungry. He'd been hungry before, but he hadn't been on the run from the Sioux. Hell's bells, he was surrounded by a marauding band of Indians who wanted his scalp.

When the rising sun turned the sky pink, they watered the horses and started off. The trees thinned out as they reached the plain, and Jack began to mentally lay out their reconnaissance square. He figured they could ride about two miles every forty minutes or so, which meant calculating how far he wanted to go in any one direction. Keeping a wary eye out for a puff of dust in the distance, they rode north for approximately two hours. He estimated that it was about six miles. One more hour made it nine miles, and then they turned west. So far, so good. But he kept his fingers crossed anyway.

The sun was merciless, like sitting inside a firepit full of red-hot coals. Jonna never seemed to get hot, but as the temperature rose, she didn't say much, and after their third hour on horseback, she said nothing at all. They drank sparingly from their hoarded supply of water, passing the canteen back and forth each time they stopped to rest the horses.

Every dust devil Jack saw made his heart stutter. Jonna paid no attention to them, or so he thought, until one puff of dust caught her attention and she stopped suddenly, lifted her nose, and sniffed the air.

"Maybe smoke," she explained. "Maybe not."

Major Jack Corder would note the direction of the smoke and ride to check it out. Sioux-escapee Corder would sit tight and pray. It was definitely smoke—*dark* smoke. And it was drifting to the east.

"Maybe campfire," she said.

He frowned. A campfire was of concern. A prairie fire would pour black smoke into the sky, and while a prairie fire was no fun to battle, at least you knew it was burning on a prairie. A campfire, on the other hand, could be anywhere—a military post or an Indian camp.

For the next mile, he kept his attention on the sky. The smoke dissipated, and after another two hours, they completed the second leg of their square. They'd been riding since sunup and had come across only an occasional twisted pine tree and a patch of sagebrush. Time—and water—were running out.

They approached a low-rolling hill, and Jack pulled his horse to a stop and studied the terrain. Behind them were scrubby pines and outcroppings of rock; ahead, it looked like more of the same. Except… He squinted against the blinding sun. Except for that patch of green ahead of them. Green meant water.

Green could also mean people. But which people—Indian or army?

"Let's get closer," he said. "Then wait for dark."

Jonna nodded.

"Unless we starve to death before dark," he muttered.

"Not starve," she said.

"No? Why not?"

She didn't answer. Then, from a pocket in that deerskin dress she wore, she pulled out a fistful of something, seized his hand, and dumped whatever it was into his open palm.

"Huckleberries! Where'd you find huckleberries?"

"Grow in woods. I find last night."

He lifted her hand, cupped her fingers, and poured in half the berries. "Breakfast, lunch, and supper, all in one mouthful."

She laughed. It wasn't funny, he acknowledged. They would starve going from huckleberry bush to huckleberry bush, and where they were now, there were no bushes at all. A flatter, more inhospitable stretch of ground he'd never seen. He popped his handful of berries into his mouth.

Huckleberry bushes were the least of their problems. Out here on this plain, they could be seen for miles. Jesus, they were probably being watched this very minute. Made his skin prickle.

They completed the second leg of their exploratory square and had just turned to the south when something caught his eye. He'd give a month's pay for a pair of field glasses right now. Shielding his eyes with one hand, he squinted into the glare. "What's that ahead?"

"Rocks," she said. "Many rocks."

"Nah. Rocks don't just pop up in the middle of a prairie like that." But… He kneed the horse forward a few yards. Maybe it *was* rocks. Whatever it was looked to be maybe an hour away.

He glanced at Jonna and laughed out loud. She was eating her scant handful of huckleberries one by one, carefully plucking one tiny berry at a time from the small pile in her palm and dropping it into her mouth.

"At that rate, it'll take you all day to eat them."

"True," she said. "Enjoy good thing slowly."

That was maybe the longest sentence he'd ever heard her utter. "You speak any English while you were with the Sioux?"

She shook her head. "I hear inside my head, but forget how to speak."

"Do you *think* in Sioux?"

"No. Think in English. Think many things in English." She popped another huckleberry into her mouth.

"Well, I'll be damned," he murmured.

"Be damned," she echoed. "Bad English."

That made him chuckle. By now he was convinced that what lay ahead of them was, in fact, a jumble of rocks. Big rocks. He figured they'd reach them around the time it got dark. The question was, who else might be heading for them? He glanced at the sky and shook his head. It'd be a race to get there before it got so dark they couldn't see their hands in front of their faces. But they didn't dare ride any faster because that would kick up a trail of dust any child could follow.

Okay, they'd take it slow and easy. And just in case, they'd circle around the rocks and come in at an angle. Hell's half-acre, maybe it didn't matter. If somebody *was* there, he was watching them right this minute, and there was no place to hide. He prayed whoever it was wasn't armed.

The darker it got, the closer they came to the odd outcropping of rocks, and the more Jack began to sweat. They veered wide to the east, and when they could scarcely see in the thickening gloom, he motioned for Jonna to dismount, and they moved forward on foot. By now he couldn't see much of anything in front of him until the pile of rocks suddenly loomed dead ahead.

Suddenly Jonna gripped his forearm. He narrowed his eyes and studied where she pointed, then almost choked. *Son of a—*

In front of the biggest rock lay a dark figure. For the second time in the last twenty-four hours, the hair on the back of his neck stood up. He groped for Jonna's hand and took a single step forward.

The figure didn't move. He slipped the jackknife out of his trouser pocket and opened the blade, then laid his other hand on Jonna's shoulder and pressed gently. "Stay here," he breathed.

He took another step forward. Still no movement. Something was wrong. Purposely he scuffed his boot in the sand and heard someone's breath hiss in, but still nothing moved. He strained his ears and heard someone's breathing rasp in and out, and all at once, he understood. Whoever it was could be sick or wounded.

Or waiting. He took another step, and the toe of his boot bumped against something solid. Not a rock. A body. Sweat started between his shoulder blades. He was close enough for whoever it was to shoot him or stab him, but nothing happened. The labored breathing continued.

He'd give a hundred bucks for a bit of moonlight right now. Maybe two hundred bucks. He dropped to one knee in front of whoever was lying there, reached one hand in front of him, and touched something warm. Fingers suddenly closed around his hand, and it was all he could do not to let out a yelp.

The fingers pulled his hand to the right, and he felt a soft fabric of some kind and then something wet and sticky. Blood. *God in heaven, he's wounded!*

"Jonna," he called.

She appeared at his elbow. He pulled her down beside him, then guided her hand to the sticky patch of blood. "Bad," she murmured. She disappeared into the dark, then returned with the canteen and her leather bag.

He found a strip of muslin, soaked it in the canteen, and felt for the man's mouth. Carefully, he laid it on his lips. "Wet lips," Jonna instructed the person. Jack noticed she repeated it in the Sioux language. He heard a moan of assent. Jonna lifted the jackknife out of his hand, and the next minute, he heard fabric ripping.

The moon rose, casting a faint light over everything. Jonna touched his arm, and he looked down to see a bare chest with a bloody hole in it. When he raised his eyes, he blinked in disbelief. He was staring at dark skin and black hair, and an Indian's black eyes were studying him. "Jesus," he breathed. It was only a kid, maybe ten or eleven years old. Cheyenne? Sioux? Didn't matter, he guessed. What was an Indian kid doing out here alone?

The dark eyes drifted shut, and Jonna rose and motioned for Jack to follow her. Close to the horses some yards away, she turned to him. "We sleep here, near horses," she said. "No danger. He is not armed. But horses valuable."

She returned to the boy, wet his lips, and laid strips of fabric on his wound. Then she moved away a few feet, positioned herself on the ground next to the black mare, and curled her body around her leather medicine bag.

Jack tramped all the way around the rock outcropping. Looked like the kid had no horse, which was odd. The biggest rock was no higher than about forty feet, and it took only fifteen steps to circle the whole outcropping. When he reached Jonna's motionless form, he glanced back to the base of the rock, then stretched out close to her. He closed his eyes, but he couldn't stop thinking about that Indian kid. Why was he out here alone with no horse and a hole in his chest?

In the morning, he opened his eyes to find Jonna sitting beside him. "Look," she said. She pointed at something, and he sat up.

The Indian boy was gone. Then he saw something that stopped his breath. The area around the rocks had been swept clean of footprints, and outlined in the dirt was a crudely drawn arrow. It pointed south.

Chapter Seven

Jack scratched his head. "South, huh? You think it's a trap? Something to lure us into an ambush?"

She shook her head.

"Riding south doesn't look too promising, Jonna. All I can see from here is sand and sagebrush and more big rocks like these."

She just looked at him.

"Huckleberries, maybe," he muttered, and she laughed. "What's funny?" he shot. "Without water, we're going to die out here."

"Not die," she said.

"Yeah? What makes you so sure of that? You ever been stranded for a whole lotta days with nothing to eat or drink?"

Again she shook her head. "Sioux eat well." She tipped her chin in the direction of the arrow drawn in the sand. "I trust."

Jack snorted. "You trust *what*?" he demanded. "Some Indian kid who'd probably kill us if he could stand up?"

"You have no faith," she said in a maddeningly calm voice. "I have faith."

He turned away in disbelief. Maybe she was suffering from sun-sickness. Maybe she was as lost and disoriented as he was, but putting on a brave face. Maybe... Oh, what the hell. What difference did it make if they died in an Indian ambush or from dehydration or starvation? Dead was dead.

But she was already mounted and moving away from him. Heading south, he noted. She must be as hungry as he was. He'd never known a woman who didn't complain if she missed even one meal, let alone half a dozen, but he sure didn't see any glowering looks or hear any whiney comments from her. He climbed on the other horse and kicked it into motion. South.

After two hot, sweaty hours under the searing sun, they stopped in what shade there was under a stunted pine tree. He unscrewed the cap on the canteen and swirled it around to dislodge the dirt. He expected a sloshing sound, but he sure didn't expect it to sound almost empty. He took a small sip, shook the canteen again, and handed it to Jonna. "We have almost no water left."

She barely wet her lips. She handed it back, and their eyes met. Dammit, she didn't even look concerned!

"You've gotta drink, Jonna."

"Not yet."

"What? Are you crazy? Drink, dammit!"

She shook her head, and that did it. He shoved the canteen at her and shook it in her face. "Drink!"

"No."

He stared at her. "Why the hell not?"

"Because I smell water."

"Oh, sure," he scoffed.

She sent him a look that was half annoyance and half amusement, shrugged, and rode on ahead of him. South, he noted. He wondered who would die first. And who would bury the survivor when the time came.

Gradually, the landscape began to change. Sprinkled here and there among stunted pines and clumps of sagebrush were swaths of some kind of bush with tiny yellow blossoms. Not wild roses, which he could identify. Not buckbrush and not serviceberry, which liked shade, not blazing sunshine.

For the next two hours, while he grew more thirsty and more frustrated, he thought about that yellow-flowered bush. Jonna rode in front of him, which was just as well because he was running out of patience and getting short-tempered.

Suddenly her horse stopped short, and she dropped to the ground and started scrabbling in the dirt. Not just scrabbling, he realized, but digging hard, sinking her fingers into the sandy soil next to a funny-looking bush with puffy white blossoms.

"Help me!" she called over her shoulder.

He slid off his horse, tramped over to her, and squatted on his haunches. She pointed to a spot closer to the strange-looking bush. "Dig there!" His hands were twice the size of hers, so he made quick work of digging a hole next to hers, but deeper. In the next minute, they joined both holes to make one large, shallow basin. As they did so, he noticed something. The color of the earth beneath the surface was darker— *much* darker, almost as if it was—

"Wet!" he shouted. "Look, Jonna, the bottom of this hole is damp!"

"Yes," she said, her voice matter-of-fact. "Water make damp. We wait."

Wait! Part of him wanted to strangle her. But when he saw water gradually seep into the bottom of the hole, he changed his mind. An hour crept by. There wasn't enough to fill the canteen, but there was enough to keep them alive. Jonna pulled two muslin strips from her leather bag and dropped them onto the wet sand. After a few minutes, they were limp with moisture, and when their color darkened, she pulled one out and handed it to him. The other she poked into her mouth.

They spent an hour kneeling by their precious excavation while the sun beat down on their backs and gnats circled their heads. The moisture he sucked from the muslin strip was gritty with sand, but never in all his twenty-seven years had anything tasted so good. He didn't care that his teeth crunched when he closed his mouth, or that dirt soiled his hands, or that he was miles away from a proper bathtub. He was alive!

He touched her shoulder. "Jonna."

She stopped digging and looked up. "Thanks." He glimpsed a half-smile.

She nodded and returned her gaze to the hole. "You are welcome, Jack."

He stared at her. "How'd you know my name?"

Her smile widened into a grin. "I…eavesdrop. That is right word?"

He felt like kissing her! Right here in the middle of nowhere, with no huckleberries and an almost-empty canteen, he felt like—

The crack of a rifle made him gag on his length of damp muslin. Winchester, if he judged right. Indians didn't have Winchesters, did they? Most tribes used older rifles captured from army patrols.

Jonna scuttled to the other side of the funny bush with white flowers, and they flattened themselves on the ground. Not much cover, but in the life he was leading now, beggars couldn't be choosers. Suddenly

Jonna rolled over and laid one ear against the ground. He flopped over onto his belly and pressed his own ear on the dirt. "Horses!" he shouted. "Hear them, Jonna? Horses!"

"Where?" she asked.

In the next instant, he realized the horsemen were unidentified and they would be caught in the open. He looked to the south, where a cloud of dust now marked the path of what he prayed were mounted soldiers and not Indians.

The dust cloud was moving straight toward them. Jack sent a silent plea to God and slowly stood up.

Chapter Eight

They were quickly surrounded by five or six men Jack wasn't sure he recognized. They wore blue military jackets, and they were dusty and travel-stained, their faces sweaty and dirt-streaked. A young, fresh-faced lieutenant leaned down toward him. Jack didn't recognize him.

"Who the hell are you, and what are you doing out here?" the lieutenant barked.

Jack bit the inside of his cheek until he could speak in a civil tone. "Who the hell are *you*?" he snapped.

The lieutenant stiffened. "I am Lieutenant Sidney Markley of the Sixth Cavalry out of Fort Kearney."

"Lieutenant Markley, I am Major Jackson Corder, also Sixth Cavalry out of Fort Kearney."

"Oh, sure ya are," the lieutenant drawled. "You're filthy, and…" He pointed his chin at Jonna. "You and your squaw are probably riding stolen horses."

Jack froze. "This woman is nobody's squaw, Lieutenant. Until four days ago, she was a captive of the Sioux."

"Oh, yeah? What's yer name, honey?"

Jonna walked forward until she stood only two feet from the lieutenant's horse, then raised her chin. "My name is Jonna Kathleen Lander."

Jack almost smiled. She must have practiced that sentence a hundred times.

The lieutenant's gaze moved back to Jack. "You look pretty scruffy for a major in the U.S. Army. You're dirty and unshaven, and I don't believe your story for one minute."

Jack grinned. "You willing to bet on that?"

"I sure am. Fifty bucks says you're lying. Fifty bucks says you're nothing but an escaped prisoner. Colonel Hawks'll clap you in jail right off."

Jack stuck out his hand. "Fifty bucks, huh? Shake on it?"

The lieutenant hesitated, then leaned down and clasped Jack's hand.

"Mind if we ride along with you back to the fort, Lieutenant?"

"Nah," the lieutenant said with a sneer. "You can tag along, you and your…companion." He wheeled his mount, signaled his cohorts, and clattered off across the sand.

Jack sent Jonna a long look and tipped his head toward their horses. Once mounted, they swung wide of the lieutenant and his soldiers to avoid their dust, and for the next four hours, they rode side by side until the wind-scarred pine trees of Fort Kearney came into view. He felt like climbing off his horse and kissing the ground.

Once inside the compound, Lieutenant Markley and his troopers headed for the stable. Jack slid off the horse and waited for Jonna to join him, then headed for his commander's office. Suddenly Jonna stopped. "What's wrong?" he asked.

She raised her head and looked straight at him. "Who is inside building?"

"Colonel Martin Hawks, the commanding officer.

This is his office."

For the first time since they had escaped from the Sioux camp, he saw fear in her eyes. "Jonna?"

She nodded, squared her shoulders, and drew in a long breath. Hot damn, she was scared! He'd never seen Jonna unsure about anything, much less frightened. Ever since the night they'd ridden away from the Sioux camp, while he gritted his teeth and shook inside, she'd looked calm and sure of herself. And then suddenly, he understood.

She hadn't wanted to live among the Sioux, but she *knew* the Sioux. She didn't know anyone here at Fort Kearney except him. She didn't know anything about living on an army post. She didn't even know the language too well. Must feel like diving into a river when you didn't know how deep it was.

"You're safe here, Jonna. This is what you wanted, right?"

She raised her chin and nodded.

"Then come on," he murmured. He took her arm and marched her up the wooden steps into the colonel's office.

"Martin?"

Colonel Hawks looked up from the desk, then jolted to his feet. "Jack! Is that you?"

"It sure is, Colonel."

"You look awful, Jack. Where've you been for the last week?"

"I've been an unwilling guest of the Sioux. And don't ask for details." He stepped to one side and gestured at Jonna. "Colonel Hawks, I'd like to introduce Miss Jonna Lander. She was also a guest of the Sioux."

The colonel's eyes widened as he took in her deerskin dress. "Jonna...?"

"Lander," she supplied.

He stared at her. "You any relation to Andrew Lander?"

Jonna caught her breath. "Yes! He is my brother." When she had been captured, Andrew was only four years old; she had spent eight years wondering if he had survived. "My brother, he is alive? You know him?"

"Well, I'll be damned. I certainly do know him, young lady. He's told me all about your capture, Miss Lander. Welcome back to civilization."

She took a hesitant step forward. "Where is Andrew?"

"Your brother is on a special mission for the army. Should be back in a week or two."

"Into Nez Perce country?" Jack asked.

"That's right. Gotta pray for the kid."

Jonna's eyes widened. "Is dangerous?"

The colonel coughed. "Well, maybe not dangerous for a skilled translator like your brother."

"Translator! What's he translating, Colonel?" Jack asked.

"That I can't tell you yet, Jack." He turned his attention back to Jonna. "Now that you're here, Miss Lander, no doubt you'll need a place to stay. My wife would be pleased to offer our hospitality."

Jonna looked up and exchanged a long look with Jack. Her eyes looked different, and it took him a moment to register what he was seeing. Fear. But that made no sense. Up until the last ten minutes, he'd never seen Jonna the least bit scared of anything. And, he reminded himself, if it weren't for Jonna he wouldn't be standing here in Colonel Hawks' office. He signaled the colonel that he had more to say.

"Yes? What is it, Jack?"

"Matthew Sullivan is dead, Colonel. We were both captured by the Sioux and forced to run a gauntlet. Matt didn't survive."

"Oh, dammit to hell," the colonel grumbled. "Sergeant Sullivan was a good man. A good soldier." He gazed out the grimy window for a long moment, then brought his attention back to Jack. "You two go along, now. Put your horses in the stable and take Miss Lander to my residence. Then get some rest, Jack. And a bath," he added. "I have to say you look mighty trail-worn."

Chapter Nine

Jonna took a deep breath and followed Jack up the seven steps to the front porch of Colonel Hawks' large white-painted house. She remembered a house like this one; she had lived in one as a child. It had a big kitchen and two upstairs bedrooms; the summers were stifling, and the winters were snowy and bitter cold. That's why Papa had wanted to go to Oregon. She closed her eyes. That's also why Papa was killed. And Mama, too.

It felt very strange being here among her own people at last; everything was unfamiliar. Even the smell of the house was strange. All at once, she was so frightened she could scarcely breathe.

"Scared?" Jack murmured.

"Y-yes."

"After what you've been through, I guess being here on an army post would feel kinda strange."

She nodded and pressed her lips together. It felt more than strange. It felt like she was dreaming. Did she really belong here?

The front door swung open and out stepped a short woman wearing a blue-checked gingham apron. She had wavy gray hair and sharp eyes. Blue eyes like hers.

"Jack!" the woman screamed. "Good heavens, you look dreadful! Where in the world have you been?" She threw her arms around him and smacked kisses on both cheeks. "My lord, you smell like a rotten apple!"

Jack took Jonna's hand and pulled her forward. "Martha, this is Jonna Lander. She's Andrew Lander's sister."

The woman's eyes narrowed. "What on earth are you wearing, child? It doesn't suit you at all!"

"Jonna's been a captive of the Sioux for the last eight years," Jack explained. "She probably knows very little about fashionable dresses."

Martha's grey eyebrows went up. "The Sioux! Oh, my dear, how dreadful!"

"We're both tired and hungry, Martha. For the last four days, we've eaten only a couple slices of jerky and a handful of huckleberries."

"Huckleberries!" She studied Jack's filthy trousers and then her gaze moved back to Jonna's deerskin dress. After a long moment, she stepped forward and took both Jonna's hands in hers. "You are welcome here, my dear. Fashionable dresses are not the least bit important."

Jack sent Jonna a long look and tipped his head toward the door. "I've got my own quarters, Jonna. Maybe I'll see you at supper." He sent Martha a hopeful look and turned away.

When the front door closed behind him, Jonna drew in a shaky breath. She had waited eight years for this day, to return to the life she remembered. Now, faced with this colonel's kindly wife in a big house that smelled of flowers and furniture polish, things she barely remembered, she suddenly felt unsure of herself.

"Well now, child," Martha said. "You'll be needing all manner of things, I imagine. But first, you must be mighty hungry after four days with only jerky and huckleberries to eat."

Jonna nodded. The woman conducted her to a warm kitchen, sat her down at a small yellow-painted table, and rattled pots and pans until a plate of scrambled eggs appeared before her. She stared at them. "I have not tasted eggs from chicken since…"

Martha's gray eyebrows went up. "No? Did you not have eggs with the Sioux?"

"Only duck eggs. And bird eggs," she added.

"What about coffee?" Martha asked.

"We make from berries. Very bitter."

Martha laughed. "I'll bet it was. Well, try some of this." She filled a ceramic cup with a dark liquid and urged Jonna to taste it.

At the first swallow, Jonna wrinkled her nose. "Also bitter," she said.

Martha smiled. "You'll be wanting to add some milk, then. Maybe some sugar as well. That's how I like it, but Martin calls it dishwater."

Jonna watched her dribble some milk into the cup and add a spoonful of sugar, then tasted it again. "Better!"

"Now," Martha said, "you finish your breakfast while I heat up some water for a bath. After four days on horseback, you must be filthy."

She gobbled the scrambled eggs and downed half a pot of coffee while Martha filled a wooden tub on the back porch with steaming water. Then the gray-haired woman stepped back into the kitchen. "Bath's ready," she announced.

Jonna hesitated. During her years with the Sioux, she hadn't bathed in anything but cold streams, and the sight of steam rising from this inviting tub of water made her skin tingle. She took a deep breath, stripped off her deerskin dress, and stepped in. When she sat down, warm water sloshed over her legs, and then her entire body was submerged! While Martha bustled back and forth adding more hot water, Jonna scrubbed every inch of her dirty skin, then dunked her head into the tub and washed her hair. Finally she leaned back and closed her eyes.

She wasn't dreaming. She was really here, really among her own people. Part of her still didn't believe it. She'd spent years thinking of this day, dreaming of a place where she could eat American food and sleep in a real bed instead of on a lumpy pallet on a teepee floor. Where she could speak her own language. Now that she was actually here, splashing water over her body in a warm bathtub in this beautiful big kitchen, it seemed unreal. Maybe she was still dreaming.

Being here was strange for another reason—she could not really speak the language. She thought in English, and in her mind, she could form whole sentences in English, but she had not spoken a single word of the language she used to know until the night she and Jack escaped from the Sioux camp.

She opened her eyes and looked around. She must not only learn to speak in English; she must learn how to act, what to say. She had no idea how to begin.

She splashed out of the tub and grabbed the folded towel Martha had left for her. Well, she had learned how to live with the Sioux; she prayed she could learn how to live among her own people. She was here now, thanks to Jack. Now she could have what she'd dreamed of for those eight years. Still, she felt off-balance.

Martha reappeared in the doorway. "Now," she

said with a smile, "wrap that towel around you and come with me." She led Jonna through the warm, fragrant kitchen and up a flight of polished wooden stairs into a small room with ruffled curtains on the windows and a bed covered with a puffy blue quilt. She then swung open the door of a tall carved wood armoire.

"When my daughter went back east to her teachers college, she left all sorts of garments behind. I think you might put them to good use. I think you're about the same size as my Samantha, so let's see what we can find."

Jonna gasped at the sight before her. There were dresses and skirts and shirtwaists and petticoats, even shoes! American girl clothes. Jonna stared at the woman, then at the bulging armoire, and a sick feeling settled in the pit of her stomach. Now she would be expected to wear long skirts and ruffled dresses like other American women. But she did not feel like an American woman!

"Please," she said quietly. "Please burn deerskin dress."

Martha laughed. "I will do exactly that right this minute. While I'm gone, you pick out something to wear. There're underclothes in that chest of drawers in the corner."

The door closed, and Jonna found herself alone. Underclothes! She hadn't worn underclothes for many years! She ran her hands over the underdrawers and cotton chemises and ruffled petticoats until she was dizzy. So many choices! She settled on a petticoat that didn't look too stiffly starched, tied it around her waist, and pulled open a dresser drawer crammed with underdrawers and lacy camisoles. She knew older girls wore garments like these, but she was not an 'older girl.' When she was captured, she had been eight years old. She was unsure what went underneath a grown-up girl's petticoat.

She studied every item of clothing and finally pulled on a sturdy pair of cotton drawers and a camisole with a pink ribbon drawstring. Everything felt scratchy against her bare skin. Then she chose a simple blue skirt made of some crinkly fabric and a pale blue shirtwaist with white buttons and long sleeves, drew them on over the strange-feeling underclothes, and turned to stare at her reflection in the mirror.

She couldn't stop staring at the girl who looked back at her. She smiled, and then she laughed out loud. But after a moment, tears flooded her eyes. Life among her own people involved so many decisions! She was starting to realize this was going to be much harder than she had ever imagined.

****

Jack found his quarters as he had left them, clean but messy. He always skimped on bedmaking, reasoning that it didn't much matter since he bunked alone. A freshly ironed dress shirt hung next to his blue military jacket, and a clean pair of twill trousers lay across the bed.

He shucked his trousers and the deerskin shirt, then stood at the tiny sink, lathered his cheeks, and shaved off an itchy five-day growth of whiskers. After a quick spit bath, he swiped his wet hand over his hair. Probably still smelled kinda ripe, but he was in a hurry.

When he was dressed, he tramped down the wooden steps and strode toward the mess hall where a young soldier was exiting. "Hold up there, Private!"

"Yessir?"

"You know a Lieutenant Sidney Markley?"

"Oh, yessir. He's new at the post. Likes to play poker."

"Where could I find him?"

The private pointed behind him. "Over at that barracks, sir. Braggin' how he captured some renegade Indians."

"I'll bet," Jack muttered. He headed for the barracks. Sure enough, a poker game was going on. Lieutenant Markley was hoarding a pile of bills on the table in front of him, and that made Jack smile.

"Lieutenant Markley?"

The lieutenant leaped to his feet and snapped a salute. "Yes, sir?"

"You mean 'yes, sir, Major,' don't you?"

"Uh…"

"Better yet, you mean 'yes, sir, Major *Corder*,' don't you?"

"Yes, sir, Major Cor—"

"Don't recognize me, do you, Lieutenant?"

The lieutenant looked blank. His poker-playing buddies were watching with interest, and now they began to murmur to each other. Jack ignored them.

"You owe me fifty bucks, Lieutenant."

"I do?"

"You do," Jack said. "When you questioned my rank yesterday, we made a bet, remember?" Markley stared at him.

"Pay up," Jack ordered.

"Uh, well, at the moment—"

"Lieutenant, with all those greenbacks you've

collected, I'll bet you another fifty bucks the money you owe me is sitting right there in front of you."

"Well, I—"

"A bet is a bet, Lieutenant Markley, so count it out. Now!" He used his snap-to-it voice.

"Y-yes, sir."

Jack walked out with fifty dollars in his pocket and a satisfied feeling inside. All the way down the steps, he could hear the guffaws of the lieutenant's poker-playing buddies.

Chapter Ten

Late the next afternoon, Jack sat on the colonel's front porch, a glass of bourbon in his hand. "Tell me something, Martin. Where'd you get a clown like Lieutenant Markley?"

The colonel gave the porch swing a push. "Promise you won't laugh now."

Suspecting this would prove interesting, Jack kept his mouth shut, sipped his drink, and waited. Colonel Hawks swirled the bourbon in his glass around and around. "I hate to admit it, but I ended up with Markley during a poker game." He lowered his voice. "Don't tell Martha."

"You mean I missed a poker game?"

"Well, yes. You know Silas Knowles, right? Colonel Knowles?"

Jack nodded. "Crackerjack card player."

"One night Silas and three other officers—one of them was young Andrew Lander's commanding officer—we got together for a little game. The long and the short of it is that I lost a hand. Junius Cruickshank, remember him?"

Jack nodded.

"Junius bet against me, and I lost. The loser had to take Lieutenant Markley."

Jack tipped his chair onto its two back legs and propped his boots on the porch railing. "That ought to teach you a lesson, Martin."

"About playing poker?"

"No, not about poker, Martin. About sending an ass like Markley off on a patrol."

Colonel Hawks grinned and topped up their glasses. "Anything else I should know, Jack?"

"Yeah. It's about Jonna Lander."

"Figured. I saw the way you were looking at her when you two walked in."

Jack's chair rocked forward onto all four legs. "I have no interest in Jonna. But I am concerned about how she's going to adjust after living with the Sioux for so many years."

"Sure you're concerned," the colonel murmured. "You think maybe a young woman who's been living with Indians for eight years might have forgotten how to conduct herself in polite society. Is that it?"

Jack laughed. "You call an army post 'polite society'?"

Colonel Hawks chuckled. "Well, hell, Jack, it's as polite as we can make it, given that it's six hundred miles from the nearest afternoon tea party. And," he added under his breath, "it's an army post that's got Lieutenant Sidney Markley in the ranks."

"Yeah, I see what you mean. But—"

"Listen, Jack. My wife is no fool. She tells me Jonna is studying *Miss Jefferson's Book of Etiquette*. She'll do all right. Martha says she's smart as a fox."

"As a fox," Jack muttered. "Jonna's also convinced she's always right." He didn't add that Jonna usually *was* right. At least she'd been usually right in the days before they reached Fort Kearney.

The colonel grinned. "Martha also tells me the post

is holding its annual summer ball come Saturday. You watch Jonna Lander. I bet she'll do just fine."

I'll watch her, all right. And I'll keep her out of Lieutenant Ignoramus Markley's path.

He got to his feet. "Thanks for the bourbon, Martin."

"Always glad to give advice to my officers," the colonel said with a grin. "Especially those who need it the most."

Jack just looked at him.

****

He wasn't prepared for the change he saw in Jonna at supper the next evening. Was this the same Jonna who'd doctored his cuts and shared her water and stolen that black mare from under the noses of a bunch of Cheyenne? Instead of the deerskin dress, she now wore a blue skirt and a shirtwaist, and instead of a single thick braid that hung down her back, her dark hair was gathered loosely at her nape and tied back with a blue ribbon.

He found himself staring at her as if he'd never laid eyes on her before. She sat directly across from him at Colonel Hawks' dining table, spooning small helpings of mashed potatoes and snow peas onto her plate and keeping her eyes no higher than the china serving dishes. She didn't look too comfortable. For sure, she looked like a fish out of water. Bet she hadn't worn drawers or a petticoat under duds like those since she was a girl. Guess she was learning how different her life was going to be from today on.

He felt kinda sorry for her. He'd spent four days watching her with his jaws clenched. Four days and four nights. Now, it looked like *her* jaws were clenched.

After Martha served her dessert of rice pudding and butterscotch cookies, she collared Colonel Hawks, tied a red gingham apron around his waist, and shooed Jack and Jonna onto the front porch. Jonna settled herself in the porch swing, and Jack eased himself down beside her and pushed the swing into a gentle back-and-forth motion.

It was a warm night, with just enough breeze to ruffle the leaves on the aspen trees, and the song of an evening sparrow filled the awkward silence. Finally he couldn't stand it one more minute. "Jonna? You doing all right?"

She didn't answer for so long he thought maybe she hadn't heard him. "Yes," she finally said. "I am all right."

"All through supper you looked...I don't know...different somehow. And you hardly said more'n three words."

She laughed. "I know only three words."

"I thought this wasn't gonna be easy for you. Maybe I should have warned you."

"True, is not easy, Jack. But I learn fast."

"Guess we were kinda busy during those four days we were tryin' to stay alive."

She smiled suddenly. "We did stay alive."

"Are you sorry now that you're here?"

She shook her head. "Not sorry. I am grateful. But...is still hard."

He shoved the swing into motion again. "Anything I can do to help?"

"Yes. Can be friend."

They rocked in silence for some minutes. "I want..." she began. "Want always you are honest to me. *With* me," she amended.

"You have my word, Jonna. I will always be honest with you. You might not like it, but I'll always tell you the truth."

She nodded. "Want coffee?"

"Yeah, sure." He'd rather have a shot of the colonel's bourbon, but coffee would have to suffice.

"I learn to make today. In pot with water. Tomorrow learn more, maybe rattled eggs."

"Scrambled, you mean?"

"Yes, scrambled." She stood up, and that's when he saw the moccasins on her feet. They reminded him of something he'd learned about Jonna the night they had escaped from the Sioux camp. She would go only so far to adapt to things that were unfamiliar to her. And she would go at her own pace. *Good for her!*

She stepped through the screen door and returned in a few minutes with a brimming china cup of coffee in her hand. She settled herself beside him on the swing, and he sipped the brew in silence, wondering why he couldn't think of a blessed thing to say.

"I ask something," she said suddenly. "You will come if…if…" She searched for a word. "If need help?"

"You mean if *I* need help? Or if *you* need help?"

"Both." She stuck out her hand. "Is bargain?"

Jack grinned. "Is bargain." He lifted her small hand in his and solemnly shook it.

"Will also be honest?"

"You mean tell you the truth?"

"Yes. Speak truth."

He chuckled. "I'm known on this post for being not only honest but being damn blunt. Doesn't always go over too well."

"What means 'blunt'?"

"Blunt is when you don't pretty up something you say."

He caught the glimmer of a smile. "Jonna is strong."

Yeah, but Jonna hasn't been around other people— other non-Indian people—for a lot of years. Got to wonder how thick her skin is.

They rocked away in silence for a good quarter of an hour, and then she brought the swing to a halt and stood up. "Would like to sleep under trees tonight, not in soft bed."

He got to his feet. "Was kinda nice, wasn't it? Even though we were just trying to survive."

"Yes," she said, lifting the empty coffee cup out of his hand. "Was nice when not afraid."

He gave her a long look and turned toward the porch steps. "Thanks for the coffee, Jonna."

When he crawled into his bunk that night, he lay awake for a long time, thinking about Jonna's small feet in those deerskin moccasins.

Chapter Eleven

A needle of fear crawled up Jonna's spine, and she wadded the huck dishtowel into a knot. "Ball? What is ball?"

Martha patiently smoothed out the towel and handed her another platter. "It's a dance, my dear. 'Ball' is a fancy name for a dance. Military posts like to give fancy names to things because they're so far from civilization."

"What people do at ball?"

"Why, they dance, of course. And they have refreshments—usually cookies and lemonade. And the officers' wives do a good deal of gossiping among themselves."

Jonna's stomach tightened. Would she be expected to dance at this ball? And talk with other women? The thought sent knives poking into her belly. "Are there children?"

"Oh, children are not allowed. A ball is for the officers and their wives who live at the post. And guests," she added. "You will be a guest."

Jonna sucked in her breath. "No," she said. "I will not be guest."

The plate Martha was rinsing slipped out of her hand, but Jonna managed to catch it before it struck the counter. "Not be a guest?" the older woman said. She dunked two more plates in the sudsy dishwater. "But my dear, whyever not?"

Jonna sucked in two more slow, deep breaths. "Because I do not know dancing. I do not know any person except you, and husband, and Jack Corder."

Martha nodded. "I can understand your reluctance, Jonna. But it would please the colonel and myself if you would join us."

Jonna shook her head. She could not do this. She could not be around people and not know what to say or how to act. A long silence descended, during which Martha continued to scrub plates in the soapy dishwater, and Jonna dried one after another and stacked it in the china cabinet. Finally, Martha toweled her hands dry, turned to Jonna, and propped her hands on her hips.

"I understand, my dear. Really I do. This whole week must have been difficult for you, and I admire the way you have met the challenges. It must seem never-ending, all the things you have to learn."

Jonna nodded. "It feels like tall mountain, and I am short people. Person," she corrected.

Martha turned back to her pan of soapy dishwater. "I am sure it does feel like a mountain, my dear. But I have watched you all this week, and I must say you have done well. Extremely well. I believe you are a very intelligent young woman. And," she added, "I believe you have courage."

Jonna said nothing for a full minute. Then she reached out and touched Martha's shoulder. "You are kind to me. You help me. Teach me much. If you and colonel wish, I will attend dance. But I will not do dancing."

Martha laughed, then wrapped her soapy hands

around Jonna and hugged her.

That evening after supper, Martha took her by the hand, climbed the stairs to the small bedroom, and swung the armoire door open. "Blue should be your color since your eyes are such a deep blue. But your skin is so suntanned, I think…" She stroked her chin. "I think you would look very pretty in pale yellow."

She rummaged through the hanging garments and withdrew a dress of yellow checked gingham with a wide ruffle near the hem and a narrower one around the deep square neckline. Jonna had to smile. She was learning something about American women. They could be just as stubborn as women among the Sioux! Just as stubborn as she herself was. That thought made her laugh out loud.

Martha sent her a puzzled look and patted her hand. "You will look beautiful in this dress, Jonna. *Very* beautiful."

She didn't care whether she looked beautiful. She only wanted to please Martha, who had been so encouraging, and her husband, Colonel Hawks, who was helping her learn many new words. So she would take a deep breath and attend this ball.

Martha whisked the yellow dress out of the armoire. "I'll just press out these wrinkles, my dear." While the sadiron heated on the kitchen stove downstairs, Jonna could hear Martha humming.

She didn't feel like humming. She felt like escaping.

****

Jack stood at the tiny sink in his quarters, studying himself in the mirror. He hated wearing his full-dress military uniform. On a warm summer evening like tonight, the tightly woven jacket would be suffocating, and he'd just as soon not wear his medals, either. But Colonel Hawks frowned if any of his officers showed up at one of his annual wingdings in anything but dress blues.

He splashed on some bay rum aftershave, checked that all his buttons were buttoned, and drew in a fortifying breath. The reception hall would be stifling, especially when the dancing started, and he always felt sorry for the musicians who would be working hard in a hot ballroom. Blowing a trumpet or scraping away on a violin must be sweaty work.

The minute he stepped up onto the wide veranda of the reception hall, he heard music, along with bursts of laughter and the buzz of a dozen conversations. When he walked in, Martha broke away from two tall, elegantly dressed officers' wives and flew toward him with both hands outstretched.

"Jack! How good of you to come this evening!"

He brushed his lips over her cheek. "I am honored, Martha. As always."

Two dimples appeared. "You are no such thing," she said with a laugh. "Don't you dare lie to me!"

He grinned at her. "I'd have to work hard to think up a lie you wouldn't spot, Martha."

"Good. Now you come with me. I want you to meet the newest addition to our corps of officers."

"We've met," Jack said shortly.

Martha laughed. "Oh, not *Lieutenant* Markley, Jack. I mean his wife, *Mrs*. Markley. Despite her taste in husbands, Lucinda Markley is a very nice woman."

He gritted his teeth but allowed Martha to drag him across the floor toward a group of chattering ladies who sat on the sidelines arranging and rearranging their skirts.

"Lucinda," Martha called when they drew near. "I want you to meet Major Jackson Corder, one of our most decorated officers."

A very young, very plain woman, almost invisible amid a puff of pink silk ruffles, raised her head. "I am pleased to meet you, Major."

Jack bent over her hand and got a whiff of cloyingly sweet perfume. "I am pleased as well, Mrs. Markley."

She tipped up her rather sharp-featured face. "Perhaps you know my husband, Sidney? Lieutenant Markley?"

"Yes, indeed," he said dryly. "I most certainly do."

She clasped her hands under her chin. "Sidney is just the bravest man in the whole army!"

Jack tried not to roll his eyes. "In what sense, ma'am?"

"Why, only last week, he single-handedly captured two renegade Indians. Surely you must have heard about it."

"I did, as a matter of fact. In great detail."

Martha gave his arm a tug. "Major Corder, you promised me a waltz, remember?" She smiled at Mrs. Markley and propelled Jack toward the refreshment table. "You know I hate waltzing, Jack. Forgive the fib, but I thought I should rescue you before—"

"I exploded," he finished.

Martha laughed. "Jack, you are a most perceptive man! Now, you will forgive me if I greet our other guests?"

Other guests, huh? Yeah, he could tell something

was up tonight. The minute he walked in, he felt an odd sense of expectation in the air. Maybe some visiting colonel from another post. Or had Martha planned some sort of surprise?

Colonel Hawks eased his portly figure up beside him. "Evening, Jack. Quite a crowd, wouldn't you say?"

"Martin, how come everyone seems so antsy tonight?"

"They're waiting."

"Waiting for what?"

The colonel frowned. "Martha didn't tell you?"

"Tell me what? All Martha did was drag me over to meet Lieutenant Markley's wife."

"Well then, I'll tell you what everyone is waiting for. Brace yourself."

At that moment, there was a flurry of activity around the entrance, and a crowd began to gather. The entire room fell silent except for a single male voice. "Holy Jehoshaphat!" he said in an awed tone.

A stunning young woman in a ruffled yellow gingham dress took a tentative step into the room, and the crowd surged forward. Her long, dark hair was tied back with a yellow ribbon, and the loose waves fell to her shoulders. Jack stared at her along with every other male in the room and felt his heart bellyflop into his stomach.

Martin leaned toward him. "Recognize her?"

"Nope."

The colonel poked his arm. "Look closer."

All at once she looked up, and a fist punched him in the gut. *Jonna?* He didn't believe his own eyes.

The music started up again, and what looked like a

whole regiment of officers descended on her. As they closed in, he saw a flicker of fear in her eyes, and without thinking, he found himself moving toward her. He elbowed his fellow officers aside, and when he reached her, she looked up and sent him a shaky smile. He held out his hand. Then, without a word, he opened a path through the crowd and walked her out onto the veranda.

It was cooler out there. The air smelled of pine trees and some sort of flowery scent. Jonna, maybe.

"Jack," she breathed. "I did not expect so many persons. I mean people."

In only a week, she'd learned to speak in long sentences? One week? One short week? He wondered what she would learn in the *next* week.

He couldn't stop staring at her. "Jonna…"

"Yes?" she said. "I am American now?"

He swallowed. "You were always American, Jonna. Just not so…" Not so beautiful his mouth went dry just looking at her. "Uh, would you like to go back inside and dance?"

She shook her head. "Not yet. I will not dance. I will sit with ladies inside. Learn things."

He almost laughed. He found a couple of rickety wooden chairs, and they sat without talking for an awkward few minutes. Her face was a study. He'd never seen Jonna look so uncomfortable unless it was the day she first arrived at the fort. Then she had looked uneasy. Now she looked downright scared.

"I warned you this wasn't gonna be easy, remember?"

"Yes, I remember. Is *not* easy. Learning to speak correctly not easy. This dancing not easy."

"As I recall, you were dead set on getting away from the Sioux. Are you sorry?"

"No," she said quickly. "Only sometimes…" She broke off and studied her hands.

"Care to define 'sometimes'?"

Jonna took a long, slow breath. "This, tonight, is worst. I do not like to be with many people all at once. I do not know what to say."

"You don't really have to say much, Jonna. All you have to do is dance with whatever man asks you. You don't have to *talk* to him."

She sent him an exasperated look that said *you're a man, you can't possibly understand.* "I do not know dancing, Jack."

"Well, hell, seems to me that's easy compared to learning to talk English again."

She sent him That Look again. It was getting under his skin. "Is *not* easy. Talking English also not easy."

"You know, I figured all this would be hard for you. Guess I thought you had enough gumption to do it."

"What means 'gumption'?"

"Having gumption means trying like hell when you're scared," he said carefully.

She said nothing for a long minute. "I have gumption," she said quietly. "Is not kind of you to…" She searched for a word. "…poke at me."

"Yeah, guess not. Didn't know you were so thin-skinned. That means over-sensitive," he added.

Jonna jumped to her feet. When he stood up, she moved in close to him and jabbed her forefinger into his chest. "You are not nice man, Jack!"

"The hell I'm not! Maybe there are some things

you don't want to hear."

She jabbed his chest again. "I hear everything you say. Some things not nice."

He stepped back, out of forefinger range. "Maybe you need to hear them anyway. You ever think of that?"

She didn't answer, just turned away, and moved toward the reception hall. He caught up with her, walked her back inside, and guided her over to the chattering women seated on the sideline. He headed straight for Lucinda Markley. She might be that ass Sidney Markley's wife, but she had a kind face.

"Mrs. Markley, this is Jonna Lander. Jonna is…visiting the post."

Mrs. Markley moved over to make room and gestured for Jonna to sit beside her. Jonna sent him a long look, and he retreated across the room to the refreshment table so he could keep an eye on her.

Martin stepped up beside him and offered a glass of lemonade. "Wouldn't you say that girl is a wonder?"

"That girl is a shock, that's for sure."

The colonel chuckled. "Every man in the room, even the married ones, think so, too."

"How did she—?"

"Dunno, son. Men have been asking that ever since Eve ate that apple!"

Jack shot a glance across the room where Jonna was sitting beside Lucinda Markley, smiling at something the woman said. Then, on the far side of the room, he saw Lieutenant Sidney Markley begin to circle toward his wife. Jack watched the man approach the seated women and then stop. But he didn't stop in front of his wife. He stopped in front of Jonna! Lucinda looked startled, but Markley paid no attention. He pulled Jonna to her feet and propelled her onto the dance floor. He moved in close, slipped his arm around Jonna's waist, and pulled her roughly toward him. Jack set his lemonade glass on the table and started across the floor.

Suddenly Markley jerked and snatched his hand away, then moved in close again. Just as he yanked Jonna against his chest, Jack muscled his way between them and swept Jonna into his arms.

"Don't talk," he murmured. "Just hang on." He whirled her away and back out onto the veranda.

"You all right?" he asked. She still stood in his arms, but he didn't care. "Jonna?"

Tears glistened on her eyelashes. *Damn him! He's frightened her.* But once again, she surprised him. "I do not like him," she said. "So I poke with pin."

"Huh? Is that why he jerked?"

"Yes. Hatpin is sharp. Martha give to me."

He chuckled. "Guess I don't need to protect you like I thought," he said.

"Yes, you do, Jack."

He studied her face. "Why? If you've got Martha's hatpin, you don't need—"

She looked up. "Yes, you do," she repeated.

"You still wearing that knife around your…" He glanced at the bare skin above the neckline of her yellow dress. "Around your waist, maybe?"

She nodded.

"Kinda hard to get at, wearin' a dress, isn't it?"

"I do not wear under dress," she said. "Wear around…" She pointed somewhere below her waist.

"Your…um…your thigh?"

When she nodded, he threw back his head and

laughed.

"Is not funny, Jack."

"Sure it is. I just spent ten minutes sweating, and you—"

"Are not sweating."

"Yeah." He wondered why he didn't feel like laughing anymore.

"You teach me to dance?"

"Uh…well, sure." He reached out his arm, pulled her toward him, and drew in a deep breath. She smelled like some kind of flowers, and all at once, the last thing on his mind was teaching her how to dance.

Chapter Twelve

The musicians were playing a two-step. At least he thought it was a two-step. It could have been a Russian hopak for all he knew.

"What about my feet?" she whispered.

"You've got two of them," Jack said.

"I mean what do I *do* with feet?"

At the moment, he hadn't the remotest idea. "Um, I think you just move them back and forth with me. Real slow."

"You *think* so?" She tipped her head up and looked at him with a frown. "You do not *know*?"

"I did an hour ago. Now I'm not so sure."

"You are joking me!"

"Wish I was, Jonna. The truth is I'm feeling a little off-balance this evening."

"Ah. Shoes hurt?"

"My shoes don't hurt, no." *It's my brain that's hurting.*

"It is me?"

Oh, yes. One hundred percent yes. "Sort of."

"What means 'sort of'?"

"It means…it means a little bit. A small amount."

"Ah, I understand. One-half cup of flour is 'small amount'."

"Huh? You been baking cakes?"

"No. Cooks. Cookies," she corrected. "With sugars

on top."

"You mean sugar cookies." *If this isn't the most inane conversation I've ever had with a woman, I'll jump in the nearest horse trough.*

She said nothing for a full minute, then looked up at him with accusing blue eyes. "You are not teaching feet!"

Nope, he sure as hell wasn't 'teaching feet.' He was trying not to breathe in the faint, flowery scent of her hair. *Not only that, Corder, you're busy learning some things about yourself.* In his entire twenty-seven years he'd never felt tongue-tied on a dance floor. What was now bumbling around in his brain was the difference between the Jonna of a week ago, a girl with a dirt-streaked face sucking on sand-encrusted strips of muslin, and the Jonna of tonight. Jonna, who was warm and alive in his arms. Jonna, who smelled like flowers.

He noticed his fellow officers hovering three deep on the sidelines, waiting for a chance to cut in, but it was Colonel Martin Hawks who stepped into his path and swung Jonna out of his arms. Jack breathed a sigh of relief. No soldier would risk cutting in on his commanding officer!

He drifted back to the refreshment table with a thirst for something stronger than lemonade. He knew Martin kept a bottle of bourbon stashed somewhere, and by the time he found it and glugged down two hefty swallows, he felt a bit more in control. But when he focused on the dance floor again, he saw it was not Colonel Hawks who held Jonna in his arms but Lieutenant Sidney Markley.

He tried to talk himself into feeling philosophical about it, but it didn't work. Jonna was young and female and so beautiful it made breathing difficult, and he had no right…

Then he noticed a white-faced Lucinda Markley sitting on the sidelines, watching her husband. The lieutenant had an odd half-smile on his face, and he was talking a mile a minute, but it was obvious Jonna wasn't paying the least attention. Then Markley suddenly pivoted, and Jack saw Jonna's face. Her eyes were shut tight, and she was frowning in a way he'd never seen before.

He gritted his teeth, and all at once, he couldn't stand it one more minute. He started across the floor, and when he got close enough, he "accidentally" bumped into Lieutenant Markley and pulled a startled Jonna free. He waltzed her to the doorway and out onto the veranda.

She sent him a smile he'd never forget. "Now I know everything about dancing."

Everything? What is "everything"? He couldn't resist one question. "Did you learn to waltz?"

"I learn many things tonight, Jack. Waltz was not one of them."

****

At breakfast the next morning, Jonna startled the colonel and Martha with an announcement. "I need to do something."

Martha's gray eyebrows rose. "Do what, my dear?"

Colonel Hawks set his coffee cup on the saucer with a sharp click. "Maybe you need to give her a bigger hatpin, Martha. Keep Sidney Markley in line.

"No," Jonna said. "Hatpin big enough. I need to be busy."

"Busy! But, my dear, you're busy all the time,

helping me in the kitchen, gathering the eggs every morning, studying your etiquette book."

"Not enough," she said quietly. "I want to be real part of life here."

"What do you have in mind, Jonna?" the colonel asked.

You have place for sick soldiers?"

"A hospital?" the colonel asked. "We have an infirmary at the post, if that's what you mean."

"Yes, infirmary. I know healing. I can help at infirmary."

"My dear," Martha said with a frown, "are you sure about this?"

"I am sure, yes. Who is at infirmary?"

"Only two doctors and one orderly."

"What does orderly do?"

The colonel cleared his throat. "Well, the orderly changes dressings and administers medicine and—"

"I can do," Jonna announced.

"But…but the orderly is a soldier here at the post," Martha said. "Not a woman."

"Why not woman?"

Colonel Hawks grinned. "She's got a point, Martha. None of the officers' wives have any nurse's training—"

Martha sniffed. "None of the officers' wives would set foot in the infirmary, Martin. Not one of them would get her hands dirty doing something useful. Except maybe Lucinda Markley."

"And me," Jonna said. "I would get hands dirty."

The colonel studied her for a long moment. "Well, why not? You could ask Doc Brownell about it. Maybe he and Doctor Solman could use some help."

Jonna gulped a last swallow of coffee, got to her feet, and untied her red gingham apron.

Martha watched her with a frown. "Don't you want to finish your—"

But Jonna was already out the door and down the porch steps.

"—breakfast?"

The colonel laughed aloud. "Let her go, Martha. She probably knows more remedies for what ails a person than the doctors."

Martha buttered a hot biscuit. "That girl is going to be hard to keep up with, Martin."

"Yep," the colonel said. "I saw that right off."

****

Jonna flew across the parade ground so intent on her mission she didn't see Jack until he stepped into her path. "Where are you going in such a hurry?"

"To infirmary."

His eyebrows went up. "You feeling sick?"

"No. Not sick."

"Then how come—?"

She propped her hands on her hips. "You are full of questions! Every time I say something, you have another question. I do not like."

"Kinda touchy this morning, aren't you?"

"Touchy? What is 'touchy'?"

Jack grinned. "Touchy means…well, it means out of sorts. Angry."

She pinned him with narrowed blue eyes. "Was not angry until you stopped me," she said carefully.

"Well then, how come you're 'not angry' and on your way to the infirmary this morning?"

Jonna just looked at him. "Do you always ask so

many questions?"

"No, not usually. It's just that—"

"Is bad manners," she interrupted. "Etiquette book says so."

"Now, just a damn minute, Miss High and Mighty! I ask questions because I'm interested in how you're getting along."

"Why?"

He gritted his teeth. Man, Jonna could poke his temper into a burn easier than anyone he'd ever met. "Because I'm interested, like I said."

"Then do not be interested." She started past him, but he caught her arm. "Listen, Jonna. Martha and the colonel are trying to help you adjust to life here on the post. I'm trying, too."

"That I know. But you...you are nosing. I mean nosy. Is none of your business if I am sick or why I go to infirmary."

He huffed out a breath. "Well, dammit, you might be right there. Sure is hard to be halfway friendly or helpful if you're gonna bite my head off every time I ask—"

"What means 'bite head off'?"

Oh, hell. "It means get mad. Angry. It means to speak sharply."

"I do not want to bite head off, Jack. I want to go to infirmary."

"Right," he snapped. "You have a real clever way of circling around a question without answering it, you know that?"

She looked up at him and smiled. "Yes, I know that." She brushed past him and continued on her way.

"What does your etiquette book say about that?" he

shouted.

"Book says always to say 'please,'" she called over her shoulder.

He had to laugh. Never met a woman who could outmaneuver him so fast and make him so damn mad while she was doing it. And still keep him coming back for more. Now, why was that?

The question nagged at him for the rest of the day.

****

The infirmary was a small white-painted building with a shake roof and rough wooden steps. Jonna paused at the entrance to catch her breath and try to quell her jitters. She shouldn't be nervous. She knew a great deal about tending ailing people, from warriors with arrow wounds to women in childbirth. She knew the Sioux way of treating the sick, but maybe the methods used by American doctors were different. Maybe the American doctors would laugh at her. Maybe...

She gave herself a mental shake. She would not let her fears stop her. She could offer her knowledge and her skills, even if she did learn them from the Sioux. Then she would be part of life here at Fort Kearney, would she not? She took a deep breath, walked inside, and nodded at the young soldier at the desk.

"Doctor Brownell is here?"

He looked up and frowned. "You ailing, miss?"

"No."

"Then how come you want to see the doctor?"

She drew herself up as tall as she could and looked straight into the soldier's eyes. "Doctor Brownell," she repeated. "Is important."

"Oh. Oh, sure, miss." Without another word, the

young soldier marched off down the hallway.

Her heart began to race. She knew this was the right thing for her to do. She must be more than a guest of Martha and Colonel Hawks. She must learn how to be part of life here at Fort Kearney.

In a few minutes, the soldier returned, accompanied by a portly man in a stained white coat. "Yes, miss? What can I do for you?"

She tried to smile, but her lips wouldn't obey. "Can give me work to do," she said.

A frown creased the doctor's broad forehead. "Work? What kind of work?"

"Can help with caring."

The frown deepened. "Can you, now?" He studied her face. "You're that girl Colonel Hawks took in, aren't you?"

She nodded. "I am Jonna Lander. When I live with Sioux, I learn much. I know how to help with sick people."

"Lived with the Sioux, huh? I'll bet you know more about nursing than most of our orderlies. Why don't you come this way, Miss Lander? I'll show you around."

She hid her smile, stepped past the goggle-eyed soldier, and followed Doctor Brownell down the hallway.

****

Later that day, Jack learned Jonna was helping out at the post infirmary. That figured. Jonna probably knew remedies the doctors had never heard of. Doc Brownell was lucky to have her. Then he had to laugh. He'd bet she wouldn't take no for an answer, and the doc had finally given in and taken her on.

For the rest of that week, he caught no more than a flash of Jonna's blue denim skirt as she marched across the parade ground to the post infirmary, and when Martha invited him for supper on Sunday, he couldn't wait to hear how she was doing. He shaved, put on a clean shirt, and even picked some wild roses for Martha. But when he climbed the steps onto the colonel's wide front porch, he suddenly felt a twinge of nerves.

Nerves! Jumpin' juniper, that made no sense. He'd taken supper with the colonel and his wife dozens of times these past months, so why should he be nervous tonight? He tapped on the front door screen.

"Roses!" Martha sang. "Oh, Jack, how thoughtful!"

"Picked 'em this morning."

"Come right on in and sit yourself down," she ordered. "We're having roast chicken and stuffing!"

"You didn't slaughter your favorite egg-laying hen, did you?" he joked.

"Heavens, no. This isn't *chicken*-chicken. It's some kind of *wild* chicken Jonna trapped in the woods."

"In the woods!" He spun to confront the colonel. "Martin, Jonna shouldn't leave the post without an escort."

"She had an escort," the colonel returned.

Jack frowned. "Good God, not Lieutenant—"

"What do you take me for?" Martin shot. "I wouldn't trust Sidney Markley within ten feet of Jonna. Her escort this morning was *me*."

Jack hid his relief and scanned the dining room. "Where is Jonna?"

"Still at the infirmary," the colonel volunteered. "Probably teaching the doctors how to stitch up wounds like the Indians do. Next I expect she'll be in the surgery, showing them how to make incisions."

Jack didn't laugh. He knew Jonna liked learning things. He also knew she was usually convinced she was right about everything. That was admirable when she really *was* right about something, but she didn't know diddly-squat about life here at an army post. Sometimes being so sure she was right about something just made her pigheaded and stubborn.

"Doc Brownell is quite taken with her," the colonel said. "Of course, Brownell's married, but Doctor Solman isn't. He's also quite taken with Jonna."

Jack said nothing. Martha pointed at the dining table, and he sat down across from the colonel. Martha sent him a twinkly-eyed look. "Sooner or later, the young single men on this post will come courting, Jack. Some might be serious; others will see whether they can sweet-talk her into a kiss. And then—"

"Then," her husband interrupted, "we'd better get a preacher from Mason City out here."

Jack heard the back door close. "There she is now," Martha said. "Jonna? Jack's here. He's taking supper with us tonight."

There was a long pause, and then he heard Jonna's voice. "Oh."

Jack frowned. *She sure doesn't sound happy about that! Guess I better watch my step.*

Martha excused herself and disappeared into the kitchen while Jonna's light footsteps receded up the staircase.

"Women," the colonel breathed. "God bless 'em all, especially my Martha. She's one in a million."

Jack nodded and accepted the glass of wine the

colonel offered. "Jonna," Martin added, raising his glass, "isn't far behind."

His first swallow of wine went down just fine. When Jonna appeared in the doorway, he gulped another mouthful, and a wave of warmth traveled all the way down to his toes. She wore a plain blue skirt and a blue gingham shirtwaist, and she was the prettiest thing he'd seen on this godforsaken post in a long, long time. Without thinking, he rose to his feet.

She settled on the chair across from him, and right away, he noticed the worried look on her face. "Lucinda Markley invites me for tea," she announced.

"Really!" Martha exclaimed. She exchanged a long look with the colonel. "I wonder why."

"She expects baby. Wants to talk."

"When?" Martha asked.

"February, might be."

"I mean when are you invited for tea?"

"Day after day," Jonna said. "I mean tomorrow. Tea is tomorrow."

Jack had made no secret of his dislike for Lieutenant Markley. He didn't know enough about Mrs. Markley to make a judgment, but a niggle of unease zinged up his spine. Maybe Mrs. Markley was just being friendly, but for some reason, he had a bad feeling about it. Maybe Lucinda Markley was a sharp-tongued gossip who'd like nothing better than tearing into Jonna like an angry buzzard because her husband had shown an inappropriate interest in her.

Or maybe the wine was making him fuzzy-headed, and he wasn't thinking clearly. Nevertheless, after supper and a generous slice of Martha's lemon meringue pie, he took his coffee and walked out onto the front porch with Jonna. When she settled herself in the porch swing, Jack paced back in forth in front of her.

"You like Lucinda Markley?" he asked.

She nodded. "She is nice lady."

"What about her husband, Lieutenant Markley?"

"Is not nice," she said quickly.

He stopped and bent toward her. "Markley is more than 'not nice,' Jonna. I'd watch out for him."

"Yes, I watch."

"He gonna be at this tea tomorrow?"

She shook her head. "Only ladies at tea. Wives of officers."

Oh, boy. Lucinda Markley might be a nice person, but he couldn't help wondering why she'd married a snake like the lieutenant. Maybe she wasn't as nice as she seemed. He didn't know about the other officers' wives. They'd probably be jealous of someone as young and pretty as Jonna.

"You, uh, sure about this tea thing?"

"Yes, am sure. Want to know other ladies. They will be friends."

He shook his head. "Jonna, sometimes not everyone is as nice as Lucinda Markley. Sometimes…" *How the hell do I warn her that jealous women can be real cats with real claws?* "Uh, sometimes women on an army post get kinda…um, kinda set in their ways."

"What mean 'set in ways'? What do you try to say, Jack?"

He groaned under his breath. "I'm trying to say I don't think you should go to this tea tomorrow."

"I *am* going to tea," she said, an edge in her voice. "Not your business."

"Well, that's true, Jonna. It isn't any of my business who you have tea with. But remember that night when I promised to always tell you the truth?"

She nodded and looked up at him but didn't say anything.

"Well, here's the truth. There're two laundresses working here at the post," he said. "They wash and iron the officers' uniforms. Sometimes they also do laundry for the officers' wives. And...well, they talk some. What they say about some of those wives isn't too flattering."

"Ah, I understand. Sioux women the same."

"Well, then? You still going to tea?"

"I go to tea. Make friends."

"Well, hell, remember I warned you." He turned away and tossed the rest of his coffee over the porch railing.

Jonna sent him a long look, lifted the empty cup out of his hand, and walked into the house without a word.

Chapter Thirteen

The next afternoon, Martha brushed her lips across Jonna's cheek and sent her off with a plate of sugar cookies to what she privately confided to her husband was the lion's den. When the front door closed, she settled on the settee in the parlor with the shawl she was knitting.

Martin gave her a long look. "Stop your worrying, Martha."

She sent him a withering smile. "Martin, you have no idea what cats women can be!"

"Sure don't," he agreed. "Don't much like cats, Martha. That's why I married you."

She threw the ball of blue yarn at him. "Oh, you…that's just like a man!"

"And thank God for that," he murmured under his breath. "Want some of this bourbon?"

She ignored his offer. "Jonna hasn't a mean bone in her body, Martin. I can't say as much for many of the officers' wives."

"You think maybe the Indians beat the meanness out of her?" he joked.

"No," Martha snapped. "They probably treated her with respect. I'm not so sure about the army wives." She glanced at the man sitting beside her. "Bourbon, you say? Well, perhaps just a small sip."

****

Jonna made her way down Officers Row, the plate of sugar cookies in her hand. She was concentrating so hard on keeping the cookies from sliding off the plate she almost collided with a horse walking through the post gate. The rider pulled it up short, and the animal shied away from her. "Jesus, Jonna, watch where you're going!" Jack dismounted and marched toward her, his mouth pressed into an unsmiling line.

She laid one hand on the napkin-swathed plate of cookies and looked up. "Jack! I almost drop cookies!"

"You weren't paying much attention, Jonna. That's not like you. Where are you going with the cookies?"

"I go to tea at Lucinda Markley's house. I watch cookies, not feet."

"Nervous?"

She hesitated. "Yes. Have not been this frightened since night we rode away from Sioux camp."

Jack nodded and fell in beside her. "I bet this is worse."

"Yes, is worse. When we escaped, I knew what to do. But I have been thinking. At tea with American ladies, I do not know what to do."

"Never could understand why women have tea parties. I've got my suspicions, though. Wanna hear them?"

"This feels like diving off cliff into dark canyon."

"That sounds about right. I felt the same way on my first army patrol."

"What did you do?"

He chuckled. "Loaded my revolver and kept a sharp eye out."

"This..." She tipped her chin at the plate of cookies. "...is my revolver. But even with revolver I am still afraid."

"Hell, Jonna, if you're scared, why do it? Why go drink tea with a bunch of gossipy women if you don't have to?"

She shook her head. "You do not understand, Jack. I want to live here at Fort Kearney. So I must learn how to fit in." She gave him a long look, then turned away.

"Can't talk you out of it, huh?" he said at her back.

"No." She walked on.

All the houses on Officers Row were small and in need of paint, and they all looked exactly the same. Lucinda said she lived in the fourth house, where a scraggly patch of yellow flowers bordered the path, and a large American flag hung on the porch. She rapped on the door, waited, then rapped again.

After what seemed like a long time, Lucinda appeared, wearing a rustly pink silk dress, and gave a whoop of delight. "I'm so very pleased you could join us! Do come in, Jonna. The other ladies are waitin' in the parlor."

She drew in a deep breath and hesitantly moved into a stifling room where three women she didn't know had spread their skirts over two green brocade settees facing each other. The room smelled of lavender and something sweet.

"Ladies," Lucinda announced, "let me introduce Jonna Lander, from—? Why, my goodness, Jonna, I don't know where you come from."

"I do not remember name of place," Jonna murmured.

"Never mind, then. Over there on the sofa is Dolly Brownell, and next to her is Nellene Schwammer. She doesn't like the nickname 'Nellie,' so we call her Nell."

Dolly and Nell inclined their heads but did not smile.

"And," Lucinda continued, "sitting across from them is Sophronia Tipton. Sophronia comes from Boston."

"Everyone calls me Sophie," the woman said. "Do come sit by me, Miss Launder."

"My name is Lander," Jonna corrected in a quiet voice. "Not Launder."

"Jonna brought cookies to have with our tea," Lucinda announced. "Wasn't that nice of her?"

"Yes, indeed," the woman called Sophie said. "I expect Colonel Hawks' wife made them," she added. The other two women nodded but said nothing.

"No," Jonna said. "I make."

The one called Nell twitched her green silk skirt. "You mean you can cook?"

"Of certain. I mean, of course."

"Isn't that amazing, Dolly?" Nell poked the woman next to her. "Surprising, is it not?"

"Quite," Dolly said.

"Oh, come now, ladies," Lucinda said, setting a silver tea tray down on a side table. "Most young women out here in the West can cook. Some," she added with a smile, "are expert cookie-makers."

"Well, *I* cannot cook," the sharp-faced one in the green dress said. That was Nell, Jonna remembered. "Back home in New Orleans, we always had a cook."

"But Nell," Lucinda pointed out, "we are not in New Orleans now. Milk?" she added quickly. "Sugar?"

"Both," Nell and Sophie said together.

"Jonna?"

"Neither," she managed.

"Neither!" the one called Dolly said loudly. "Why, goodness me, aren't you the Puritan."

"I do not know what is 'Puritan,' " Jonna said.

"Dolly," Lucinda said suddenly. "Tea?"

"Of course. That's why I'm here, is it not? To have tea and meet…what was your name again?"

"Jonna. Jonna Lander."

"Speak up, girl! Joanna, was it?"

Lucinda's face changed color. "Jonna Lander," she said clearly. "L-a-n-d-e-r. Do have one of *Jonna's* cookies."

"Jonna," Sophie said, helping herself to three of the biggest cookies. "That's a really odd name. Is it French?"

"I do not think so," Jonna answered. "I am named after father. He came from Ireland."

Sophie bit into a cookie. "Pity," she said in a disparaging tone. "One's family lineage is *so* important. However, your cookies are surprisingly acceptable."

"Ladies," Lucinda said, raising her voice. "Y'all are guests in my house, and I expect you to show good manners. Jonna, please have some tea." She handed her a delicate china cup.

"Nell? Dolly? Would you care for a cookie?"

Jonna bit her lip. Lucinda's three guests were being mean on purpose, even though Lucinda Markley was going out of her way to make her feel welcome. The other ladies did not like her, and she did not know why. She couldn't help wondering why Lucinda's friends spoke with forked tongues. She also wondered why a nice woman, a kind woman like Lucinda, would marry a man like Lieutenant Markley.

She studied the faces of the women gathered in

Lucinda's parlor. They were all attractive—more attractive than Lucinda, who was rather plain-looking. Jonna wondered what their husbands were like. She knew Dolly's husband, Dr. Brownell. He was a good doctor, a good man. But Dolly. . . Dolly had a sharp tongue. Sophie said mean things on purpose. And the one called Nell was even meaner.

She straightened her spine. Very well. She could be sharp-tongued, too. She had learned many things in the eight years she lived among the jealous wives of Sioux warriors. Carefully, she set her teacup on its saucer and drew in a long breath.

"I wonder," she began, "I wonder how you make beautiful dresses." She gestured at the array of full skirts puffing over the settee upholstery.

"Well," Nell began, "on an Army post this far from civilized life, I have learned how to sew my own dresses."

Jonna made a show of inspecting Nell's green silk skirt. "Yes, I see." She shook her head. "Bad stitches do not show much."

Lucinda gasped and clapped one hand over her mouth. But her eyes were dancing, and a slight nod told Jonna it was acceptable to fight back.

Sophie smoothed her hand over her lavender dimity skirt. "I purchase all *my* dresses ready-made," she announced. "From Berman's in Chicago. I don't suppose you have even heard of Berman's, Joanna. They are very exclusive. They ship all my orders by Wells Fargo."

Jonna drew in a deep breath. "Then," she said in feigned confusion, "why do they not fit better?"

Sophie paled. "I beg your pardon?"

But Jonna wasn't finished. "Your dress too tight over your chest."

"Perhaps a good seamstress could adjust the fit," Lucinda said quickly. "You could ask one of the laundresses."

Sophie blinked her small brown eyes. "Why, thank you for your concern, ladies. Lucinda, I notice *your* dress is a bit tight."

"Well," Lucinda said with a laugh, "y'all are sharp-eyed for certain. Actually, my dress fits snugly because I am…I am expecting."

While the ladies oohed and ahhed over that news, Lucinda caught Jonna's eye and winked. Then Dolly, whose crinkly brown dress was pulled so tight across her ample chest a button threatened to pop off, made the mistake of criticizing Jonna's blue gingham skirt. "I see you prefer a drab, understated style of attire, Joanna."

"Jonna," she corrected. "My name is Jonna, not Joanna. And I do not choose skirt."

"Well, my heavens, who *does* choose your wardrobe?"

Jonna hid a smile. "Colonel Hawks' wife chooses clothes."

An embarrassed silence fell, followed by uncomfortable laughter. "Jonna," Sophie said loudly, "you are turning out to be a worthy opponent."

The others nodded.

"I do not wish to be opponent," Jonna said, looking from one to the other. "I wish to be friend."

"And that," Lucinda said, rising to her feet, "is exactly what you shall be!"

The women were full of advice, but it was obvious

to Jonna they didn't know what they were talking about. Jonna *did* know, and for the next two hours, the ladies listened in fascinated silence as Jonna described remedies for morning sickness and how to ease the pains of labor.

She did not tell them the knowledge she was sharing was what she had learned from the Sioux women.

When she returned to Colonel Hawks' house, she found Martha and the colonel sitting side by side on the porch swing. "Well," Martha inquired as she climbed the steps, "how did it go?"

"Tea good," she answered. "Ladies not nice."

"Oh, my," Martha said under her breath. She sent her husband a significant look and set her knitting aside. "I should have warned you."

"You did warn me," Jonna said with a laugh. "Jack, too. Next time, I listen."

The colonel chuckled. "You willing to share the details?" he asked.

Jonna sank onto the rocking chair next to the swing. "Lucinda Markley is kind person, but other ladies have tongues that wag at both ends."

"Two-faced, you mean," Martha clarified.

"Mrs. Tipton, Sophie, was worst. Mean in spirit."

"That figures," the colonel muttered. "Her husband's pretty spineless."

"What mean spineless?"

"No backbone," he explained.

"What about Nell Schwammer?" Martha asked. "I never liked her husband, George. He acts too big for his britches."

"Britches?" Jonna said. "Oh, you mean trousers."

"Too big for his trousers doesn't sound right," the colonel said with a laugh. "His wife must be just as bad. Probably not too civilized."

Jonna grinned. "I know 'civilized,' " she said with a smile. "Means polite. Not like tea ladies."

Martha sent her husband an I-told-you-so look. "Well, what *about* Nell Schwammer?"

"She very angry lady. Bad temper. She is jealous Lucinda expecting baby."

Martha's grey eyebrows went up. "Is she, now? That's news to me!"

"Might explain Lieutenant Markley's interest in Jonna," the colonel said.

"Might, yes," Martha said. "But Martin, how many young, pretty, single women have you seen at the post lately?"

"You mean in addition to our two laundresses?"

"*Including* our laundresses," Martha clarified. "Both of them are young and unmarried, but pretty? As pretty as Jonna? I don't think so."

Jonna frowned. "Woman must be pretty to wash clothes?"

The colonel raised his bushy eyebrows. "Fair point. Lieutenant Schwammer, Nell's husband, spends more time hanging around the laundry shack than drilling new recruits."

"But his uniform is always clean and ironed," Martha murmured. She lifted the ball of yarn in her lap and unwound a few lengths.

Jonna watched her hands. "Nell smiled and smiled. I do not trust."

"What about Dolly Brownell, Dr. Brownell's wife?"

"Dolly very serious. I think not happy."

"That might explain why she's so interested in Jack Corder, might it not?" Martha sent her husband a quick glance. "Or am I just imagining things?"

The colonel stood up. "My dear, you never 'just imagine things.' A more sharp-eyed woman doesn't walk this earth."

"Sharp-eyed?" Jonna asked. "What is sharp-eyed? Like sharp tongue?"

"He means I notice things most people miss," Martha said.

"Ah. See like hawk."

The colonel grinned. "Sounds like your tea party was plenty interesting."

Jonna nodded. "Is true. I learn many new words. And," she said with a laugh, "even with ladies saying unkind things, I win. I will enjoy next time tea."

Chapter Fourteen

The next morning, Jonna had just finished changing the dressing on a wounded soldier's arm when Dr. Brownell stepped into the ward. "Jonna, someone is waiting to see you."

She looked up in surprise. "To see me? Here at infirmary?" She followed the doctor down the hall to find Lucinda Markley pacing back and forth in front of the young soldier sitting behind the desk.

"Lucinda! What is wrong?"

"Oh, Jonna, I am sorry to disturb you, but…" She glanced at the soldier and tipped her head toward the doorway. When they were out of earshot, Lucinda turned to her, twisting her hands in her ruffled pink skirt. "You're the only one who can help me."

"Help with what?"

Lucinda bent toward her and lowered her voice. "Help with my morning sickness. I can't keep anything down but dry crackers, and the sutler's supply is running low."

"Morning sick—Oh, you mean vomiting? Is that right word?"

Lucinda nodded. "Yes, vomiting. In the morning mostly, but sometimes I feel sick all day long. When you described those Indian remedies at tea last Sunday, I knew you could help me."

Jonna nodded. "You need tea of yerba santa."

"Yerba—? What on earth is that?"

"Is herb," Jonna explained. "Grows near streams. Sioux women use leaves in special tea for sickness."

"Could you get me some of these yerba leaves?"

"Yes." Jonna smiled at her. "I will get."

Lucinda grasped both her hands. "Oh, thank you, Jonna. I am so very grateful. And in exchange, perhaps I could help with English lessons."

"You would help?"

Lucinda laughed. "Yes, I will help. I promise."

Jonna swallowed hard. "Will bring herb soon. First must find where herb grows."

"Could you come for tea on Saturday? We could start your English lessons then."

Jonna nodded. "I will bring herbs for sickness."

Lucinda turned to leave, then hesitated. "My friends were rude to you last Sunday. I want to apologize for them. But despite their bad manners, I hope you and I will become good friends."

Jonna nodded and touched her hand. "You are friend already. And teacher," she added with a smile. Lucinda's brown eyes grew shiny, and she pressed Jonna's hand.

That night at supper, she told Martha and the colonel she planned to explore some of the creeks to gather yerba santa leaves.

"Absolutely not!" Martha said.

"But must find—"

The colonel cleared his throat. "Jonna, it is not safe for you to leave the post alone and ramble along some creek. I will provide an escort."

"But I can ride horse!"

The colonel's eyebrows rose. "A horse?"

She nodded. "Yerba santa not easy to find. Maybe travel far."

Martha bit her lip. "Not too far, I hope."

"With an escort," the colonel repeated.

The following morning, after a breakfast of bacon and sourdough biscuits, which Jonna made, she walked out onto the porch to find Jack Corder waiting at the bottom of the steps with two saddled horses. "Jack! Why are you here so early?"

"I'm your escort. Colonel Hawks doesn't want you riding away from the post on your own."

She gestured at the horses, both roan mares. "Where is black horse?"

"Getting saddle-broke. Not smart for the army to have a horse nobody but you can ride. I still can't believe you stole it right from under the noses of those Cheyennes."

Jonna smiled. "You have much to learn, Jack."

He rolled his eyes. "You know something, Jonna? A man doesn't like to have his nose rubbed in things he doesn't know."

"Ah. Then I will not remind you how to steal black horse."

He clenched his teeth and mounted his horse. They passed through the post entry gate and headed north. The early morning sun was warm, and the air smelled of pine trees and dust.

"There's four creeks within a ten-mile radius of the fort," Jack said. "Salmon Creek's about a mile from here. We should check that one out first."

"Creek has shady places?"

"Shady places? Some. You looking for shade?"

"I look for yerba santa. Grows in shade."

"Yerba santa, huh? Never heard of it."

Jonna laughed. "Am not surprised. You like herb tea?"

"Nah. Tastes like medicine."

"It *is* medicine. Good for sickness in morning."

He reined up and stared at her. "Morning sickness! Jonna, for God's sake, are you—?"

She laughed. "Not for me. For my friend, Lucinda Markley."

Jack's eyebrows rose. "You're friends with Lieutenant Markley's wife?" he asked with a quick look at her face. "That's kinda surprising."

"Yes, I am friend. Lucinda expects baby. Need herb tea for sickness in morning."

"Lieutenant Markley's wife is expecting a baby?"

She frowned. "You are surprised?"

He blew out a long breath. "I don't like the lieutenant much. I kinda figured his wife might feel the same."

Jonna nodded. "I do not like lieutenant *at all.* But Lucinda is friend. She needs yerba santa, and she will teach me more English."

He shook his head. "Looks to me like you're learning English pretty fast."

"Not fast enough, Jack. Ladies at tea make fun of me."

"Did they? Well, that figures," he muttered. "Jealous old biddies."

She shot him a look. "What are 'old biddies'?"

"Women who are…" He searched for a word. "Not young and pretty."

Jonna nodded. "Ah. Then these women are 'young biddies.' Not old, just rude."

"Hell, Jonna, they're just jealous."

She sent him a glance. "Jealous? What jealous mean?"

"Full of envy," he said.

She laughed. "No, envy not possible. All ladies have beautiful dresses."

"Just not beautiful manners, huh?"

She nodded. "No, not nice manners."

"That figures, too," he said under his breath. He knew something about what went on at Lucinda Markley's tea last Sunday because Sidney Markley had been running off his mouth about it. He'd give a month's pay to know the details. Colonel Hawks had stonewalled him, and when he'd asked Martha about it, she gave him a twinkly-eyed look. "Jonna more than held her own," she'd said. What the heck did *that* mean? Sure wish he'd been a fly on Lucinda's wall.

They rode in silence for the next hour, then Jack drew rein and pointed ahead. "See that green spot over yonder? That's Salmon Creek."

The minute they drew rein, Jonna drew a small burlap sack from her skirt pocket, slipped off her horse, and disappeared into the tangle of cottonwoods and willow trees along the creek bank.

"Jonna?" he called after her.

"Yes?"

"Watch out for poison ivy."

"Fireweed, you mean."

"And watch for…" Oh hell, there's probably nothing that grows or crawls or flies Jonna doesn't know about. He'd guess what she *doesn't* know about are "lady things" like silk dresses and corsets and such. That struck him funny. Jonna wouldn't give a flying fig about silk dresses or corsets.

She emerged from the trees, shaking her head. "No yerba santa."

"Coyote Creek is about four miles farther on," he said. "Good fishing."

"Oh?"

"Yeah. Trout, mostly. Little ones."

"How little?"

He chuckled. "Hardly a good mouthful."

She looked up at him with a grin. "But you have big mouth!" she joked. She remounted her mare and rode on ahead of him. Jack blinked. He never realized Jonna had much of a sense of humor, but she was turning out to be one surprise after another.

By now the sun was high overhead, and the air was hot and still. Out here on the plain, it felt like an oven. They approached Coyote Creek at an angle to avoid a small waterfall. Unfortunately, that's where the shade was.

The creek was more overgrown than Jack remembered, with tangled clumps of vine maples and young willow trees along the bank. Jonna grabbed her burlap bag, jumped down from her horse, and disappeared into the brush. His first instinct was to watch her, make sure she didn't slip and fall in the creek. On second thought, Jonna had probably explored more creeks in this territory than he had. Sure felt strange being with a woman who knew more about the land than he did.

A sharp cry brought him half out of the saddle. "Jonna?" He'd halfway dismounted when he heard her voice again.

"I find herbs! Lots of them!"

"Need any help?"

That brought a whoop of laughter. Guess not. He remounted and waited for her to emerge from the brush.

But she didn't.

"Jonna?"

No answer.

The back of his neck prickled, and he slipped his boots out of the stirrups. "Jonna!"

"Yes?" Her voice sounded far away. He crashed into the brush and worked his way upstream where the waterfall tumbled over a rock ledge. He found her standing under the cascade of water, one hand twisting her hair off her shoulders. Fully clothed, he noted. And getting completely drenched.

"Do you not feel heat?" she called.

"You mean do I feel hot and sweaty and like I'm gonna melt?"

"Yes."

Without answering, he waded into the creek and splashed upstream to where she stood under the waterfall. Jonna stood next to him, turning this way and that in the water until her blouse and blue denim skirt were sopping wet. Plastered to her skin that way, the garments revealed every dip and curve of her body, and suddenly he couldn't breathe.

He turned away to let the cool water spray over his back, then ducked his head under the falls. When he emerged, he found Jonna with her skirt rucked up above her knees, wringing out the water.

Not smart, Corder. Don't look. Don't even think about it. When she splashed out of the creek, he forced himself to look away.

"Did you find that herb you were looking for?"

"Yes, yerba santa," she said. "Look!" She held up the burlap bag, now bulging with leafy fronds of something green poking out the top.

"Looks like some kinda of weed."

"No, not weed. I dry leaves, then make tea. Good for mothers."

"What's it taste like?"

She wrinkled her nose. "You would not like."

"Good thing I'm not expecting a baby, then," he joked.

"Also good for headache," she said.

"The only headache I've got is—"

He snapped his mouth shut. Was Jonna a headache? He drew in a deep breath. No, Jonna was *not* a headache. He kept asking the colonel how she was adjusting to life at the fort, but when it came to Jonna, Martin was annoyingly close-mouthed. "How come you're so interested?" the colonel had asked.

"No particular reason," he answered. The colonel shook his head and smiled.

Now he watched Jonna slog over to mount her mare in that waterlogged skirt. She managed to get her foot into the stirrup, but she was so weighed down by the sopping garment she couldn't heave her body into the saddle. After her third try, Jack walked over, planted one hand on her backside, and shoved her up onto the horse. Her wet skirt was cold and clammy, but putting his hand on her made him feel hot all over.

They rode back toward the post for a good half hour before he hazarded a question. "How many cups of tea will that bag of yerba whatever make?"

"Many."

"Enough to last nine months?"

She shook her head. "Should not need much after early months. If she does…" She sent him an assessing look. "…I will return here for more."

"With an escort," Jack reminded.

"Not need. Now I know where—"

"With an escort!" he repeated.

She stared at him. "Why?"

"For God's sake, Jonna, you can't ramble all over these plains like you're still living with the Sioux! You want to get kidnapped?"

She pressed her lips together. "Do not shout at me!"

He made an effort to lower his voice. "You're not safe out here alone."

She studied her saddle horn and said nothing.

"Do you understand?" he asked.

"I understand. I do not like, but I understand."

He spent a few tense minutes studying the hazy mountains in the distance. "I guess after living with the Sioux all those years it's hard for you to think like a white woman. Hard to know what you should do and what you shouldn't."

"Yes," she said shortly. "Is difficult."

"Yeah. Thought so. You're probably used to knowing how to do things."

She twisted her head to look at him. "Most difficult is bossy companion!"

He snorted. "Hell, Jonna, I'm just trying to keep you safe. Colonel Hawks asked me to be your escort when you leave the post."

"You mean he *ordered* you?"

"No. What difference would it make if he did?"

She stared at the trail of hoofprints they were

following back to the post. "Would like more if you *wanted* to." She spurred her horse forward.

He studied her rigid spine, blew out a long breath, and closed his eyes. Guess he'd never really understand a woman like Jonna. She was the most puzzling female he'd ever encountered. And the most maddening. Sometimes when he was with her, his jaw ached from gritting his teeth. Other times…well, he wouldn't think about the other times.

But damned if he hadn't riled her up this morning. Now she'd probably ask the colonel for anyone *but* him for an escort. The thought of someone like Lieutenant Markley riding out alone with Jonna sent a knife into his belly. *He* wanted to be the one riding with her. He thought hard about that all the way back to the post.

When they rode through the gate and over to the colonel's house, Jonna dismounted, and Jack led both horses away. She flew up the porch steps to find the colonel and his wife rocking in the swing.

"I find herbs!" she announced, holding up her burlap bag.

Martha laid her embroidery in her lap. "Jonna, you're soaking wet! What *have* you been doing?"

"Took bath in creek, under waterfall. Jack wet, too."

"Jack! You mean you *both* took a bath?"

The colonel laid his hand on her arm. "Hold on a minute, Martha. Jonna, are you telling us—"

"That you and Jack took a bath *together*?" Martha finished.

Jonna looked from the colonel's wife to the colonel and back again. "Not together, no. Me first."

The colonel nodded. "You mean that little waterfall

on Coyote Creek? Hardly big enough for a real bath, is it?"

"Martin!" his wife hissed. "Such details are irrelevant!"

"Look at her boots, Martha," he murmured. "They're wet. Nobody takes a real bath with their boots on."

"Oh."

Jonna looked puzzled.

"Martha," the colonel said with a chuckle. "Her clothes are wet because she didn't take them off."

"No," Jonna said slowly. "Not proper."

Martha smiled suddenly. "Come inside, my dear. You need dry clothes and some hot tea."

Chapter Fifteen

Jack turned both horses over to Seamus at the stable and walked on to his quarters. His shirt was still damp from standing under the waterfall, so he left it on, but he pulled on a pair of dry trousers. Halfway to the mess hall, he ran into Lieutenant Markley.

"Been out riding, huh?" the lieutenant said, his thin mouth twisting. "Kinda early, isn't it?"

"The army doesn't sleep late," Jack snapped.

"Yeah. I'm out early because my wife's tossing up her breakfast in the chamber pot, and I don't fancy cleaning it out."

Jack gave him a long look. "For better, but not worse, is that it?"

Markley ignored the barb. "Lucinda tells me that Indian girl is bringing her some kind of morning-sickness remedy."

"That girl is not Indian, Lieutenant! She's Irish."

"Whatever she is, she's real pretty. Noticed that right off."

Jack stopped a few yards short of the mess hall and spun to face him. "You're a married man, Markley. You shouldn't be ogling other females on this post. Or anywhere else."

The lieutenant smiled. "Looking doesn't do any harm, does it, Major?"

Jack stepped in close. "You hear me, Lieutenant?

Keep your eyes on *Mrs.* Markley. That's an order!"

The lieutenant snapped a salute. "Oh, yessir, Major. I hear you loud and clear."

Jack nodded and moved on toward the mess hall. He didn't like Sidney Markley, and he trusted him even less. The man made his skin crawl, and over his years of Army service, he'd learned to trust his instincts.

"Hey, Major?" Markley's voice called from behind him.

He stopped walking but didn't turn around. "Yeah?"

"I hear my wife's gonna teach that Ind—that girl some English. Seems she's lacking in the communication department."

"Jonna Lander is not lacking in *any* department, Lieutenant. I'd advise you to keep your mind on your military duties, not on your wife's companions."

"Oh, yessir, I sure will try to do that."

Jack spun to face him. "You better do more than *try,* Lieutenant. You damn well better *succeed.* You take my meaning?" Without waiting for an answer, he about-faced and moved on into the mess hall. *Man alive, my fuse is sure short these days!* He wished Jonna had never agreed to gather those herbs for Markley's wife. He didn't want Sidney Markley anywhere near her.

Jack's unease about Lieutenant Markley came to a head on Sunday when he and Colonel Hawks were relaxing with a glass of bourbon on the colonel's porch. "Jonna's planning another excursion to Coyote Creek tomorrow to gather those herbs she's using for Mrs. Markley," the colonel said. "Lieutenant Markley has volunteered to be her escort."

Jack's boot hit the floor with a thump. "No!"

The colonel's salt-and-pepper eyebrows went up. "Whaddya mean 'no,' Jack?"

"I mean *no*, Martin. I don't want Lieutenant Markley anywhere near Jonna."

The colonel frowned. "Some reason?"

"I don't trust him around her."

Colonel Hawks topped up their glasses, then sent Jack a penetrating look. "You mean because his wife's expecting and some men gets antsy while they're waiting nine months for the baby to be born?"

Jack shook his head. "Even if Markley's wife wasn't expecting, I wouldn't trust him around Jonna. She has no experience with men—"

"What about Indian men?" Martin asked.

"She has no experience with Indian men, either. The Sioux chief had adopted her, and he kept her well protected."

"Kinda unusual, isn't it? Wonder why."

"He planned to award her to some brave who distinguished himself in battle. Jonna didn't want that. That's why she escaped."

"With you."

"Might have been with Sergeant Sullivan, but I was the one who survived the gauntlet. She got away just in time, too. Some Sioux brave wanted her, but she didn't want him."

"If she was smart enough to hook up with you, what makes you think she's not smart enough to deflect Lieutenant Markley's unwanted attention?"

Jack gulped a mouthful of bourbon. "She's smart in Indian ways, Martin. She might not know how to evade the unwanted advances of a snake like Sidney

Markley."

"I see." The colonel sipped away at his bourbon. "Would you be volunteering to escort her every time she leaves the post?"

Jack nodded. "Yes, I sure am."

"It's a deal!" the colonel said with a grin. "I was prepared to twist your arm, but you saved me the effort."

Jack touched his glass to the colonel's. "You're a real fox, Colonel."

Colonel Hawks grinned. "Would you stay for supper?"

Before he could answer, Martha burst through the screen door. "I've set the table for four, Jack. And don't say you're not joining us."

****

Jonna muddled a handful of dried yerba santa leaves in the bottom of Lucinda's bone china cup, added boiling water from the teakettle, and stirred. "Drink when cool," she said.

"I can't tell you how much difference this tea is making," Lucinda said. "I no longer dread mealtime, and preparing supper for Sidney doesn't make me toss up my breakfast."

Jonna nodded. "Am glad. Is correct?"

"*I am* glad is better English. And you could say *is this* correct."

"*Is this* correct," Jonna repeated. "More words, same meaning."

Lucinda nodded. "You could also say '*the meaning is* the same'."

For the next hour, Jonna continued to steep Mason jars of yerba santa tea and trade sentences back and forth with Lucinda. Finally, she glanced at Lucinda's mantel clock and rose. "I go now. Martha makes supper."

"*I must* go now," Lucinda corrected with a laugh. "Martha *is making* supper."

Jonna nodded. "Martha *is making* supper. Is correct?"

"That is correct," Lucinda said, her thin face lit with a smile.

On her way back across the parade ground, she practiced the phrases she had learned. When she arrived at the house, she found Jack rocking away in the porch swing with the colonel.

"Jonna, you been over at Lucinda Markley's brewing up that magic tea?" he asked.

She opened her mouth to answer, then thought for a moment. "Yes," she said carefully. "I have been at Lucinda Markley's house. I brew healing tea for her."

"Whew!" he exclaimed. "That's more words than I've ever heard you string together before!"

"Yes, more words," she said with a smile. "You understand?"

Jack saluted her with his bourbon. "I understand very well, Jonna!"

"Now, when brother—when *my* brother comes, I can speak more with him. Is good."

"I gather Lieutenant Markey was not at home?"

"Yes, Lieutenant not…I mean, *was* not at home."

The colonel gave the swing a push. "Every single day Jonna asks me when her brother is returning to the post, and I have to tell her I don't know. He and his guide have been gone almost a month now."

Jack shook his head. "A month! The Nez Perce are

generally peaceable, but there's always the possibility of something unforeseen happening. How old is your brother, Jonna?"

"Andrew four years—Andrew *is* four years younger. I am now sixteen, so he is twelve years."

"Twelve! Martin, you sent out a twelve-year-old kid to deal with the Nez Perce?"

"Andrew Lander is no ordinary kid, Jack. He's a gifted linguist. Don't know how he picked it up, but he can speak the lingo like he's half Indian. Besides, young Lander doesn't belong to this post. He's actually assigned to Fort McHenry. Colonel Hardesty loaned the boy to me for a special detail."

"Is it dangerous?"

The colonel shot a surreptitious glance at Jonna. "Some. But an Indian uprising would be even more dangerous. There's an armed soldier and an Indian guide with young Lander. Personally, I think that kid alone is keeping half the territory from getting scalped."

"But a month is a long time! What about a rescue party, Martin? I'll lead it."

"No need, Jack. Appreciate the offer, but Andrew always turns up sooner or later. I'm not worried about him."

"When my brother returns, he will be surprised," Jonna said carefully.

"He sure will," Jack murmured. "He probably won't recognize you."

She shook her head. "My brother will recognize."

Jack wasn't so sure. It was getting so half the time *he* no longer recognized Jonna.

Chapter Sixteen

The following morning, as Jonna finished bandaging a deep cut on a soldier's shoulder, Lucinda Markley stopped by the infirmary. "Lucinda! You are not ill, are you?"

Lucinda smiled. "I haven't had a speck of morning sickness since you brought me those tea leaves. But…well, my supply is running low, and I was wondering if—"

"Yes," Jonna interrupted. "I can gather more yerba santa. I will bring tomorrow."

Lucinda grasped both her hands. "Bless you, my friend. I am truly grateful."

When she finished her duties for Dr. Brownell, she untied her apron and threaded her way past the juniper bushes and sugar pine trees to the colonel's office to request the escort he insisted on. Just as she reached the door, heavy footsteps sounded on the stairs behind her.

"Ah, Jonna," a silky voice called.

She turned to find Lieutenant Markley. Her heart plummeted into her belly. "Lieutenant."

"You lookin' for Colonel Hawks?"

"Yes. I gather herbs for your wife."

He nodded and stepped closer, his narrow face flushed. "You weren't planning to ride out alone, now were you?"

"No. Colonel Hawks provides escort for me."

"Does he indeed?" The lieutenant's thin face lit up. "Then you're in luck. I was on my way to saddle up my horse. I'll bring a mount for you, as well."

"No, I do not think—"

"I insist. It's the least I can do since those herbs are helping my wife." Before she could object, he turned on his heel and tramped off toward the stable.

"Wait!" she called. But the lieutenant strode on and paid no attention.

She hurried across the parade ground to the house, only to discover the colonel was not at home. Martha confessed she hadn't seen him since breakfast. Before she could think what to do, the lieutenant was back, leading two saddled horses. He gestured for her to mount, then stepped behind her and spread his hands around her waist.

She shrugged out of his grasp. "I have ridden since I was eight years old, Lieutenant. I mount by myself."

Instantly, he lifted his hands away. "I forget you lived with the Indians. Guess you can ride pretty good, huh?"

"Yes, I can."

By the time he swung up on his horse and fumbled for the reins, she was in the saddle and riding away from him. "I can sure see that," he muttered.

She headed across the plain toward Coyote Creek, and soon the lieutenant caught up with her. He rode at her side without speaking, but she began to feel more and more uneasy. All at once, she changed her mind.

"I will gather herbs another day," she announced. She started to rein up, but the lieutenant reached over and grabbed her bridle.

"Today's as good as any," he said. He tugged her

mount forward.

"No, it is not," she said. "Release my horse."

He said nothing, just continued pulling the animal along.

"Lieutenant Markley," she said loudly. "I want to return to fort."

"No, you don't, Jonna. Now just relax and do what I say."

Jonna glanced behind her, calculating the distance back to the post gate. She could drop to the ground and run, but she could never outdistance a man on horseback. While she tried to think, he continued to pull her mare along. If she could wrestle the reins out of his grip, could her horse outrun his gray mare? He had double-wrapped her reins tight around his fist, and now he was dragging her mount farther and farther from the post.

"Tell me about this creek," he said. "I hear it's got a nice cool waterfall."

She thought for a minute. "Yes, waterfall is nice." She shot a glance at his flushed face. "I bathe there," she added on purpose.

"Do you, now?" He turned a smiling face toward her. "Now that's something I'd like to see." He yanked her horse forward and picked up the pace. When she spied Coyote Creek ahead of them, Jonna waited until they reached the cottonwood trees along the bank, then pointed to a thick tangle of brambles and indicated she would dismount.

"Anything you say," he murmured. "I'll be right behind you."

Without a word, she slipped off her horse and disappeared into the trees. She watched the lieutenant dismount, and when he started after her, she melted away into the underbrush. He listened for a telltale rustling in the bushes, and when he heard nothing, he plunged into the brush after her.

Quiet as a cat, she moved along the creek bank, listening to the lieutenant crash around in the undergrowth some distance away. She couldn't help smiling. Making no noise, she doubled back toward the horses. Still listening to the lieutenant thrash among the brambles, she glided toward his horse, slipped a prickly cocklebur under the saddle blanket, and quietly mounted her mare. Snatching up the reins, she drove her booted feet hard into its sides and put her head down against its neck.

****

Jack grasped the liveryman's shirt front. "Seamus! Say that again?"

The pudgy Irishman stepped back. "Uh, well, Major, that lieutenant, you know, the one with the smart mouth and no horse sense?"

"Yeah. Lieutenant Markley. What about him?"

"Well, a little while back, he came barrelin' in here like he owned the place, grabbed that gray he favors and a roan mare, saddled 'em up in a hurry, and—Hey, there's more, Major! Don'tcha wanna hear it?"

Jack tossed his saddle on the nearest horse, stuffed his boot in the stirrup, and thundered out the open stable door. He knew Jonna would head for Coyote Creek, and for the first time in over a year, he used his spurs. Halfway to the creek, he saw a telltale puff of dust and headed straight toward it.

The closer he got, the clearer his vision grew. A single horse was racing toward him, kicking up a cloud of prairie dust. "Jonna!" He dug in his spurs and raced toward her.

She streaked past him, then circled back, and he pulled his horse up to meet her. "Jonna," he shouted. "Are you all right?"

"Yes, I am all right." Her mount danced close to his. "I am glad to see you, Jack."

"Where's Lieutenant Markley?"

She tipped her head over one shoulder. "In bushes. Beside creek."

"I'll kill him," he muttered.

"No," she panted, "do not. Let his horse do it."

"His horse?"

She nodded. "I put prickly burr under saddle." She reined away.

Jack stared at her back, then spurred forward and fell in beside her. She said not one more word until they reached the post gate, where she slid out of the saddle and laid the reins in his hand. "Lieutenant Markley will be delayed."

An hour later, a sweaty Lieutenant Sidney Markley limped into the stable, leading a winded gray horse. Jack was waiting. He'd purposely shed his military uniform, and now he stepped forward, yanked the gray's reins out of the lieutenant's hand, and handed them to Seamus. Then he grabbed Markley's dusty blue shirt and ripped it open. Brass buttons sprayed all over the straw-covered stable floor. Jack smiled and drew back his fist.

****

At suppertime, Colonel Hawks and Jack sat on the colonel's porch, sharing some bourbon. "Damnedest thing, Jack," the colonel said as he rocked away in the swing. "Lieutenant Markley has asked for a transfer."

"Yeah?" Jack said, his voice careful.

"'Course I'm not going to inflict that man on another army post. Not right away, anyhow."

"Some reason?" Jack asked mildly.

"Yes. His wife's gonna have her baby in a few months. Doesn't seem like the right time to trade one houseful of furniture at this post for another houseful of furniture at a new post."

"Guess not," Jack said. "Think he'll keep out of trouble until then?"

"Oh, I'm quite sure he will. Something seems to have scared the man out of his cocky bravado."

Jack focused on the nearest pine tree. "That so, Martin? Wonder what it was?"

The colonel hid a smile and sipped his bourbon. "I couldn't begin to guess. Maybe the mosquitos this time of year."

"Damned pesky little beggars," Jack said. "Never know where they're gonna bite next."

Without a word, Colonel Hawks leaned forward and touched his glass to Jack's.

Chapter Seventeen

Before the sun rose the following morning, Jonna was awakened by pounding on her bedroom door. "Jonna? Jonna, wake up!"

It was still dark outside, but Martha sounded upset. The colonel's wife was never up this early unless...*Unless something was wrong.* She tossed back the blue quilt, climbed out of bed, and flung open the door. Martha was not smiling, and Jonna caught her breath. "What is wrong?"

"I don't know, my dear. Martin was roused out an hour ago by a soldier banging on our front door. Now the colonel wants to see you in his office."

Hurriedly she pulled on her blue denim skirt and a gingham shirtwaist, skimmed down the stairs and out the front door, then sped through the pine trees to the small log building Colonel Hawks used as his office. When she burst through the door, she saw three soldiers gathered around the colonel's desk. She recognized Jack, but the other two had their backs to her. Both wore filthy uniforms.

The colonel stood up, and some sort of look passed between him and Jack. "Gentlemen," he said, "may I present Miss Jonna Lander."

Both strangers turned around, but neither spoke. Then the shorter one passed his hand over his eyes and uttered a single word. "Jonna?"

"Yes, I am Jonna Lander. Who are you?"

The boy blinked and again passed his hand over his eyes. "Jonna, don'tcha know me?"

She stared at him. His face didn't look familiar, but his eyes were the same dark blue as her father's, and— Her hand flew to her mouth. "Andrew? *Andrew*?"

"Yeah, it's me," he said.

She didn't recognize his voice, but his eyes, now shiny with moisture, were the same eyes she remembered from long ago. He took a step toward her. "Colonel, you sure this is my sister?" he asked in an uncertain voice.

Jack stepped forward. "I'm sure, son. Jonna and I did some traveling together in Sioux territory. If you're Andrew Lander, this woman is your sister."

"Oh, my God," the youth said. "Oh, my God. *Ohmigod*." He stared at her.

"Drew?" she whispered. Then she gave a cry and flung both arms around him.

"Andrew! Andrew, you're alive!"

"Sure am," he said. "And you... After all these years, I thought for sure you were—Gosh, Jonna, I thought you were dead!"

"I am not dead." She wept. "I am not dead! I am here!"

He studied her face. Finally, he lifted his hand and traced his forefinger across her cheek. "You sure grew up nice, Sis," he murmured.

A laugh burst from Jack's mouth. "She also grew up feisty as hell."

She glared at him. "I am not feisty, Jack."

"And argumentative," he added.

"I am *not* arg—" Both the colonel and Jack

laughed. Young Andrew nodded. "That's my sister, all right. She was always talkin' back to Ma and Pa."

Jonna could not stop looking at him. He was tall and slim, and an unruly shock of dark hair straggled over his forehead. "The last time I saw you was before—" She swallowed hard. "You were only four years old! How did you—?"

"I hunkered down in a ditch so the Indians wouldn't see me, and I stayed real quiet. Ma started to scream, and I put my hands over my ears and closed my eyes. After a while, I didn't hear anything, and it was gettin' dark, so I climbed out of the ditch and crawled into the back of our wagon. Ma and Pa were both dead, and I was plenty scared. When it got light, I started walkin'."

Jonna clapped her hand over her mouth. "But you were only four years old!"

"Didn't have a choice. Long about dusk, a fellow on horseback found me and took me to some fort somewhere—I'm not real sure where—and they sent me to a town that had a church. The preacher kept me, and I grew up. Just like you did."

Jonna flicked a glance at his companion. "And now you are here with this army man? But you are only twelve years old!"

"Nah, I'm thirteen now. My voice changed and everything."

The colonel pulled a large white handkerchief from his trouser pocket and blew his nose, then waved his hand at the other man. "Jonna, this is Corporal Lance Singleton. Your brother and Corporal Singleton have just now returned from a special mission for the army."

Jonna gasped. "Andrew is in the army?"

"Andrew works for the army," the colonel corrected. "Your brother is a special detail translator. Along with Corporal Singleton and an Indian guide, they've just returned from the Nez Perce encampment in Oregon Territory to negotiate a—"

"An understanding," Corporal Singleton said quickly. "With the Indians, such things as a lasting peace are a delicate balance of intimidation and diplomacy."

Jonna tore her gaze away from her brother to focus on the tall man at his side. "Was this mission dangerous?"

"Yes, miss, it was dangerous. That's why Drew is an asset. He looks too young to be much of a threat."

"But *you* don't," Jonna said. "You would look like big threat."

Jack playfully punched the corporal's shoulder. Dust puffed from his uniform. "Big threat," he joked."

"Believe me, Miss Lander," the corporal said, "I am a very peaceable man."

"Until he gets mad," Andrew said with a grin. "Then you better watch out!"

"Not much gets Lance mad," Jack said. "Except for bad food and muddy trails and—"

"Runaway pack animals," Andrew said with a grin.

"And know-it-all travel companions," Corporal Singleton said with a grin.

"Gentlemen," Colonel Hawks said, "would you join us for breakfast?"

"You bet, Colonel," Andrew blurted. "I've been hungry for the last two hundred miles."

The colonel nodded. "Come on over to the house. My Martha's an excellent cook, and Jonna isn't far behind."

"Jonna can cook?" Andrew exclaimed. "She wouldn't go near a cookfire when we were comin' out West!"

"I am older now," Jonna said quietly. "And Mrs. Hawks has a real stove!"

Jack clapped Corporal Singleton on the back. "Come on over to my quarters, Lance. You, too, Andrew. You can wash up there. Can't have you puffing dust all over Jonna's flapjacks."

Half an hour later, the sky turned a rosy peach color, and Jack, Lance, and Andrew Lander tramped across the parade ground and up the colonel's porch steps. Colonel Hawks directed them to the dining room, where Jonna was laying out plates and silverware. The colonel's wife bustled out of the kitchen to welcome them, seated them at the lace-covered dining table, and filled mugs with hot coffee. When she came to Andrew, she hesitated. "Perhaps you would like a glass of milk?"

"Milk!" Lance blurted. "Drew's been drinking coffee ever since he joined up with me. How old were you then, Drew? Nine? Ten?"

"I was eleven," Andrew replied. "But I've been drinking coffee ever since I was six or seven because that's what the teachers at my school drank."

"Teachers?" Jonna blurted. "You went to school?"

"Sure. That place the church sent me was some kind of school, so I learned to read and write and do sums...and drink coffee!"

Jonna disappeared into the kitchen, then set platters of crisp bacon and flapjacks on the table. Jack noted that Lance Singleton had a hard time keeping his eyes off her. Even when she took the chair next to her brother, Lance didn't stop staring at her. It made the back of his neck itch.

He couldn't say why that bothered him, but it did. Lance was his oldest friend. They had enlisted together, and for the past seven years, they'd served under various commanders, sometimes together, sometimes at different posts. As far as he knew, Lance had never before looked twice at any female.

He downed a gulp of coffee. Lance Singleton was one of the few men he respected, but he had to admit his friend's obvious interest in Jonna nettled him. It was plain she had no interest in anyone at the table other than her brother, but whenever she rose to fetch the blue speckleware coffeepot or fill the platter with more fluffy flapjacks, Lance's gaze followed her.

"Colonel Hawks," Lance said when Jonna reappeared, "we found the Nez Perce trying to walk a fine line between the American Army and the Nootka and the Salish tribes living near them."

"Were they hostile?" the colonel asked.

"Nope. Drew here spoke to them in their own language, and they listened respectfully. They even invited him to join the tribe! They didn't invite *me*," Lance added with a grin, "just Drew."

"Guess I look harmless," Andrew said. "Too young to be a threat, but—"

"Smart enough to speak their language," the colonel finished. "I'd say both you and your sister are pretty intelligent."

"Well, sure, Colonel. Jonna was always real smart."

"Smart enough to survive eight years of captivity with the Sioux and live to tell about it," Jack said.

"Smart enough," Jonna added with a quick glance at him, "to help us both escape."

Andrew's blue eyes widened. "Gosh, Sis, how'd you manage that?"

"Carefully," Jack answered.

"Intelligently," Jonna added.

Jack caught her eye. "And with great courage."

Her dark eyebrows went up, and she held his gaze for a few seconds, but she said nothing.

After breakfast, Andrew stayed to talk more with Jonna while Jack and Lance set off through the trees for his quarters. "Man alive," Lance said as he stepped off the colonel's front porch, "Drew Lander's sister is an eye-popping beauty!"

"Yeah," Jack acknowledged. "She's smart and sensible and—"

"Pretty enough to make your mouth water."

An inexplicable stab of unease poked at him. "Next thing I know you'll be requesting a transfer from Fort McHenry."

"Yeah. Maybe I will." He sidestepped to avoid a bushy pine tree.

Jack jerked. "You want a bunk for tonight?"

"Sure do, Jack. Darn nice of you to offer."

"Then forget the transfer idea."

Lance came to a halt. "Huh? Why should I forget it? Maybe Drew would like to be posted near his sister, and where he goes, I go. Drew and I are a team."

"Maybe," Jack allowed.

"You have some special interest in Jonna Lander, do you?"

"Nope."

His friend's broad forehead wrinkled into a frown.

"She's the first female I've ever seen you get all het up over, Jack."

He stopped dead. "I'm not 'all het up' over Jonna. Half the time we don't even like each other." That was a lie, but Lance didn't need to know that.

"Be okay if me and Drew ride over once in a while so…uh…he can visit with his sister?"

Jack sent him a long look. "Does Drew ride a horse?"

"Well, sure, he rides—"

"Then he can ride over and visit his sister any time he wants, can't he? He doesn't need you to nursemaid him."

"Huh? Kinda touchy about it, aren't you?"

Jack didn't answer, and they walked on through the pine trees in silence. "Seems to me," Lance said after a moment, "you're kinda testy this morning, Jack. Something on your mind?"

"Nope."

"Does Jonna know you feel protective of her?"

"Nope. And don't you go telling her!"

Lance raised both hands. "Okay, okay. Look, I'll make a bargain with you, Jack. I won't tell her you feel protective toward her if you won't object if Drew and I request a transfer to Colonel Hawks' command."

"No deal." Jack tramped up the three wooden steps to his quarters, thrust open the heavy wooden door, and pointed to an empty bunk. "All yours, Lance. Drew can take the cot in the corner."

Lance grinned. "Thanks, Jack. I always knew you never hold a grudge."

"No grudge, Lance. Just cautious. I don't want to see Jonna hurt."

Lance hid a smile. "Understood, my friend."

While Lance caught up on his sleep, Jack kept himself busy, inspecting squad details and supervising drills, then wandered half-heartedly around the post. Around supper time, he and Lance walked over to the mess hall, where they found Drew.

"Golly, Major," the boy said, eying his plate of beans and cornbread. "I sure want to thank you for rescuing my sister from the Sioux."

Jack laughed. "Actually, I did no such thing, Drew. Your sister rescued *me*. Without her, neither of us would have escaped. Or," he added, "lived to tell about it."

Drew chortled and stirred his beans around with his fork. "That's kinda funny, Major. Jonna says without *you* she wouldn't be here at Fort Kearney, learning to speak English and make flapjacks."

"Your sister," Jack said with a grin, "exaggerates a lot."

"No, she doesn't, Major. Leastways, she never did before. But I sure did. I got paddled every time I fudged about how many eggs our hen laid."

"Well, then, Drew," Lance interrupted, "maybe you could ask your sister if she'd like to go on a picnic next Sunday."

"Ask her yourself," Drew shot. "You scared of her or somethin'?"

Chapter Eighteen

Three days later, Andrew Lander and Lance Singleton rode away from the post and headed back to Fort McHenry. Jonna stood at the gate and waved until they disappeared into shimmering heat waves, then threaded her way through the pines to Lucinda's house for her English lesson. The air smelled pungent and green as she rapped on the front door.

Lucinda, straining the seams of her pale green dimity dress, proposed that they forego their usual grammar practice in favor of informal conversation. "I'll start, shall I?" She described her girlhood in South Carolina, then told Jonna how she met and married her husband. "Sidney was so dashing, Jonna. You understand what 'dashing' means?"

When she nodded, Lucinda burbled on, tipping the contents of the china teapot into their cups. "Then Sidney came courting—you understand 'courting'?"

Jonna shook her head.

"Well," Lucinda continued with obvious relish, "courting is when a man pays you special attention. He brings you flowers and asks you to dance at balls. Has any man ever brought you flowers, Jonna?"

"No," she said. "Only horses."

"Horses! Mercy me, surely you are joking?"

"I am not joking. When a Sioux brave wants a wife, he brings horses to her father."

Lucinda stared at her, then dropped her eyes and studied her teacup. "You poor dear. Then you have never known the joys of love, have you?"

"My brother Andrew loves me," Jonna replied.

"I mean the love of a man. A man who w*ants* you. You understand 'wants'?"

"N-no. 'Wants' what?"

Lucinda giggled. "*Wants* in the sense of, well, *desires*. He wants to be joined with you. In marriage. *Physically* joined."

"Oh." Jonna had only a vague idea of what "physically joined" meant, and then suddenly she understood. "Joined" must mean the physical connection between a man and a woman as practiced by the Sioux. Sleeping next to each other. And touching. And...*Oh. Oh, my.*

"Well," Lucinda went on, "it was perfectly thrilling when my Sidney first kissed me. It was like...like a big dish full of stars raining down on my head."

Jonna listened in silence. No man had ever poured a dish of stars on her head. "No man has ever touched me except for Major Corder, and that was because we were riding away from the Sioux camp on only one horse." She closed her eyes. "We were hot and hungry and tired and filthy, and we smelled funny."

"Why, that doesn't sound romantic at all," Lucinda said.

"No, it was not. We thought only of surviving."

"My goodness, that is perfectly dreadful! I would absolutely die if Sidney ever visited me when he smelled funny. He says I always smell like violets! Isn't that sweet?"

For the twentieth time, Jonna wondered how a

genuinely nice woman like Lucinda could marry a man like Sidney Markley. "Lucinda," she said slowly, "why did you want to marry a soldier and live at an Army post?"

"Well, Sidney was so charming, he simply swept me off my feet. I traveled part of the way from South Carolina on the train, you see. Sidney met me in St. Louis, and we were married. Then we came on to Fort Kearney by stagecoach. Now *that* was truly exciting!"

"Why?" Jonna asked. The minute the word left her lips, she wanted to snatch it back. No doubt Lucinda was about to describe Indian attacks, and she did not want to be reminded of her parents' death.

"Oh, my," Lucinda breathed. "My darlin' Sidney made it exciting! We had the stagecoach entirely to ourselves, and we…well…I blush just remembering it."

What on earth could a man and a woman do in a stagecoach that was jolting and swaying over a rough road? She shook her head. Perhaps she had not understood.

Lucinda gently touched her arm. "Jonna, have you not experienced *anything*?"

"I have experienced many things," she said. "Some of them I do not recall with pleasure. Scraping deerskin until it is soft and stitching it into shirts and moccasins. Burying potatoes in hot coals to bake. Drying buffalo meat."

Lucinda stared at her. "You did all those things?"

"All those things and more."

"I never did a lick of work until I came out West with Sidney. At home, we always had servants who did the cooking and the sewing and housecleaning." She looked at Jonna with her brown eyes full of pity. "I imagine with all that work you were doin' at that Indian camp there was no time for courtship, was there?"

That made her laugh. "There was plenty of time, but I had no interest. And because I was the adopted daughter of the chief, he asked for so many horses for me, the braves got discouraged and chose other wives."

"Surely you don't mean—"

"A girl's price is paid in horses. You call it something else."

"We call it a dowry. That's what a woman brings to her husband."

"What does the man bring?"

"Well…" Lucinda hesitated. "Actually, the man brings nothing at all. I think Papa might have been glad Sidney came along because I have six sisters, and all of us were hankerin' for husbands."

"And Lieutenant Markley chose you."

Her friend hesitated. "Not exactly. You see, I was the oldest, so naturally I was married first. But Sidney was very happy about my extremely generous dowry."

Jonna wondered if her friend suspected her "darling Sidney" was…what was the word? Too friendly with other women. She released a long breath. She was learning much more than new English words from Lucinda. She was learning about things she had always wondered about, things between a man and a woman. Surely that was what Mama and Papa had— many, many dishes full of stars. Someday she wanted to have a dish of stars, too!

When she thought of Mama and Papa, she felt like crying. All these years, she had been afraid to care for anyone for fear she might lose them, but now there was Drew, her precious baby brother. And when you love someone, really love someone, you can't let yourself think about losing them.

The sun's rays began to warm the still air in Lucinda's parlor, and Jonna drew in a deep breath. She wanted to continue her conversation with Lucinda, but she did not want to hear any more about Lieutenant Markley. She couldn't say this to her friend, so she sipped her tea in silence.

"Tell me about Major Corder," Lucinda asked suddenly.

"Major Corder? What about him?"

"Do you like him?"

"Yes, I do like him. It was difficult to leave the Sioux camp, and Major Corder did things that took courage. I am grateful to him."

Lucinda took her hand. "Is that enough, Jonna?"

"Enough for what?"

"Enough to live on for the rest of your life. Surely you have thought about it?"

Jonna frowned. "Thought about what?"

"Thought about the rest of your life. About finding someone you want to be with for the rest of your life. Someone like Major Corder."

"No, I have not. Ever since we reached this army post I have been busy learning all the things I need to know. I have no time to think about Major Corder."

Which wasn't actually true. She thought quite a lot about Jack Corder. But she could never talk about him as part of her English lesson. Besides, most of the time she and Jack ended up arguing about something.

Chapter Nineteen

"A picnic?" Jonna kicked the porch swing into motion, hoping the back-and-forth movement would stir up some cool air on this stifling afternoon. "I have never been on a picnic."

"Yeah, Sis, a real American picnic," Drew said. "Me an' Lance found a real pretty spot on a creek 'bout a mile downstream from where you pick those herb-things. Next Sunday." He twisted his lanky body toward her. "How 'bout it?"

"Well…"

Lance poked Drew's arm. "Oh," the boy added, "and Jack, too. He an' Lance are old friends from way back."

"You rode all the way over from Fort McHenry to invite me to go on a picnic?"

"And Jack," Lance reminded. "He wouldn't take kindly to being left out."

Jonna nodded. "Colonel Hawks's daughter is coming home from teachers college next week. Her name is Samantha. Maybe she could come, too?"

"Oh, sure, Sis. That'd be someone for Jack to…uh…"

Jonna frowned. "For Jack to what?"

Lance cleared his throat. "Someone for Jack to talk to."

She almost laughed out loud. "Jack does not like

anyone deciding who he talks to or does not talk to. Jack likes to make his own decisions."

"Yep," Lance said with a grin. "That's Jack, all right."

"So how about the picnic, Jonna?" Drew asked. "Next Sunday around noon, okay?"

****

On Saturday morning, Colonel Hawks sent a four-man detail to Sand Point to meet the train bringing his daughter home. All that morning, Martha flitted between the kitchen, where she was icing her daughter's favorite chocolate cake, and the front porch, where the colonel sat pretending to read *Last of the Mohicans*. Jonna spent part of the day moving into the smaller bedroom at the opposite end of the hallway, then helped out at the infirmary, rolling bandages and scrubbing enamel pans.

But her mind was a whirl of uneasy doubts and questions. She was more than apprehensive about meeting the colonel's daughter. What if she was like Lucinda's friends, who didn't even try to hide their dislike? If Samantha was educated at a college, would she laugh at Jonna's English? Maybe she would resent her place in the colonel's household.

As the day dragged on to late afternoon, when the stagecoach was expected, she found herself wishing she could talk to Jack and quell her flutters.

She returned to the house around four o'clock and watched from the front porch as Samantha Hawks, a tall, willowy girl with long blonde curls, flew across the parade ground and threw herself into her parents' waiting arms. Martha cried, and the colonel blew his nose while his daughter jumped up and down and laughed with joy. "I'm home! I'm really home! And now I'm a teacher, Momma! A real teacher!"

"Come and meet Jonna, honey," Martha urged. "The girl I wrote you about, remember? She's been staying in your old room."

Samantha, wearing a stylish dark blue traveling suit that flared about her ankles, flew up the porch steps, both hands outstretched. "Jonna! I'm so pleased to meet you! Momma wrote all about you, so I feel I know you already."

Jonna drew in a breath of flower-scented perfume and returned Samantha's exuberant handshake. "Hello, Miss Hawks. Welcome home!"

"Oh, it's so glorious to be here! Everything smells so green and fresh, not like the smoky old streets of Boston." She spun back to Martha. "Oh, Momma, I've been so awfully homesick."

"Where's your trunk, Sam?" the colonel asked.

"More to the point," Martha said, "are you hungry?"

The girl laughed with delight. "A wagon is bringing my trunk tomorrow, and yes, I am absolutely famished!"

While their daughter devoured scrambled eggs and fried potatoes, Colonel Hawks and his wife peppered her with questions and gazed at her adoringly. Watching them made Jonna's throat ache, so she kept herself busy bringing fresh toast and refilling coffee cups.

Later that afternoon, she again walked over to the infirmary to check on two inmates who had come down with measles. When she returned to the house for supper, she found Jack sitting in a straight-backed chair, tipped onto its two back legs, and the colonel rocking in the porch swing. Both were sipping whiskey. She moved past them, walked straight to the kitchen to help Martha with supper, and tied on her red-checked apron. Already the house smelled of roasting chicken.

To Jonna's surprise, the supper of chicken and mashed potatoes and gravy made Samantha cry. "Oh, Momma, I haven't tasted gravy—real chicken gravy— for years!"

"Surely they fed you at that teachers college?" the colonel said.

"Oh, yes," she said, mopping tears off her cheeks with the colonel's handkerchief. "But it was never like Momma's cooking. *Nothing* is like Momma's cooking!"

"Sam, how does it feel to be home?" Jack asked.

Sam? Jack knows her well enough to call her Sam?

Samantha smiled at him. "Oh, my heavens, it feels perfectly lovely!"

"I guess the trip all the way from Boston was pretty tiring, huh?"

"It was exhausting, Jack. Four days on the train to Sand Point. Only now am I starting to feel more like a human being."

"You interested in going on a picnic Sunday?"

Samantha looked up at him, her green eyes sparkling. "A picnic! Oh, I'd love to go on a picnic!"

Jack nodded. "Good. Think you and Jonna could fry up some chicken?"

"Of course we could! And I'll make a potato salad," Samantha volunteered.

"What are Lance and Andrew bringing?" Martha inquired.

Samantha's eyes widened. "Lance and Andrew? Who are Lance and Andrew?"

"Corporal Lance Singleton," Jack answered. "And Andrew Lander, Jonna's kid brother. I think you'll like them, especially Lance."

Samantha sent him a sharp look. "Oh? Why Lance especially?"

Jack looked momentarily uncertain, and Jonna had to laugh. Apparently Samantha didn't like having things decided for her any more than Jack did.

"Lance Singleton is from New York," Jonna volunteered.

Martha laughed. "That means he's got some 'couth,' as we say out here in the West. But it's true— Lance has had more book-learning than most soldiers."

Jack's eyebrows rose. "How did you know Lance is from New York, Jonna?"

"Because he told me, how do you think?"

"Oh, yeah, I see."

She sent him an exasperated look. "No, you don't, Jack. Lance told me because I asked him."

"Why did you ask him?" Samantha asked.

"I asked him because I wanted to practice my English, and I assumed he—"

"Sure," Jack said dryly. "Lance would love you to practice your English on him."

"Why, Jack," Samantha said with a laugh. "You sound positively jealous."

Jack groaned. "I am not jealous of Lance Singleton," he snapped.

Colonel Hawks laughed aloud. "Here's a good English sentence for you to practice, Jonna. It's from Shakespeare. 'Methinks he doth protest too much.' "

Jack bit the inside of his cheek. "Mind your own business, Martin."

One thing Jonna noticed immediately about Samantha was her slim frame. Apparently attending school in Boston meant doing more studying than eating. But she did envy the girl's education. Only Jack seemed unimpressed by Samantha's teacher's certificate. But then, not much impressed Jack.

She couldn't help wondering what *did* impress him. Samantha's pretty blonde curls? Martha's caramel cake? Jack was hard to figure out sometimes. Often she couldn't tell what he was thinking, and she *always* wanted to know what people were thinking. Especially Jack.

After supper, she climbed the stairs to her new bedroom and settled on the bed with one of the colonel's books of poetry when someone tapped at her bedroom door. When she opened it, she found Samantha smiling at her.

"Oh, good, you're awake," she said. "I hope I'm not disturbing you, Jonna. I wanted to say something to you, something I couldn't say at supper."

Jonna's breath caught. "Come in, Samantha. I have no chair to offer you, but—"

"I have two chairs in my room, Jonna. You should have one of them."

"But—"

"Hush! I came to thank you for something. Giving you a chair is the least I can do."

Jonna stared at her. "Thank me? For what?"

Samantha looked down at the braided rug on the floor. "For coming to Fort Kearney. Momma was so bereft when—"

"Bereft? What does bereft mean?"

"Bereft means sad. Unhappy. I know Momma was really sad when I went away, and I worried about her. Papa was not much help because I think he didn't really understand a mother's sense of loss when her only child leaves home. So…" She laid her hand on Jonna's shoulder. "I want to thank you for coming to stay with Momma and Papa."

Jonna swallowed. "I-I had nowhere else to go. You know that Jack and I escaped from the Sioux camp together, don't you? He brought me to this army post, and your mother and father took me in. They have been very kind to me."

Samantha smiled. "It must have seemed strange to you at first."

Jonna nodded. "Every day since I arrived here has felt strange," she said slowly. "At first, I was surprised that Jack and I had really escaped. Then I was surprised that your father and mother gave me a place to stay. Your mother offered me your bedroom, your old dresses, even your old nightrobes. And they helped me learn English again and how to behave, and—" Her voice broke.

"And then you found your brother," Samantha finished. "Oh, Jonna, I am so glad. Truly I am! I have always wanted a sister, and here you are! Now, tell me about this Lance Singleton and our picnic on Sunday."

****

After breakfast on Sunday morning, Jonna and Samantha donned aprons and bustled about the overheated kitchen, frying chicken, peeling potatoes, and boiling eggs for potato salad, and chopping up the last of the pickles Martha had put up the previous summer. Martha stood at the counter, spreading caramel frosting on the apple cake Jonna had baked. "You could feed half the army on this picnic," the gray-haired woman muttered.

Samantha wrapped both arms around her mother. "Not half the army, Momma. Just five hungry picnickers." They packed everything up in a wicker picnic hamper. Jonna added two Mason jars of lemonade, and they walked over to the stable where Jack, Lance, and Andrew were waiting with the horses.

Lance looked admiringly at Samantha's split riding skirt and ruffled pink shirtwaist and shiny leather boots. Jonna smoothed her hand over her plain blue dungarees and gingham shirtwaist and was disconcerted to find Jack watching her. When she raised her eyebrows in a question, he looked away.

They rode through meadows dotted with red and yellow wildflowers, then south along a stream bordered by gray-green willows and cottonwood trees. It was a scorching summer day, the sun blazing out of a clear blue sky and not even a breath of a breeze. Both Jonna and Samantha wore wide-brimmed sunhats.

When they came to a flat area along the stream, Drew settled the lemonade jars in the creek to keep them cold while Jack spread a blanket in the shade of a cottonwood tree, plopped the picnic basket in the center, and invited Samantha and Jonna to sit down. Lance opened the hamper and handed out small plates and forks. "Miss Hawks," he began, "I understand you are a teacher?"

Samantha laughed. "Oh, good heavens, call me Samantha. And yes, after two years at Boston Teachers College, I am now a certified teacher."

"Do you know where you will be teaching?"

"Yes, I do know where, Mr. Singleton."

"Lance," he corrected.

"Lance," she amended. "I have been hired to teach in Maple Falls. That's in Oregon, near Baker."

"Baker!" Jack shot. "Sam, that's over a hundred miles from the train station at Sand Point!"

"True," she said in a quiet voice. "But you know I ride extremely well, thanks to you. A hundred miles is a mere three-day ride."

"Four," Jack amended. "Five, if it's raining."

"Oh well, if it's raining, she would no doubt choose to stay dry in Baker," Lance said. "Or take a stagecoach."

Jack noticed Lance was not looking at Sam. He was looking at Jonna. "No stagecoach runs from Baker," Jack snapped. "She could maybe catch a train at the railhead in—"

Samantha jabbed her forefinger into his shoulder. "Please, Major Corder, do not refer to me as if I were absent!"

Lance guffawed. "Yeah, Major Corder, she's sitting right next to you!"

Jonna caught her brother's grin at this exchange and shrugged. It was too pretty a day to waste it in talk. She stretched out full-length on the blanket and pulled her sunhat over her face.

"Want some lemonade?" Drew whispered.

"No. I want to lie here and smell the sunshine."

"Huh! You always were funny that way, Sis."

"What way?" she said lazily.

"I dunno, kinda—"

"Poetic?" Jack supplied in an undertone.

Jonna didn't utter a word. Lance raised his eyebrows, then watched Sam paw through the picnic hamper. She pulled out a fried chicken drumstick, offered it to Lance, and pulled out another one for herself. Again Jack noticed his friend's glance rest not on Sam but on Jonna, and a dart of annoyance snaked up his spine.

"Hey, Sis?" Andrew said in the sudden quiet.

"Yes?" she said, her voice drowsy.

"Whaddya do over at that infirmary place you go to every day?"

"Whatever is needed."

Lance leaned over her inert form. "What sort of 'needed' would that be?"

"Just what I said, Corporal Singleton."

Jack bit back a grin. Lance wasn't used to Jonna's forthright way of speaking. Maybe it would discourage him.

"You mean changing bandages and giving medicine and things like that?" Lance asked.

"Yes," Jonna said. "Things like that."

Sam sent him an amused look. Well, *someone* was enjoying this one-sided conversation, but it sure wasn't him! Jonna's brother was looking off over the tops of the cottonwoods and trying not to smile. Lance, however, was undeterred.

"Miss Lander, what do you do when you're *not* helping out at the infirmary?"

"Practice my English," Jonna said shortly.

At that, Sam laughed outright. "Andrew, your sister is very straightforward."

"Oh, yes, ma'am. She's always been that way. She can spell real good, too!"

Sam turned her attention to Jack. "You've always been that way, too, Jack."

"What way?" he grumbled.

"Straightforward."

"Jack is not 'straightforward,' " Jonna said from under her sunhat. "He is bossy."

"Now, wait just a min—"

Sam laid her hand on his arm. "It's true, Jack. I remember when you were teaching me to ride. It was always 'Do this. Don't do that.' "

"Exactly," came Jonna's voice.

Lance shifted his gaze away from Jonna. "So Jack taught you to ride, Miss—Samantha? That sounds interesting."

Jack smiled to himself. He'd succeeded in pulling Lance's attention away from Jonna and back to Sam. But his triumph didn't last long.

Sam stuck a fork in the container of potato salad. "I kind of grew up under Jack's wing because Papa was the post commander, and he was usually too busy to pay much attention to me. Jack taught me how to play horseshoes when I was too little to even lift the darn things. And he taught me how to dance a Virginia Reel and how to sing 'My Darling Clementine' and how to make coleslaw, and—"

"How to make coleslaw!" Lance shot.

"Why sure," Jack drawled. "Everyone should know how to make coleslaw. You never know when somebody gonna's throw a cabbage at you!"

Even Jonna laughed at that. Still, Jack noted, his old friend's gaze kept going straight to Jonna, reclining under her sunhat. *Hell and damn.* Then he caught Sam's laughing eyes and swore under his breath.

145

"Have some chicken, Jack," Samantha said in an amused voice. "Jonna fried it specially for you."

Lance jerked his attention to Jonna. "She did, huh? How come?"

"Why?" Sam said airily. "Because Jack likes fried chicken."

The four of them lazed away the better part of the warm Sunday afternoon in idle conversation, then packed up the picnic basket and headed back to the post. As they rode, Jack studied Lance and then Sam, hoping to see a spark of mutual interest. *Nada.* Sam drank in every green willow tree and oohed and aahed over every wildflower-swathed meadow, but never once did she look at Lance with any interest. To make matters worse, instead of noticing the fine figure Sam made on her mare, Lance hung on every brief word that came out of Jonna's mouth.

He gritted his teeth. Some poet once wrote something about the best-laid plans, but rather than puzzle out which poet, Jack chose to puzzle out his friend Lance. How come he wasn't interested in the pretty blonde girl riding beside him? All Lance Singleton had done since they left the post was study Jonna's face, her capable hands, the thick dark braid that hung down her back, and everything else about her.

They rode slowly, enjoying the cooler air now that the sun had tipped behind the distant mountains. Jack rode ahead on his favorite black mare, the one Jonna had stolen from the Cheyenne camp. Jonna and her brother rode side by side, talking about her life at Fort Kearney. Lance kept edging closer to Jonna's roan mare.

They had almost reached the post entrance when Jack suddenly reined up short and raised one arm.

Chapter Twenty

"What's wrong?" Lance said at his elbow.

"Indians," Jack muttered.

Jonna and Samantha reined up behind him. "What kind of Indians?" Samantha asked.

Jonna shaded her eyes. "Sioux." She gripped the saddle horn so tightly her knuckles whitened.

"You sure, Sis?" Andrew asked.

"She's sure," Jack answered, his voice clipped. "She knows the Sioux."

"They're on foot," Lance said quietly. "Maybe five of them. Their horses are off to the left."

"I wonder what they want?" Samantha said in an undertone.

"Something we've got that they don't," Jack said slowly. "I hope it's not Jonna."

"Yeah," Lance muttered. "They're blocking the entrance gate."

Jack motioned the two women to stay back, then slowly stepped his mount toward the Indians. Lance and Andrew moved up on either side of him. Four yards from the Sioux braves at the gate, Jack stopped. Without looking around, he issued an order. "Jonna, pull your hat down to hide your face."

Three of the Indian men walked forward. "Andrew," Jack murmured. "Hope you can speak their language."

"I can," Drew said quietly.

"Lance, let Andrew parley with them. See what they want."

"Agreed." He nodded at Drew. "Go ahead, my friend."

Jonna understood every word Drew and the Sioux brave said, and she quietly translated for Samantha beside her. "They want something. Some kind of help."

"Help?" Sam whispered. "Are you sure?"

Jonna nodded, and Drew and the brave continued to talk. "They want a doctor!" she gasped. "They want Drew and a doctor to go with them to their camp and…" She cocked her head, listening. "…treat a boy who is injured."

Samantha shook her head. "My heavens, Jonna, anyone would be crazy to go with them."

There was more talk, and then the cluster of Sioux braves suddenly moved away from the post entrance, and Jack stepped his horse through the gate. Drew and Lance advanced alongside him, and Samantha and Jonna, keeping their heads down, walked their mares close behind them.

When they were all safely inside the compound, Jack spoke to Jonna over his shoulder. "Get Colonel Hawks. Sam, walk your horse into the stable yard, then go tell Martha what's going on. Got that?"

"Yes."

"Lance, if the colonel decides to send a doctor with these braves, he'll want you and Andrew along. You okay with that?"

"Sure," they both replied in unison.

Jonna's heart catapulted into her stomach, and she had to bite her lip to keep from crying out. *Not Drew.*

Send Lance, but not my brother.

Drew moved his horse next to her. "It'll be okay, Sis. Lance and me have done this lots of times."

She bit her lip. "You will be careful?"

"I'm always careful, Sis. And I speak good Sioux, I really do." He reached down, squeezed her hand, and reined away across the parade ground.

Jonna raced for the colonel's office.

Ten minutes later, a visibly uneasy Dr. Alexander Solman met the five Sioux braves at the post entrance. Lance and Drew rode behind the doctor's horse, and when her brother reached the gate, Jonna galloped up. "Wait! I will go also!"

Jack stepped into her path, grabbed the bridle, and yanked her out of the saddle.

"What are you doing?" she screamed.

"Hush up!" He marched her into the stable, but he didn't let go of her arm. Inside, he yanked her around to face him. "Are you crazy? You can't go back to a Sioux camp!"

"Jack, you have no right—"

"Jonna, shut up!"

"I won't shut up! Drew doesn't know the Sioux like I do, and neither does Dr. Solman. If that injured boy dies, they won't let him return. Or Drew or Lance, either."

"You're not going with them."

"You don't understand, Jack. I want to go with my brother. You can't stop me."

"You're real wrong there, Jonna. I can stop you, and I will. Don't push me. If I have to, I'll tie you to the porch post. You're not going back to the Sioux." He was shouting now, and Jonna stared at him.

"Why not?" she screamed.

"Because it's dangerous. Because I won't let you set one foot outside this fort to do a damn fool thing like that."

"You don't own me, Jack! You can't tell me what to do!"

"I already did, dammit. It's too risky."

"Why should you care whether it's risky? It's *my* risk, not yours. What difference does it make to you?"

"Oh, hell, Jonna. I don't know what difference it makes, but I care whether you get yourself killed, and I'm sure as hell not going to watch you do it." He reached out and dragged her into his arms. "I'm not gonna watch you play fast and loose with your life."

"You can't stop me!"

"Oh, yes, I can." He closed one hand about her jaw, tipped her chin up, and kissed her. Hard. When he came up for air, he did it again. "I don't ever want to have this conversation again, you hear me?" he said when he lifted his mouth from hers. He gave her a little shake. "*Do you hear me?*"

She looked up at him, her blue eyes blazing, and he felt her tremble. They stood staring at each other until Jack shook his head and set her apart from him. "You're not going with them, Jonna."

Suddenly she started to cry, and that about did him in. "Jonna, I'm sorry. I'm sorry."

"You're *n-not* sorry."

He studied the stable roof for a long moment. "You're right, I'm not sorry. I'm not a damn bit sorry."

They stared at each other without speaking. Finally, she turned away and walked unsteadily toward the stable entrance. "Please give my horse an apple," she said over her shoulder.

He stared at her receding figure until he heard horses moving away from the post gate and realized he'd won. It didn't exactly feel like winning, he acknowledged. Felt more like hell.

*****

At supper that night, Jonna said exactly four words: No. Yes. And thank you. Samantha was also unusually quiet, and after a significant look passed between Martha and the colonel, the meal progressed in silence. Later, Jonna and Samantha stood side by side at the kitchen sink, washing the dishes.

"Are you all right?" Samantha asked the second time a platter slipped from Jonna's grasp and splashed back into the dishwater.

"No."

"Still mad at Jack?"

"Yes."

Samantha sighed. "Does that mean 'yes and I will never forgive him' or 'yes, but he probably saved my life,' or 'yes and—'"

"Oh, Sam, I don't know. All I know is that if anything happens to my brother, I will never forgive myself."

Sam smiled. "And you'll never forgive Jack for whatever he said to change your mind about going with them."

Jonna nodded and lifted a soapy hand out of the dishpan to brush away the tears rolling down her cheeks.

"Look, Jonna. Maybe you don't understand Jack. He's a complicated human being, and he can be maddening. But he is a *good* human being. You can trust him."

"I d-do trust him. I just don't l-like him very much."

Sam smiled. "Well, *I* like him very much, and let me tell you why. When I was growing up, I was all knobby knees and torn skirts, and I hated myself. But Jack didn't notice those things. He taught me that I was a smart and worthwhile human being."

Jonna handed her a dinner plate.

"So," Sam continued, "of course I fell madly in love with him. Jack saw that. I threw myself at him and probably would have ruined myself, but Jack saved me. He did it by preventing me from being foolish. He never laid a finger on me. He's never even kissed me under the mistletoe at Christmas."

"Oh." Jonna handed her another plate.

"As a matter of fact, in all the years I've known him, I don't know of *any* girl Jack has kissed, and believe me, there were plenty who wanted him to."

"Oh." A saucer slipped out of Jonna's fingers and plopped back into the soapsuds. Samantha went on smoothing her dishtowel over the dinner plates.

"Sam…"

"Yes, Jonna?"

"I can forgive Jack for keeping me here on the post. But…but I still don't like him."

Samantha nodded, then gave her a long look and just smiled.

Chapter Twenty-One

Six agonizing days dragged by. Every morning, Jonna had tea and an English lesson with Lucinda Markley. Every afternoon, she worked for Dr. Brownell in the infirmary. And every evening, she paced back and forth in front of the post entrance, watching for any puff of dust that might be a horse carrying Drew. During the long evenings, Martha taught her to knit afghans and how to make fudge and divinity, and Sam showed her how to wind up her hair and pin it into a bun. She even learned the words to "Streets of Laredo" and "Clementine."

Finally, late one scorching afternoon, as she walked down the infirmary steps, she spied a distant spiral of dust far across the plain. She raced to the post gate and watched as horses emerged from the haze. The next thing she knew, Jack was standing beside her.

"One of those riders is a Sioux brave," he murmured.

"Do you see Drew?"

He didn't answer for so long, Jonna punched his arm. "Jack, do you see—?"

"Yeah. He and Lance are riding behind Dr. Solman, and that Indian is carrying something in front of him."

Jonna narrowed her eyes. "He's carrying a child!"

"Looks like a young boy. Could be he's—"

"He's injured!" They watched in silence as the riders approached, and then Jack swung the wide wooden gate open and moved aside. Dr. Solman spurred toward him.

"Got a sick boy here, Major. Minutes count, so don't want to stop."

Jack waved him through, along with the Sioux brave carrying the boy. Lance and Andrew brought up the rear. As the doctor passed by Jonna, he leaned down to speak to her. "Get Dr. Brownell. Got to do an amputation."

She raced toward the infirmary. Dr. Solman spurred after her and signed for the mounted Indian to follow him.

A tired-looking Andrew Lander pulled his horse to a halt and dropped to the ground.

"You look plenty dusty," Jack said. "You okay?"

"Mostly hungry," Drew said with a grin.

"Jonna about wore a path from the colonel's house to the gate, watching for you."

"Women worry too much!" the boy said.

Jack laughed at that. "I dare you to say that to your sister!"

Drew groaned. "*You* tell her that. You're bigger'n me."

An hour later, Lance walked back to the gate. "Jehoshaphat," he said in a tired voice. "Am I glad that's over! Poor kid broke his leg, and by the time the doc got to him, it was infected. Real bad infection. That Sioux brave is the kid's father, and he was scared and plenty hostile. If it wasn't for Drew, none of us would be here to tell about it."

Jack nodded. "The colonel says Jonna about drove

him crazy with her worrying."

"Yeah?" Lance grinned. "That's real flattering, Jack."

Jack snorted. "She wasn't worrying about *you,* pal. She was worrying about her brother."

Lance's grin faded. "Oh. Sure."

Jack chuckled. "Come on, my friend. I bet you and Drew could use some supper and some sleep."

"What I could *really* use," Lance said with a laugh, is a stiff shot of Old Bailey's!"

****

Jonna missed supper and didn't return from the infirmary until well past midnight. When she finally walked through the back door into the kitchen, Martha gasped. "My lord, child, you look worse than you did when you first arrived!"

Samantha emerged from the parlor. "Would you like some hot tea?"

"Oh, yes, please. And...could you add some whiskey?"

Martha's gray eyebrows went up. "We saved some supper for you, Jonna. You must be starving."

Jonna released an uneven breath. "I am too tired to be hungry, Martha. It has been an awful day."

"Oh, my dear!"

Samantha handed her a small glass of whiskey. Jonna gulped a swallow, then choked and coughed and sputtered until Martha pounded her on the back.

"Can you tell us what happened?" Samantha asked.

"No, I can't. It was...dreadful." She downed another swallow of whiskey. "That poor boy," she whispered. "He had broken his thigh bone falling off a horse, and when his father realized something was wrong, the boy was raging with fever from an infection. By the time Dr. Solman got him back to the infirmary, gangrene had set in. They had to amputate the leg."

"Oh!" Samantha's hand flew to her mouth. "How awful!"

Jonna gave a shaky sigh. "Yes, the boy's pain was awful. His father's desperation was almost worse. No one could understand much of what he was saying, and Dr. Solman and Dr. Brownell couldn't waste time explaining things, so they went ahead and..." She shuddered. "...chloroformed the boy and took his leg off."

She stopped to down another gulp of whiskey. "There was blood everywhere, *everywhere.* The boy's father screamed and wailed, and it took two soldiers to drag him out of the room and keep him from attacking the doctors!"

"Oh, my," Martha whispered. "Oh, my heavens."

Samantha added more whiskey to Jonna's glass. "Then," she continued, "when the boy's father saw the leg they'd sawed off, he went crazy. He started chanting and shouting and weeping...it was terrible to hear him. Dr. Solman had to pry his hands away from his son's body before the anesthesia wore off."

Shaking her head, she closed her eyes. "I was so busy trying to..." She hesitated. "...stop the bleeding and not be sick, that I didn't have time to cry."

Samantha squeezed her shoulder. "Are you feeling all right now?"

"I don't know. I am steadier now, maybe because it's over. Maybe," she added with a soft laugh, "it's the whiskey."

"Maybe," Samantha suggested, "it's because you

have very strong nerves, Jonna!"

"Do I?" Jonna said, her voice tired. "I do not feel strong. Not after today."

Martha lifted the whiskey glass out of her hand. "You sit down and have a bite to eat, now. Then Lance Singleton is waiting on the porch to see you."

Jonna forced down a bowl of chicken soup and half a sourdough biscuit, then stepped out onto the porch to find not only Lance but Jack. He surged out of the porch swing. "Jonna! Are you all right?"

"No," she said, her voice unnaturally calm.

"I'm not surprised," Lance said. "I've been telling Jack what went on in the infirmary today. Pretty awful, wasn't it?"

She nodded and sank down on the swing next to Jack. She looked dazed, and he could feel her entire body shaking. He edged close enough to touch his arm to hers.

"I thought that kid's father was gonna go berserk," Lance said. "I could hear him all the way out in the hallway."

"He *did* go berserk," Jonna said dully.

Lance swallowed. "Yeah. I was worried about you."

"*Me!* Why me? I was worried about that young Indian boy."

Jack shook his head. Part of him was secretly pleased at Lance's clumsy show of sympathy. Another part of him sensed Jonna's distress and wanted to ease her pain.

Lance looked at her with real concern in his eyes, but he said nothing. Smart of him to shut up, Jack thought. He pushed the swing into a gentle rocking motion.

Lance leaned forward. "Gosh, Jonna, I'm sure sorry you had to—"

"Lance," Jack interrupted. "She already knows you're sorry, so stop telling her."

"Oh. Oh, sure. Well, I'm sor—"

Jonna shut her eyes. "Stop talking, Lance. Please, just stop talking." Lance snapped his jaw shut and passed his hand over his chin. Jonna drew in a shaky breath, and then she surprised Jack by settling her hand on his arm and kicking the swing into motion again.

They rocked back and forth in silence, but her uneven breathing told him she was more unnerved than she was letting on. He could feel her body trembling next to his. He felt like slipping his arm around her shoulders but some instinct told him she wouldn't want that. What she needed was a shot of whiskey.

"Lance, go inside and ask Martha for half a glass of the colonel's whiskey."

"Oh, sure thing, Jack." When the screen door whapped shut behind him, Jonna flinched.

"Sam already gave me some whiskey before I came outside."

"Did it help?"

"No. I still feel awful."

"Yeah, I'm not surprised. Drew's asleep in my quarters," he said to take her mind off her ordeal. "Said he could sleep for a week."

"He doesn't have a week. He and Lance are due back at Fort McKinley tomorrow."

He tried not to grin. *Good.* Lance meant well, but he was upsetting Jonna more than soothing her. "You gonna be all right, Jonna?"

"Yes, I think so. If Lance doesn't talk too much and you keep rocking this swing."

Jack chuckled. "I can guarantee rocking the swing, but sometimes I can't shut Lance up."

She gave a choked laugh as the screen door opened.

"Whiskey," Lance said, pressing a glass into Jonna's hand. He dropped noisily onto the chair across from them.

"Thank you," she murmured. Jack noticed she didn't drink it, just held the glass in her hand. "I've already had some whiskey," she murmured to Jack.

"Enough?" he asked quietly.

"I don't know yet. I still feel like I have rocks in my stomach."

Lance leaned forward again. "When I feel like that, I try to get some sleep."

"Good idea," Jack muttered. "Lance, maybe you could check on Drew. He's over in my quarters."

"Your quarters? You check on him, Jack. I'll sit with Jonna."

The swing rocked forward and then back, but neither man moved. It made Jonna smile, so she sipped her whiskey and waited. When she laid her hand on Jack's arm again, Lance bolted to his feet and, without a word, clunked down the porch steps and ambled off across the parade ground.

"That worked," she breathed. She lifted her head to down another sip of whiskey.

Jack laughed. "Feeling better?"

She nodded. "I don't really like the taste of whiskey. I just like the way my chest feels when it goes down."

"Same here." He lifted the glass out of her hand and downed what was left. "But do me a favor and don't tell the colonel." He touched her shoulder and stood up.

Jonna looked up at him and tried to smile. "Thank you, Jack."

The next morning, after breakfast in the mess hall, Lance and Drew rode off to Fort McKinley. And all the rest of that day, Jack thought about Jonna's small hand on his arm.

****

After Drew left, Jonna spent hours at the infirmary, caring for the Indian boy. By late afternoon, her back ached from bending over to sponge off his sweaty face, and her head pounded as if horses were stomping through her brain.

At suppertime, Samantha walked over with a cheese and bacon sandwich and a Mason jar of hot coffee. "How is the boy doing?"

Jonna sighed, bit into her sandwich, and swallowed before answering. "As well as can be expected, Dr. Solman says. The boy still imagines that his leg is attached, and it hurts. The worst part is that he's frightened."

"Does he know he is safe here?"

"He remembers his father shouting and carrying on, and he doesn't understand why he is not here with him."

"You speak their language, don't you? Can you make him understand?"

Jonna took another bite of the sandwich. "I try."

After Sam's visit, Jack turned up. He took one look at Jonna and walked her out of the boy's room into the hallway. "Have you been here all day?"

"Yes, since breakfast."

"You look worse than that kid in there. Have you eaten anything?"

"Sam brought me a sandwich and some coffee. But I wish I had—"

"Some whiskey, I bet," he said with a laugh.

"No! Well...yes."

"Martha's invited me to supper. How about meeting me on the colonel's porch in half an hour?"

Jonna nodded and tried to smile, then turned back to the room where the young Sioux boy lay.

"Wait a minute!" Jack suddenly said. "I learned something about amputees during the War."

"You did? I know nothing about them. A Sioux brave with gangrene usually died."

"Might try applying heat."

"Heat?"

"Yeah, you know, hot towels or something. Eases that phantom pain amputees have."

"I will do that, Jack. Thank you."

"Has his father turned up?"

She shook her head.

"Funny thing about Indian men. All men, maybe. They can hardly stand to see someone they care about in pain. They don't mind watching an army buddy get shot or stabbed, but even Indian men can't stand to hear a woman screaming when she gives birth."

"I'm not sure I could, either," Jonna said.

"Supper's in an hour," he said with a wry smile. "But if you want some whiskey, come early."

****

Four days later, the boy's father rode up to the post

gate and signed that he wanted his son. Dr. Solman objected, but Jonna could understand why he was demanding his son's release, so the doctor really had no choice. Hurriedly, she gave the boy instructions for caring for the stump of his leg and sent him off with half a dozen clean towels and some antiseptic salve.

She watched the Indian brave ride through the post gate with his son mounted in front of him and said a silent prayer. Suddenly, the boy twisted around to look at her. He lifted one hand and signed his thanks, then leaned back against his father's chest and looked ahead.

Her throat tight, Jonna watched until she could no longer see the dust raised by the retreating horse. She felt uneasy about the boy's future. Among the Sioux, young boys were expected to become expert riders to fight their enemies on horseback. With only half his leg, she wondered how the boy could even stay mounted.

She dragged herself up the porch steps to find Colonel Hawks and Samantha sitting in the swing, enjoying tall glasses of lemonade. "Jonna, you look done in!" the colonel remarked. "Sit yourself down and have some lemonade."

Samantha jolted out of the swing. "You look completely exhausted." She motioned for Jonna to take her place. "I have some news!" she sang.

"Oh?" Jonna said in a tired voice. "What news?"

"You'll never guess who has invited both of us to tea on Sunday. Lucinda Markley!"

Jonna could only nod. "Lucinda invited me for tea when I first arrived. Later she helped me with my English."

"She must be pleased at your progress," the colonel

said. "It's plain you've got a brain in that pretty head of yours."

"I have a lovely sprigged dimity dress you could wear," Sam offered.

At the moment, she could no more think about sprigged dimity or afternoon tea with Lucinda than turning cartwheels through the pines. "I don't know, Sam. Right now, I do not feel very civilized."

"You should be proud of yourself, Jonna!" Colonel Hawks said. "Both Dr. Brownell and Dr. Solman tell me you were of significant help during the boy's surgery and afterwards. You helped save that Indian boy's life."

"Do say you'll come to tea with me tomorrow," Sam begged. "I don't know Lucinda Markley very well."

Jonna studied her friend's eager green eyes. Sam had such a sweet, easy way about her, always pleasant, always cheerful. She was sure Lucinda would like her. Maybe Sam's sunny spirits would cover up her own disinclination to talk to Lucinda's friends. "All right, Sam, I will come to tea with you. I am sure it will be enjoyable."

But "enjoyable" could not begin to describe what happened that Sunday afternoon.

Chapter Twenty-Two

Jonna and Sam climbed the four porch steps of
Lucinda Markley's small frame house and tapped on
the front door. She would give anything to avoid this
tea. Tired and shaken after the ordeal at the infirmary,
she would much rather go for a long walk or bake bread
or read one of the books she'd found in the colonel's
library. But she didn't want to disappoint Sam, so she
had donned the yellow dimity dress Samantha insisted
she wear, lifted her chin, and walked across the parade
ground beside her.

The door swung open, and a visibly pregnant
Lucinda Markley appeared. "Jonna!" she exclaimed,
grasping both of her hands. "Oh, I did hope you would
join us, and here you are! And Miss Hawks! Samantha,
isn't it? Y'all are very welcome."

The three women Jonna had met before at
Lucinda's were already seated in her friend's
comfortable front parlor. Dolly Brownell, Dr.
Brownell's wife, spread her purple silk skirt on the
brocade settee next to Nell Schwammer. Sophronia
Tipton occupied one end of the green velvet sofa
opposite Nell and Dolly. The over-warm air in the
parlor smelled of perfume.

"Ladies," Lucinda sang, "y'all remember Jonna
Lander, do you not? And this is Samantha Hawks,
Colonel Hawks' daughter." Murmured greetings

accompanied the introductions, and Sophronia twitched her stylish lavender dress aside to make room for them on the green velvet sofa.

Samantha sat down and brushed aside her ruffled blue skirt to make room for Jonna while Lucinda set a silver tea tray on the coffee table and lowered her considerable bulk into a maple rocking chair. "Ladies, I declare, never in my life have I ever felt so ungainly! My waistline seems to expand almost overnight."

"Well, Lucinda," Sophronia said in a voice tinged with envy, "if you must insist on bearing a child out here at this desolate Army post, you shouldn't complain."

Lucinda's cheeks turned pink, but she made no reply, just went about filling the rose-flowered china teacups, settling them on their saucers, and handing them around.

Nell Schwammer smoothed the folds of her pale green silk dress. "I'm quite sure *my* husband Arnold would never wish *me* to bear a child out here in this untamed wilderness."

"But sometimes," Samantha ventured, "a child just *comes*, whether planned or unplanned."

"My dear girl," Sophronia retorted, "are you married?"

"Well, no, I am not," Sam admitted.

Nell leaned forward, her thin face flushed. "Then I suggest you keep your opinions to yourself."

"Why, Nell," Sophronia admonished, "that is rather harsh."

"It is not harsh at all, Sophie. It is merely realistic." Nell's lips tightened.

"As you all know," Dolly Brownell said, "my

husband is a doctor. I assure you, ladies, there are ways to avoid conceiving a child. If one chooses to, that is." She sent Lucinda a long look.

Jonna swallowed a sigh and met Samantha's gaze. Sam rolled her green eyes toward the ceiling. "Oh, I see," she murmured.

"Ladies," Lucinda said quickly, "shall we enjoy our tea?" She handed Nell a flowered china plate heaped with oatmeal cookies. "Perhaps you would pass these to the other ladies?"

Without a word, Nell snatched three cookies from the plate and handed it to Dolly. During the long minute that passed while the plate of cookies was passed around, no one said a word. Then Dolly spoke up. "Joanna…"

Jonna stiffened. "My name is not Joanna," she corrected in a quiet voice. "It is Jonna."

"Oh, yes," Dolly said with a sniff. "I remember now." She twitched her flounced purple skirt importantly. "Jonna, my husband tells me you helped save the life of an Indian boy."

"Yes, I did. Without your husband and Dr. Solman, the boy would have died."

"Why was it so important to save his life?" Dolly continued. "What's one Indian, more or less?"

Jonna stared at her. "I do not believe your husband feels that way."

"Oh, Arnold and I never discuss such things, but I am sure he feels the same."

"Then you really have no way of knowing what his feelings are, do you?" Jonna said in a quiet voice.

"Well, no. But when you've been married as long as I have, you certainly know what your husband thinks about things."

"Perhaps not," Samantha said slowly. "Even a man who has been married for years and years might have private opinions, might he not?"

"Certainly not!" Sophronia said sharply. Two spots of color appeared on her plump cheeks. "Being married means you share everything with your husband. *Especially* what he thinks about certain things."

"Ladies," Lucinda interrupted. "More tea?"

No one responded until Jonna leaned toward their hostess. "Yes, thank you, Lucinda. I would like more tea." Lucinda's three friends seemed very argumentative this afternoon. If she was attacked again, as she had been before, Jonna feared she could not trust herself to keep her temper.

"Dolly," Nell asked, an edge in her voice, "how long *have* you and Arnold been married?"

"Almost fifteen years," Dolly snapped. "And they've been *happy* years. *Very* happy years."

"I'm sure they were," Lucinda said quickly. "I will pass the cookies again, shall I? Sophronia, wherever did you find that lovely silk dress you're wearing?"

"In New York City," Sophronia answered. "Mail order, of course."

"I cannot *wait* until my old dresses fit me again," Lucinda said.

"Is your husband excited about the baby?" Samantha ventured.

"Gracious, no! Sidney never gets excited about *anything*. That's what makes him such an outstanding army officer."

"Huumph!" Dolly sniffed. "I've always believed that what makes a fine soldier is discipline under fire.

And believe me, a doctor's emergency surgery is 'under fire.' Why, my—"

"Samantha?" Lucinda suddenly turned to Sam. "I understand you recently graduated from the teachers college in Boston."

"Yes, I did, just this last month."

Sophronia reached over and poked her arm. "You do know that teachers in Oregon must remain unmarried."

"Yes, I know that."

"Don't you *want* to get married?"

Sam laughed. "Well, not right away. I want to do what I have been trained to do—teach school."

Sophronia moved her gaze to Jonna. "What about you, Joanna?"

"Jonna," she corrected again. "What *about* me?"

"Do you plan to get married? I understand that handsome corporal Lance Singleton is interested. And it's obvious you can't go on living with Colonel Hawks and his wife for *too* long."

Samantha leveled a long look at Sophronia. "Why can't she? Why can't Jonna live with my parents for as long as she wishes?"

"Well, she doesn't exactly *belong* here, does she?" Sophronia said.

Sam drew in a deep breath. "Of course, she belongs here. Why wouldn't she? Besides, I don't see that where Jonna lives is anyone's business but Jonna's."

"It's also the business of Colonel and Martha Hawks," Nell Schwammer said from across the room.

Sam smiled. "Once again, that is no one's business but theirs. Don't you agree?"

Jonna caught Sam's gaze and was surprised to see

amusement in her green eyes. How could she possibly be amused by such rude statements? But Sam just smiled at her and turned her attention back to Sophronia Tipton.

"I have done a good deal of thinking about my first year of teaching," she said rather loudly. "I intend to teach the children things that are important. For instance…" She raised her voice. "I will teach them that people should treat others as they themselves wish to be treated, as it says in the Bible. And," she added with a smile, "I will also teach them that a soft answer turns away wrath."

Lucinda choked on her tea while the other ladies looked at each other in uneasy silence.

"Why, Miss Hawks," Lucinda managed, "that is truly admirable."

"I think," Jonna began, "you forgot one important lesson, Samantha."

Samantha sent her a conspiratorial smile. "I did? What lesson is that?"

Jonna slowly surveyed the officers' wives gathered in Lucinda's parlor. "It's something my father taught me. 'The closed mouth attracts no flies.' "

Sam clapped her hand over her mouth to keep from laughing aloud. When she could speak, she met Sophronia Tipton's gaze, then turned to Jonna. "Jonna, I will make sure to include your father's teaching in my lesson about tolerance."

Sophronia twitched her skirt in place. "*My* father always said he never learned much of value in school. The teachers were all old-maid know-it-alls who had nothing better to do."

Lucinda gasped. "I'm sure that is not true of Miss

Ha—"

"Oh, but it is," Samantha interrupted with a smile. "At twenty-three, I am already considered an old maid. However, that does not disturb me. It's also true that I have 'nothing better to do,' as you so succinctly put it, Mrs. Tipton. That is because I cannot think of *anything* better to do than teach young minds about the danger of always believing they are right about everything. Why, such narrow-minded thinking is the worst kind of prejudice, don't you agree?"

Sophronia opened her mouth, but Lucinda cut her off. "Quite right, Miss Hawks. No truly well-educated person can possibly think he—or she—knows *everything*."

Once more, Sophronia opened her mouth. "I—"

"That," Sam continued, "is what is called..." Theatrically, she clapped both hands on her cheeks. "Oh, Jonna, what is the word I want?"

"The word for always believing you are right?" Jonna said in an innocent tone. "I believe that is called prejudice."

"Of course! I was going to say close-minded or even arrogant, but prejudice is more correct."

In the heavy silence that descended, Jonna tried hard not to look at Sam for fear she would laugh. The other ladies studied their teacups. Lucinda alone met Sam's eye, and then Jonna's, and she raised her cup to them in a subtle salute.

****

At supper that night, Martha made the mistake of asking about Lucinda Markley's tea party. Samantha and Jonna looked at each other across the dining table and burst into laughter. "It was...enlightening," Sam spluttered.

"And educational," Jonna added. "I learned much about the wives of army officers."

"I have often thought that women have no place on an army post," Colonel Hawks said. "Most women are not suited to army life."

"Except for me," Martha said firmly.

"And me," Samantha added. "And Jonna."

"Me!" Jonna blinked. "I do not fit in here. Not one of Lucinda's friends has ever said anything kind or even friendly to me."

"Jonna," the colonel said in a decisive voice. "You fit in *here*, in this house. You are accepted by me and by Martha and Samantha. And Jack," he added.

Martha rose to replenish the platter of fried chicken. "And you are most certainly accepted at the infirmary. I am told you are a great help to both Dr. Brownell and Dr. Solman. Dr. Brownell, in particular, values you."

Samantha smiled at her father. "Well, Dr. Brownell's snippy wife made it quite clear *she* doesn't value Jonna. Her unkind remarks set my teeth on edge."

"Who cares about the doctor's snippy wife?" the colonel said. "I've met a dozen officers' wives just like Dolly Brownell. Not even their husbands can stand to be around them for very long. That's one reason why they volunteer for extended scouting missions."

Jonna leaned back in her chair and drew in a long, shaky breath. She was beginning to feel something she had never expect to feel—out of place. Even here at the supper table with Samantha and Martha and the colonel, she wondered if she would ever truly belong. She had worked hard to fit in, to be part of life here at

Fort Kearney. Here, with Martha and Colonel Hawks, she had everything she had longed for during those long years with the Sioux. Best of all, she had found Drew.

But sometimes, in the middle of the night, she woke up wondering why she still felt vaguely unsettled. What was missing?

Chapter Twenty-Three

As the Fourth of July drew near, everyone at the post, including the laundresses, the sutler, and the mess hall cook, looked forward to the big dance the colonel and his wife hosted every year. It was the highlight of the summer, and no one would think of missing it. Martha and Jonna baked batch after batch of oatmeal and cinnamon-drop cookies and apple teacakes while Samantha rescued the huge punch bowl from the attic and stitched up gingham tablecloths and dozens of napkins on Martha's treadle sewing machine. Any soldier who could play a musical instrument was recruited for the band, and every morning, the sound of rehearsed waltzes and polkas floated from the reception hall. Invitations were sent to all the army posts within a hundred miles, including Fort McKinley, where Lance and Andrew were assigned.

Medals and uniform buttons were polished to a shine; the post barber trimmed beards and mustaches, and young women pressed their best dresses and made sure their hair was properly rolled up in curling rags.

At the colonel's dinner table two days before the dance, Martha and Samantha were working hard to convince Jonna to attend. "You absolutely must come," Sam pleaded. "Everyone at this post will be there, all the officers and their wives and—"

"I promised to visit the soldiers in the infirmary,"

Jonna protested. "One of the new recruits has pneumonia, and two more have gunshot wounds."

"Gunshot!" Martha exclaimed. "Who in the world—?"

"The Sioux now have rifles," the colonel explained. "Not much ammunition, but enough to cripple two of my lieutenants."

Martha set aside her coffee cup. "Martin, that makes me purely nervous. You send out patrols every day. What is to prevent—?"

"Nothing," he said brusquely. "This is the army, Martha, not a society picnic."

Samantha reached her hand across the table. "Jonna, surely those ailing soldiers won't take up your entire evening. You could come to the dance later."

Jonna bit her lip. "Oh, no. I…"

Sam studied her face. "Why are you hesitating?"

"Because…because I do not know any of those dances."

"Is that all?" Samantha cried. "In one hour flat, I can teach you every dance they could think of. Come on into the parlor. We can start right now."

****

July Fourth turned out to be a sweltering summer day, so hot even the cicadas were silent. But when evening fell, the air grew soft and fragrant with the scent of desert sage and Martha's Belle of Portugal roses. From the infirmary ward, Jonna could hear the faint sound of violins and guitars, but her jittery nerves kept her purposely over-busy. Finally, even the soldiers in her care began urging her to attend the dance.

Still, she hesitated. Crowds of people still made her nervous, and she knew none of the officers' wives except for Lucinda to be the least bit friendly. She never knew what to say or how to act. What if Sophronia Tipton or Dolly Brownell said something mean?

"Oh, please," Samantha begged. "Just this once."

Oh, all right, she decided. She would go. At least tonight she would know the dance steps, thanks to Sam.

She heated the sadiron on the stove in Martha's kitchen and pressed the wrinkles out of the lemon-yellow dimity dress Sam had insisted she wear. Then she pulled on a ruffled petticoat and brushed out her hair. When she was ready, she took a deep breath to quell the butterflies in her stomach and walked out the front door and down the porch steps.

Tonight her nerves were even more jangly. After that first dance, when Lieutenant Markley had been so overbearing, she had resolved never to attend another one.

But you want to fit into life here at the post, do you not? Yes, she did. But sometimes, like this evening, she wondered why it was that no matter what she did, she still felt vaguely unsettled, as if deep down something important was missing. Nevertheless, she didn't want to disappoint Martha or the colonel, so she drew in a deep breath, raised her chin, and started off for the reception hall.

****

Jack spent an hour searching for Jonna among the women gathered in the crowded ballroom. He knew she disliked large social gatherings, so he waited all evening to see whether she would walk through the door. Had she decided not to attend?

He recognized some of the officers' wives sitting

on the sidelines, but it was Lucinda Markley who caught his attention. Looking hugely pregnant in a voluminous peach-colored dress, Lucinda was sitting between two chattering women while Lieutenant Markley lurked on the sidelines, waiting to cut in on couples already skimming across the dance floor.

Samantha whirled past with first one partner, then another. Then Martha and the colonel danced by doing a spirited polka. But no Jonna.

Another hour went by. He danced half-heartedly with some lieutenant's wife whose name he couldn't remember, then with the redheaded laundress who kept his uniforms clean and pressed. A lady's-choice waltz found him partnered with the other laundress, a tiny, muscular-looking brunette whose over-starched petticoats got tangled up between his legs.

Finally, he cornered Colonel Hawks. "Isn't Jonna coming?"

"I sure thought she was, Jack."

"Any idea where she is?"

"At the infirmary, far as I know. But she promised—" He broke off and gestured across the room where a girl in a ruffled yellow dress was standing uncertainly in the doorway. She hesitated for a long minute, then stepped into the room. Jack swore every man in the room stopped whatever he was doing and stared. His mouth went dry.

This wasn't the Jonna he'd seen around the fort every day for the past six months. This Jonna had let her hair down, and it tumbled about her shoulders in dark waves. *Jupiter, what the hell had happened to her?* She looked like a shaft of sunshine in that yellow dress, and by the sudden quiet in the room, he guessed every male present thought exactly the same thing.

"Why don't you ask her to dance?" the colonel suggested.

"What?"

"I said—"

"Yeah."

The colonel chuckled. "Never seen you so flummoxed, Jack."

"What? Oh, yeah. Dance with her."

A knot of soldiers two and three deep already surrounded her. He drifted to the bar, manned by a fresh-faced private. "Whiskey," he said in a hoarse voice.

"Double, Major?" the private asked.

"What? Oh sure. Make it a double."

He scarcely registered that it was whiskey and not dishwater that slid down his throat. After two big gulps, he about-faced and leaned against the bar, studying the room. The knot of men around Jonna had formed into a clot of soldiers standing on the sidelines, waiting for a chance to cut in while a tall captain from another army post was waltzing with Jonna and desperately trying to steer her away from them. Jack noted she was easily following the captain's steps. *Where had she learned to dance like that?*

A hand touched his arm. "I taught Jonna some dance steps last night," Sam said with a laugh. "You're staring at her like you've never seen her before."

"I've never seen *this* Jonna before."

She laughed. "Girls are like that. They change. But sometimes a man doesn't see what's right in front of him." She pressed his arm. "She's been right in front of you all this time."

"Not like this, she hasn't. Not like she is tonight, Sam."

Samantha smiled. "I should be jealous that you're admiring her and not me."

"Yeah, maybe." He downed another swallow of whiskey.

"You have never once looked at me like that," Samantha said quietly. "However, I am not jealous. I am truly fond of Jonna."

With an effort, Jack pulled his attention from the dance floor to focus on Sam. "You're not what?"

"Jealous," she repeated with a laugh.

"How come, Sam? You used to be jealous of every horse I saddled."

"Because," she said happily, "I'm no longer in love with you the way I was when I was eleven years old."

"Oh. Yeah." Again his eyes followed Jonna and the waltzing captain. "You know something, Sam?"

"I know a great deal, Jack. Things I did not learn at my teachers college in Boston."

"Yeah." He took another sip of whiskey. "Want some lemonade?"

"No, thank you. Don't you want to know what I *didn't* learn at my teachers college?"

"Hmm?"

Sam poked his arm. "I did *not* learn how to tell when you'd rather be friends with a man than a paramour."

He surveyed her with a frown. "I'm afraid to ask where you *did* learn that, Sam."

She sent him an impudent grin. "I learned it from you, you dolt!"

"You did, huh?" Once more, his gaze traveled back

to the dance floor.

Sam poked his arm again. "You should dance with me, you big ox. You'll never get close to her from the sidelines." Then she was suddenly whirled away in the arms of an officer.

She was right. But as he set his whiskey glass down and turned toward the dance floor, he spied Lance Singleton striding toward him.

"Jack!" Lance said in a loud voice. "I thought you didn't like these shindigs."

The two men shook hands. "I...don't. I'm...uh...watching over the colonel's daughter, Samantha."

Lance nodded, hiding his smile. "Samantha needs watching over, huh? I see her over there dancing with some captain. I don't recognize him, do you?"

"Nope."

"You gonna cut in?"

"Nope."

Lance just looked at him. Jack shifted his gaze from Jonna to Samantha and her captain, spinning and weaving around the other dancers. Then Jonna and her partner, a muscular corporal from Fort McKinley, waltzed past. Suddenly, she stopped dead in the center of the floor, stepped out of the corporal's arms, and walked away.

The rejected officer strode after her and snaked out his hand to stop her, but she sidestepped around him. The instant she reached the sidelines, the gang of waiting males besieged her. One grasped her wrist and pulled her into his arms. That galvanized the other soldiers, and all at once, fists started flying. Jonna was caught in the melee.

Jack reached her just as the rejected corporal grabbed her shoulder. She jerked free, but the man then made a lunge for her. Jack stepped between them, pulled Jonna into his arms, and swung her away.

She said something, but he couldn't hear over the uproar on the sidelines, so he just kept moving his feet. She felt good in his arms, warm and…good. Over her head, he watched Colonel Hawks approach the squabbling soldiers, and suddenly, the two main combatants were saluting and edging toward the doorway.

"Problem's over," he murmured near her ear. She nodded but said nothing, so he continued to waltz—*this was a waltz, wasn't it?* She felt soft and alive, and all at once, he found he couldn't think clearly. He didn't want to think, really. He just wanted to keep his arms around her. Her hair smelled like something flowery, roses maybe. He closed his eyes and sucked in a deep breath. *What the hell was happening?*

For some reason, Jonna didn't feel like saying anything, either. She just wanted to stay in Jack's arms and *not* say anything. He smelled of sweat and whiskey and something like mint, and she closed her eyes and let herself drift.

She liked this man. Sometimes she didn't *want* to like him, but she did. She liked him a lot. Tonight there was something unsettling about being held in his arms, something that poked at her breastbone and made her feel as if she was holding her breath. She didn't want to look up into his face. She knew his eyes were gray. They could harden to cold steel in an instant, and when he laughed, the skin at the corners crinkled.

He made her nervous sometimes. And mad. She

hated it when he laughed at her, hated it even more when he *didn't* laugh and kept silent, as he was doing now. Jack Corder was the most...the most...

Suddenly, Lance Singleton stepped up and swung Jonna out of Jack's arms.

"Oh!" she exclaimed. "What happened? I was dancing with Jack, and then all of a sudden, I wasn't."

"It's called 'cutting in,' Jonna. Aren't you glad to see me? It's been over a week since your brother and I left for Fort McHenry."

"Has it?"

"Andrew and I rode in a couple of hours ago."

"My brother is here? At the dance?"

"He's somewhere around. Last time I saw him, he was drinking coffee over at the mess hall."

"Coffee! Oh, my, I can't get used to my baby brother drinking coffee."

"Boys grow up," Lance remarked. "Girls grow up, too. And I must say," he continued, gazing down at her, "some girls grow up prettier than others."

Jonna said nothing. Across the room, she saw Jack talking to Martha and Samantha. What would it be like to go to a college? she wondered. To travel to the other side of the country, to a city where she knew no one? She swallowed hard. She wouldn't know how to behave, but the idea of something beyond life here at Fort Kearney made her smile inside.

"Jonna, I was wondering if we might go riding together Sunday afternoon."

"Why?" she said bluntly.

"Well, uh, so we could get better acquainted."

Her gaze again drifted to the other side of the room where Jack was now dancing with Samantha and laughing about something. Sam looked beautiful in that pale green dimity dress, with her blonde hair caught up with a green ribbon.

"Better acquainted," she echoed. Did she *want* to be better acquainted with Lance Singleton? *Lance doesn't make me laugh the way Jack does. He also doesn't make me mad, the way Jack does.*

"What about Sunday?" Lance pressed.

Suddenly, she stopped dancing and stood perfectly still. *Not the way Jack does.*

"Jonna? Did I accidentally step on your foot?"

"No," she murmured. "You did not. And I would like to go riding on Sunday."

"Good."

"Bring Drew with you," she said.

"Huh?" A frown creased his forehead. "Oh, sure, Jonna. I'll bring Drew along, too."

All at once, she spied Sidney Markley making his unsteady way across the room, heading straight for her, and a shiver crawled up her spine. Lance looked up, saw the lieutenant lurching toward them, and quickly put Jonna behind him.

"Hey, pretty lady," Sidney shouted, "you wanna dance wi' me?"

"She's already partnered, Lieutenant," Lance said. "Leave her alone."

Markley visibly swayed toward him. "Sez who?"

"Name's Lance Singleton. And the lady is dancing with me."

"Oh, yeah?" Markley drunkenly shoved Lance's arm. "Get outta th' way, Lanch Sh—Shingleton. She's gonna dance with me."

Lance shifted his body to block him. "No, she is

not. Why don't you go back—"

Markley's fist connected sloppily with Lance's jaw, and the next thing Jonna knew, Lance twisted away from her to grab Markley's arm, wrenched it up behind his back, and propelled him across the floor. Couples scattered out of his path as men snatched their partners out of the way.

Jonna seized the opportunity to escape. She was halfway across the floor when Jack snaked out his arm and pulled her to a stop. "Jonna? What's wrong?"

"He's drunk!" she blurted.

"Yeah. Lance is escorting him outside." He kept his hand on her arm. "Want some lemonade?"

She nodded, her heart pounding. "Want some whiskey in it?" he joked.

She shot him a look. "Yes, please."

Jack blinked. "You sure?"

"Jack, you know I never say anything I do not mean."

"Yeah, I know," he said with an edge in his voice. He ladled out a glass of lemonade, then added a splash of whiskey. "Godawful combination," he muttered.

"Oh, I don't want it to *taste* good. I just want it to calm my nerves."

He handed her the doctored lemonade, closed her fingers around the glass, and gave her a long look. "You look kinda worried."

"I've agreed to go riding with Lance tomorrow. And Andrew," she added. "I...I do not see my brother often enough."

"Oh. Lance and your brother, huh?" He hid a smile. Sure was clever of Jonna to include her brother. Then another thought popped into his head. Why should *he* care who Jonna went riding with? He had no claim on her. Most days Jonna didn't even notice him!

For the rest of the evening, he watched the general melee that occurred each time one of Jonna's partners relinquished her. He also kept his eye on a much-subdued Sidney Markley. The lieutenant made no move in Jonna's direction, but he wasn't paying attention to his wife, either. Lucinda Markley sat awkwardly on the sidelines, her very pregnant state obvious.

He decided he'd ask her to dance, but as he started across the floor, Jonna's brother appeared in the doorway. Andrew looked like he'd rather be anywhere but here at the colonel's Fourth of July dance, and Jack had to smile. For a few minutes, the boy stood watching his sister being fought over, then he shrugged and vanished.

He remembered what that age was like, full of vague longings, awkward attempts to talk to a girl, and tongue-tied silences. He still felt that way a lot of the time, like there was some language other men knew that he didn't, and for years, he'd covered it up by being brusque. Lance and the colonel were rare exceptions. He could talk to them. And maybe Sam, he acknowledged.

He'd known Samantha Hawks ever since she was a gangly, inquisitive kid who wanted to learn everything—horseback riding, how to fire a pistol, how to care for newborn kittens, even how to catch trout. Sam had grown into a very pretty young woman, but he'd never been particularly attracted to her. He liked her well enough, but he'd never felt any physical pull toward her. In all the years he'd helped Martha, Colonel Hawks, and Sam decorate their Christmas tree, he'd never once felt the urge to kiss Sam under the mistletoe.

Long after midnight, the musicians packed up their instruments, and the guests began to drift toward the door. Colonel Hawks stopped Jack at the bar. "Martha and I have to put the refreshment table to rights, Jack. Would you take a lantern and walk Sam and Jonna back to the house?"

"Glad to, Martin. See you tomorrow."

On their way through the pine trees to the colonel's house, Sam chattered on and on about her dancing partners and her conversations with the women sitting on the sidelines.

Jonna said not one single word.

****

The next morning, Jack tramped over to the mess hall for some coffee and ran smack into young Andrew Lander. "Drew! What are you doing up so early on a Sunday morning?"

The boy grinned. "Gotta eat somethin' before the picnic this afternoon. Jonna doesn't make enough food to feed a grasshopper."

Jack stopped dead. "Picnic! You're having a picnic?"

"Lance and Jonna are goin' riding this afternoon down by some creek, and they're gonna take a picnic hamper. I'm goin', too, even though I don't really want to."

"Why not?"

"Gosh, Jack, I see enough of Lance as it is. I don't need to sit by some creek to talk to him. And besides, I don't really like picnics too much."

"Maybe Jonna wants you along as a chaperone."

The lanky young man frowned. "Whatza

chaperone?"

"A chaperone is someone who goes along on an outing to—"

"Keep the peace?"

Jack laughed and signaled the kitchen attendant for two cups of coffee. "Not to keep the peace, son. More to keep things from, well, from getting out of hand."

"How much out of hand can they get sittin' by a creek eatin' a sandwich?"

"You ever have a girlfriend, Drew?"

"Me? Heck no! Why would I want a girlfriend?"

"Wait a while, Drew. You might surprise yourself."

Drew shook his head. "Jack, you gonna explain what a chaperone does?"

Jack guided him over to an empty table. "If you want to know what a chaperone does, the explanation won't make much sense. And if you *don't* want to know, you already know what a chaperone does, in which case you probably don't want one."

Drew shot him a puzzled look and downed a gulp of coffee. After three swallows, he nodded his head. "Oh, I get it. Jonna wants me along to make sure Lance doesn't—"

"Exactly. Make sure Lance *doesn't.*"

"How come she doesn't take *you* along as a chaperone, Jack?"

He chuckled. "One reason is that a chaperone is usually a disinterested party, and I'm—" He clamped his jaw shut.

"You're not disinterested, huh?"

Jack swallowed a gulp of coffee and focused on the far wall. *Well, Major Corder, are you disinterested?*

Drew was studying him closely. He cleared his throat. "No, I'm not exactly disinterested. You don't survive four days on the trail being chased by the Sioux without developing some regard for your travel companion."

"Yeah, she told me about that. In some ways, I'm surprised you're still speaking to each other."

Jack sent him a sharp look but said nothing.

"But in other ways," Drew continued, "she talks about you like...like she used to talk about our Grandpa Thornton. Thorny, we called him. I remember how the old man cried when we started off for Oregon."

Grandpa Thorny, huh? Guess that tells me something.

"Look, Drew, you keep a sharp eye out for...trouble this afternoon, okay?"

"Trouble? What kinda trouble?"

"You know, Indians. Snakes. Poison oak." *And a lovestruck Lance Singleton.*

"Sure, Jack." Drew slurped the last of his coffee and gave him a suddenly knowing look. "I'll keep an eye on things." Then he stood up, clapped him on the shoulder, and headed for the door.

Jack let out a long sigh and watched Drew's long-legged stride until the mess hall door flapped shut behind him.

Chapter Twenty-Four

Jonna dismounted in the shade of a cottonwood, patted the neck of her roan mare, and led her to the creek to drink. Lance handed the wicker picnic hamper to Drew and tied the three horses to a low-lying branch. Then the three of them walked downstream until they found a shaded clearing in the tangle of willows and vine maples. Lance unrolled a travel-worn blanket and motioned for her to sit down.

She didn't feel like sitting beside Lance. She didn't feel much like a picnic, either, but she did like spending time with her brother. Lance might be annoyed at that, but she cared more about Drew than what Lance Singleton felt. She withdrew two Mason jars of lemonade from the picnic basket, handed them to Lance, and tipped her head toward the burbling creek.

"Oh, sure, Jonna. I'll make sure they get chilled." Whistling, he moved farther downstream, and Jonna settled herself on the blanket beside Drew. After two hours of riding under the scorching summer sun, the shade felt cool and pleasant. How, she wondered, did men on army missions stand the heat? Did Drew wear a broad-brimmed hat, as Lance did, to keep the sun from burning his nose and the back of his neck? What did her brother do on hot nights when he was away on some assignment?

It was Drew she really wanted to talk with. Her

brother was important to her, but Lance? Not so much. When the tall corporal returned from the creek, he settled on the blanket and leaned close to Jonna. "Did you enjoy the dance last night?"

"I enjoyed parts of it," she said quietly. "Other parts I would rather forget."

"I understand Colonel Hawks hosts that Fourth of July dance every year. I usually miss them because I'm out on a mission to some Indian camp or other."

She turned to her brother. "Drew, do you like being a special agent for the army?"

"Yeah, I like it fine, Sis. They pay me 'n everything." She noticed he was methodically plucking blades of camas grass and tossing them aside, and suddenly, she realized her brother was bored to death on this picnic.

"I like it fine, too," Lance volunteered. "When your brother came along, the assignments got more interesting. He's really good with different Indian dialects."

"How did you learn all those languages, Drew?"

He sent her a grin. "Dunno, really. Guess I've got a good ear for it. Colonel Hardesty at Fort McHenry says so anyway."

"That must be valuable to the army," Jonna said.

"*Very* valuable," Lance said. "Without Drew, we'd waste a lot of time trying to figure out what's really going on with the tribes."

Jonna opened the picnic hamper and lifted out a stack of napkin-wrapped sandwiches. "Which would you like, cheese and bacon or bacon and cheese?"

Drew chortled, but Lance didn't even smile. "Either one sounds fine to me," he said. "You make them?"

Jonna nodded. Drew hid a smile but said nothing and reached for a sandwich. "Are you gettin' used to life at Fort Kearney, Sis? Sure must be different from livin' with the Sioux."

She handed him a sandwich. "In some ways, I wonder if I will ever get used to it. I lived a different kind of life with the Sioux, and now…well, now sometimes I feel a bit lost."

Drew sent her a quick look. "Are you happy at this post?"

"At times," she said, her voice quiet. "Other times I feel…confused."

"Confused?" Lance said, a sandwich halfway to his mouth. "Confused about what?"

"Lance," she said quickly, "do you think that lemonade is cold yet?"

"I'll go check on it." He got to his feet and strode off along the creek bank.

Drew touched her hand. "I feel confused sometimes, too, Sis. Guess it's because of what happened to us. Sometimes it seems like a bad dream, and if I close my eyes, it'll go away. You ever feel that way?"

"Yes," she said. "Often."

"Think it'll ever go away? Being confused, I mean?"

Jonna sent him a long look and sighed. "I don't know, Drew. I thought I knew what I wanted when I arrived at the fort. I wanted to fit in, to belong. But sometimes I feel something is missing, and I don't know what it is. Do you understand?"

"Yep. I don't feel it as strong as you do, but I sure

do understand."

"I was so sure about what I wanted, so I'm surprised that being here at Fort Kearney feels like it's, well, not enough somehow."

Lance emerged from the trees with a dripping jar of lemonade, which he handed to Jonna. "Saw some medium-sized trout in the stream a ways down. On our next picnic, let's go fishing."

"You don't like trout, Lance," Drew said with a laugh.

"Yeah, but I like to fish. Too bad we didn't bring fishing lines and some hooks."

Jonna sent him a long look, then without a word, she stood up and marched off upstream. Lance and Drew stared at each other. "What did I say?" Lance asked.

Drew shrugged. "Dunno. Maybe the lemonade's not cold enough."

"She didn't take the lemonade."

Five minutes later, Jonna reappeared with something folded up in her blue denim skirt. Quickly, she knelt on the blanket and dumped a fat, shiny trout at Lance's elbow.

"What the— How the devil did you catch that?"

"With my hands," she said. "The Sioux never use hooks to catch a fish."

Lance looked dumbstruck. Drew laughed. Jonna quietly wrapped the trout in a napkin and stowed it at the bottom of the picnic basket.

"Gosh, Sis, could you teach me how to fish like that?"

"If you like. Maybe next time we have a picnic."

Lance leaned forward. "What about next Sunday?"

Jonna said nothing. As much as she liked seeing Drew, seeing Lance didn't have the same appeal.

"Drew," Lance said, "why don't you go get that other jar of lemonade I set in the creek?"

"Nah," Drew said. "You stashed it, you get it. Besides, I don't know where it is."

"Oh. Well, I guess I should…" The corporal's voice trailed off as he got to his feet and started downstream.

Drew leaned toward her. "Lance is a good man," he intoned. "Just makes me grit my teeth sometimes."

Jonna laughed.

"You like him?"

She hesitated. "Somewhat, yes."

"Me, too. I know he and Jack are friends from way back, but sometimes, I'd like to punch him. Do you ever want to punch Jack?"

"No. He makes me mad sometimes, but he's never…uninteresting."

"Jack's interesting, huh? He's sure full of advice sometimes."

Jonna's dark eyebrows went up. "Oh? Advice about what?"

Drew looked off toward the creek. "Uh, advice about bein' a chaperone. At least that's what I thought we were talkin' about."

She hid a smile. "Jack usually says exactly what he means. Sometimes that makes him hard to talk to."

"Blunt, huh?" Drew said with a laugh.

"And," Jonna added with a smile, "he's usually convinced he's always right."

"Golly, Sis. Remind you of anybody?"

She thought for a moment. "Yes! Granddad

193

Thornton."

"Exactly! Kinda reminds me of you, too." He ducked the hand she swung at him.

Lance emerged from the creek bank, a dripping jar of lemonade in his hand. "Drew, what reminds you of Jonna?"

Drew caught his sister's eye. "Just…something, huh, Sis?"

All the way back to the fort, Drew watched Lance send admiring looks at his sister. He also noticed that Jonna was paying no attention. *If this is what people mean by "courtship," it sure is strange.*

Colonel Hawks invited Lance and Drew to stay for supper that night, along with Jack Corder. Samantha and Martha were close-mouthed about the menu, except that it included scalloped potatoes, corn on the cob, and a surprise. Jonna made an apple spice cake, then set out plates and glasses and silverware while the men sat on the front porch, sipping the colonel's whiskey.

"Surely Drew is not drinking whiskey!" Jonna said in alarm.

Martha patted her arm. "Martin watered down his glass."

"Jonna," Samanatha said, untying her gingham apron. "Your brother is going to grow up. You can't stop it."

"I don't want to stop it, Sam. I just don't want him riding into an Indian camp with whiskey on his breath!"

"Does Lance drink whiskey?" Martha inquired.

Jonna frowned. "I have no idea."

"And no interest?" Sam asked with a smile.

Jonna pressed her lips together, and Martha laid a serving spoon in her hand. "Go call the men in to supper, would you? My hands are all floury."

When everyone was seated at the big walnut table in the dining room, Martha suddenly bolted back into the kitchen. "Oh, heavens, I almost forgot Jonna's *pièce de résistance!*"

"Huh?" Jack and Lance said together.

"Piece of resistance," Drew supplied.

Jonna stared at her brother. "Isn't that a French phrase? How on earth would you know that?"

Drew just shrugged.

Martha emerged from the kitchen with a small platter, which she ostentatiously set in front of Jack. "Jonna prepared this just for you."

"Looks like a trout," he said. "How come it's for me?"

"Because Lance doesn't like trout," Jonna answered.

"And because Jonna caught it in the stream today," Drew added. "She wanted to show you something."

"Show me what?"

"Show you that I can catch a trout," Jonna said.

"With no fishing pole or a hook or anything!" Drew said proudly.

Jack stared at her. "Really? Why'd you do that?"

"Because I wanted to show you that I am not unskilled just because I lived with the Sioux while other girls were learning how to waltz and cut out dress patterns. I learned many things from the Sioux. How to sew beads onto a deerskin shirt, how to dry fish, how to make pemmican and jerky, how to stitch deerskin moccasins, and—"

"Jonna, I never said you were un—"

"Can you really make pemmican?" Drew

195

interrupted. "Could you show me how?"

"First you have to kill a deer," Jack said dryly.

Jonna glowered at him. "I can do that, too," she said.

"And," Martha added, "she makes a delicious apple spice cake!"

"Golly, Sis," Drew breathed. "And you can do those waltz-things they were doin' at the dance last night, too, huh?"

"She sure can," Lance volunteered.

"Drew," Jack said. "Girls are surprising." He forked a bite of fried trout into his mouth. "And your sister is a girl who can catch a trout and cook it and look damn pretty while she's doing it!"

Jonna stared at him until he caught her eye and grinned.

****

The next morning, Lance and Drew headed back to Fort McHenry. Jonna stood at the gate, watching their horses gradually disappear into the dust until her eyes ached. Suddenly, Jack was standing at her elbow.

"Drew is a nice kid," he murmured.

Jonna nodded. "What about your friend Lance?"

"Lance is a fine man and a good friend. I've known him ever since we enlisted in the army together." He hesitated. "Maybe you're a mite interested?"

She didn't answer for a long moment. Finally, she turned toward him. "I am not interested. I am interested in what my future is going to be."

"That's understandable, I guess. You've spent half your life with the Sioux, speaking their language, learning their ways. Must seem strange to change horses all of a sudden."

She shook her head. "It *is* strange. I wanted to escape the Sioux camp. I wanted to leave that life behind because…because I didn't belong there. Now people tell me that I belong *here,* but to be honest, sometimes I don't really feel I *do*." She half-turned away from him. "Sometimes, I think I don't belong anywhere."

He studied her back. "You know, when you first arrived at the post, you were convinced you knew exactly what you wanted. And up until now, you've been pretty good at getting it, about fitting in and all that. Are you saying maybe you're finding that just fitting in isn't enough?"

She released a long breath. "Maybe. I am not sure."

Jack nodded but said nothing.

"I don't know what I really want," she went on. "Maybe I will never know. Maybe I will never really fit in anywhere. Lucinda Markley is a friend, but the other officers' wives make it clear I am not one of them."

He nodded again and hooked his boot on the gate rail. "I used to feel that way when I was growing up," he said slowly. "I lived on a farm, and the kids I went to school with all lived in town. Ma and Pa scratched out a living on land that wasn't worth a damn, and we were really poor. Other kids always had something to eat in their lunchboxes. Lots of times I didn't. Made me feel different."

"Did you feel different when you got older?" He was silent for so long she thought he hadn't heard her. "Jack?"

"Sort of, I guess. Pa died, and my mother went back to Georgia to live with her sister. That's when I joined the army."

"How old were you?"

"I'd just turned sixteen. Same as you. Believe me, I learned a lot in a hurry. On my first mission, I met Lance Singleton. He was another misfit like me, so we kinda traveled together. Lance is a good man, Jonna."

"Yes. You said that before."

He sent her a sharp look. "He's thinking of getting assigned to Fort Kearny," he said, watching her face.

"Good. Then I could see more of my brother."

"Yeah. Guess you could." But somehow, the thought of Lance Singleton and Jonna being at the same post made his gut tighten. Couldn't say why exactly except that…except that…Well, hell, Corder. Except what? You have no claim on Jonna. One minute, she's mad at you. The next minute, she's sitting beside you on the porch swing, sipping whiskey-laced lemonade and not saying a word.

He shook his head. All his life, he'd steered clear of most women except for Martha and Samantha Hawks, and they're sort of family in a way. But Jonna? Jonna was definitely *not* family. He wasn't even sure who she really was under that brave front she put up.

****

Jonna spent the following afternoon at the infirmary, ministering to another soldier who'd contracted pneumonia and a corporal with a case of poison oak so severe the man's eyes were swollen shut. When the sun went down, she started back to the house to help Martha with supper. Just as she reached the front porch, a young soldier raced up the steps behind her.

"Miss Lander!" She spun toward him. "Miss Lander, you gotta come. Miz Markley and her husband are having an awful fight, and I'm afraid she's gonna get hurt."

"Hurt? Why would she—?"

"'Cuz Lieutenant Markley is dead drunk."

Drunk! Oh, good heavens. "Find the colonel and Major Corder right away," she ordered. "Hurry!"

Chapter Twenty-Five

Samantha suddenly appeared in the doorway. "Jonna, I heard shouting. What's wrong?"

"Lucinda Markley needs help! Her husband is drunk."

"Get Jack!" Samantha said instantly.

"I sent a soldier to find him. Sam, tell Martha I'll be late for supper." She started down the steps and heard the screen door slam behind her.

Even before she reached Lucinda's house, she could hear her screams. She ran up the steps to find the front door standing wide open and a man's angry shouts and the sound of breaking china clearly audible.

"Lucinda? Lu—"

"Jonna!" her friend screamed. "Get help!"

Another crash. This time, it sounded like breaking glassware. When she walked in, she found jagged pieces of crockery and shards of broken glass littering the parlor floor. Lucinda was cowering behind the china cabinet, holding her belly with one hand and clinging to the back of a chair with the other.

Sidney Markley turned a flushed face toward her. "Get out!" he shouted, gesturing wildly with one arm. "This ish between my wife an' me, so jus' get out!"

She started toward Lucinda, but the lieutenant hurled a china teapot at her. She sidestepped it and kept walking. Lieutenant Markley smelled strongly of alcohol.

When she reached her friend, blood was oozing from a cut on Lucinda's bare forearm.

"Lucinda, you're hurt!"

"N-no. He hit me, but—" Just as Jonna reached her, she felt a sharp blow in the small of her back, and a silver tray bounced onto the floor.

"Shstay away from my wife!" the lieutenant shouted.

Jonna ignored him, grasped Lucinda's shoulder, and slipped an arm around Lucinda's thick waist. She was trembling, and her breath came in sporadic gasps. "Don't get near him," she whispered. "He'll hurt you."

"Get away from her!" the lieutenant yelled. "Damned whiney woman deserves what she gets!" He heaved a china platter at his wife, watched it smack onto the floor and shatter, then threw another one. This one hit Lucinda's chest. The next one thudded into the back of Jonna's neck.

Markley started toward her, and in the next second, his stumbling gait brought them face to face. He drew back his hand to strike her, but suddenly, he was yanked backward, and someone's fist smacked into his jaw. Markley dropped heavily to the floor.

"Jack!" She was so glad to see him tears stung into her eyes. Behind him stood Colonel Hawks. "Are either of you hurt?" Jack asked as he moved toward them.

"Lucinda's arm is cut."

The colonel whipped out his handkerchief and handed it to Jonna. She wrapped it around Lucinda's forearm, and then the colonel walked the pregnant woman through the mess of broken china and glassware, past Sidney Markley's inert form and out onto the porch, where he carefully settled her in the rocking chair.

"I'm putting your husband under arrest, Mrs. Markley. And then I'm going to transfer him to another post, so he'll not be bothering you again. However, you are welcome to stay on here at Fort Kearney for as long as you wish."

Lucinda's eyes brimmed. "Thank you," she whispered.

Jonna surveyed the mess of broken crockery. "Lucinda, I will clean all this up."

"There's no need," Colonel Hawks said. "I have two fractious privates just itching to be useful."

Lucinda looked up at her, and Jonna saw an ugly purple bruise on her neck. "Please, Jonna, go on home. I-I would like to be alone."

She felt Jack's hand at her back. "Do what she says," he murmured. "The colonel's sent for the doctor, and Martha's holding supper."

Shaken, she could not think of one sensible thing to say. He walked her across the parade ground, and when they reached the colonel's house, he handed her in through the screen door, gave her a long look, and tramped back down the porch steps.

****

"Oh, that poor woman." Martha moaned as she set a china bowl of creamed peas on the dining table.

"Lieutenant Markley was completely out of his head," Jonna said. "The colonel put him in jail."

"Not a moment too soon," Colonel Hawks added. "But that idiot Jack just waded right in. Could have got himself shot."

Shot? But Jack and the other soldiers at this fort

risk their lives every time they ride out through the gate. And Drew does, too. Any of them could be killed!

"Jonna," Sam said quietly. "You haven't eaten a bite of supper. Whatever is wrong?"

She closed her eyes briefly. "I am learning something about life. Every single day is full of danger, and I am beginning to see how protected I was living with the Sioux. The braves rode off to battle; some came back with wounds, and some didn't come back at all, but I was always kept safe. Now I am starting to see life as it really is."

"Particularly life out here in the untamed West," the colonel remarked. "Most particularly, life on an army post."

Jonna caught her breath. "Martha, how do you stand it?" She reached across the table for the older woman's hand.

Martha laid her fork on her plate with a sharp click. "How do I stand it? Well, my dear, you *don't* stand it. At night, you lie awake wondering if the man you love is dying alone on a battlefield somewhere. You worry about dying yourself when you're birthing a child. You worry about your daughter traveling back to Boston, alone in a city full of—" She swallowed. "You *don't* stand it, child. You just do the best you can."

Tears stung into her eyes. "Ever since Jack brought me here, I have felt safe. But I am learning that no one is truly safe, are they?"

"No one with half a brain believes they're really safe anywhere," the colonel said. "Life is too unpredictable."

"And," Sam said slowly, "life can be cruel. But if we huddle in our nice safe bedrooms in our nice safe houses, we might be safe, but we won't be alive, either."

Martha reached over and covered Jonna's small, slim hand with her own larger, wrinkled one. "Forgive me for saying this, my dear, but I think you are beginning to see life as a grown woman."

Jonna stared at her without saying a word. Samantha stood up and walked around the table to where Martha sat, leaned over, and wrapped her arms around her mother's shoulders. "It must take great courage to be a mother," she said quietly.

Martha patted her daughter's hand. "It takes greater courage to love someone and risk losing them, as Jonna is now realizing."

Colonel Hawks pulled out his handkerchief and blew his nose. "Jonna, you think men like Jack and your brother Andrew are brave. Courageous. But I have to tell you, we men are not half as brave as the woman who walks away from a life of luxury with well-to-do parents and gets on a train to come out here and marry a military man like me. Or," he went on, sending her a long look, "one who risks her life escaping from a camp full of Sioux warriors. Now, let's eat supper before it gets cold."

****

Over the next week, Jonna thought many times about that suppertime conversation. She visited Lucinda Markley and marveled at how calm she seemed about the impending birth of her child. She checked on two soldiers at the infirmary who were recovering from bullet wounds and learned they were anxious to ride out on patrol again. One afternoon, she stopped Jack cantering through the post gate on his way back from a patrol.

"Where have you ridden today?"

He reined up. "You don't want to know, Jonna."

"Oh, yes, I do want to know! Tell me."

He let out a long breath and looked down at her with an odd expression in his gray-green eyes. "I rode over to Fort McHenry to see Lance."

"And Drew? Did you see my brother?"

Jack said nothing.

"Well?" She propped both hands on her hips and waited. "Jack, there is something you are not telling me. I want to know what it is."

He hesitated. "Lance and Drew aren't at Fort McKinley, Jonna. They've been sent into the mountains on a, well, a kind of risky mission."

"Why is it risky? Are there Indian tribes there?"

"It's a rescue mission. Some damn preacher and his wagon full of disciples got themselves stuck up in the high country, fighting off some Indians, and now they're running out of food. One of them walked out a week ago, and Colonel Hardesty at Fort McHenry sent Lance and Drew in with a pack mule loaded up with supplies."

"Why not send army troops?"

Jack blew out a long breath. "Because the Indians in the area are hostile. Colonel Hardesty doesn't want to start a war."

She stared at him, unable to speak.

"Drew left a message for you," Jack added. "Said to tell you not to worry."

She snapped her jaw shut. "That's like telling a fish not to swim!" She thought suddenly of Martha's words at supper the other night. "*You pray they don't die on a battlefield somewhere.*" She turned away and pressed her knuckles against her mouth. She heard Jack dismount, and the next thing she knew, his arms were around her.

"I want to be b-brave, but he's my only—"

He said nothing. Just rocked her gently and let her cry. Jack was always sensible and…and caring, she thought. Somehow, he always let her know he was on her side. He was a good man. Lance was a good man, too, but, well, Jack was different. Despite all their disagreements, she liked him. She trusted him. She knew she could rely on him. Now he stood holding her close, letting her spill it all out.

When she looked up at him, he had the strangest look on his face, and her heart skipped. What was wrong? Was there something he wasn't telling her? He seemed to hesitate, but as she opened her lips to ask why, he bent his head and caught her mouth under his.

His kiss went on and on, and it felt…it felt glorious, like Lucinda's dish of stars. It was so beautiful she never wanted it to end.

When he released her, she was shaking, so she stood without moving, her nose pressed against his uniform. All she could think about was the heart-stopping feeling of his mouth on hers. It made her feel all swirly inside, as if her entire body was floating in a big bowl of whipped cream.

"How come you only kiss me when I'm crying?" she said, her voice quiet.

He chuckled. "Damned if I know, Jonna."

"Do y-you think Drew will be all right?"

He lifted his head and looked past her across the parade ground. "I think if anyone will be all right, it will be your brother."

Once again, Jonna thought of Martha's words at supper the other night. If she had real courage, like Martha, she would grit her teeth and keep going. Then she laughed softly. If she had *real* courage, she thought with a laugh, when Jack kissed her, she would kiss him back.

Chapter Twenty-Six

That night, Jonna tossed restlessly on her narrow bed, and when she finally fell asleep, she had terrible dreams. Sometimes, she heard Drew's voice calling her name. Sometimes, she was clinging to his sleeve, trying to stop him from leaving her. Each time she woke up, she found her cheeks wet. After the last dream, she rolled over, pummeled her feather pillow, and lay awake until dawn. Then she climbed out of bed, pulled on her denim work skirt and a blue gingham shirtwaist, and went downstairs to the kitchen.

Martha was sliding a pan of biscuits into the oven. "Jonna, you look plumb exhausted. Did you not sleep well?"

"No, I did not."

Martha gave her a searching look. "Looks to me like you didn't sleep at all," she said dryly.

Samantha flew in, sent Jonna a smile, and waltzed her mother around the room. "Good morning, everyone! Isn't it a glorious day?"

Martha propped her veined hands on her hips. "Sam, what on earth has lit up your lantern this morning?"

"I've been making plans for my first day of school. Isn't that wonderful? I can hardly wait!"

"Already? Why, that's a whole two months away!"

"No, Momma, it is exactly twenty-three days from

now."

"Oh, surely, it's not so soon," Martha protested.

"For me, it's not soon enough, Momma. I am really getting excited!"

"Well," her mother sniffed, "*I* am certainly not excited." She slid another pan of biscuits into the oven and banged the door shut. "I'm having a bad case of the flutters."

Samantha put her arms around her mother. "Cheer up, Momma. Jonna will be here to keep you company."

"Hummmph! No doubt Jonna will be getting married one of these days and traipsing off with some man or other."

"I wonder who she'll traipse off with," Sam mused with a covert glance at Jonna.

"Or…" She looked suddenly thoughtful. "Jonna, why don't you come to Oregon with me?"

The mixing bowl slipped out of Martha's hands and plopped into the dishpan. "What? That is a perfectly *dreadful* idea!" she said in a quavery voice. "You want to leave me with no one to fuss over? No one to teach how to make cakes and pies and put up preserves?"

Jonna stared at her, then at Sam's shining face. *It is true, I could go to Oregon with Sam.* Samantha grasped both her hands. "What do you think, Jonna?"

"I am not thinking," she announced. She picked up a stack of plates and headed for the dining room. "I am going to eat breakfast."

But she did think about it. She thought about it all that morning, and when her brain grew completely muddled, she walked over to visit Lucinda Markley.

"Oh, you darling girl," Lucinda cried. "You've

come to keep an eye on me."

"I am not keeping an eye on you, Lucinda. I am making a visit."

"You mean to say you're payin' a call," Lucinda said with a laugh. "I'll make a Southern belle out of you yet!"

Jonna lifted the tea tray out of her friend's hands. "What is a 'Southern belle'?"

"My heavens, Jonna, I keep forgettin' you're not from the South. A Southern belle is…well, she is a young woman of good family who is raised to be a lady."

"A lady? What does that mean? Aren't all of us ladies?"

"Oh, my no. A lady is someone who learns about how to talk and act with, well, with grace and charm and good manners."

"Is Dolly Brownell a lady?" Jonna asked. "And Nell Schwammer and Sophronia Tipton?"

A thoughtful look crossed Lucinda's face. "Well…"

"Lucinda, I know they are your friends, but they are often unkind. They speak with grace and charm, as you say, but the things they say are hurtful."

Lucinda touched her hand. "You are quite right, Jonna. They have directed mean remarks at you and…I am ashamed to admit I failed to put a stop to it."

"So," Jonna said, accepting a cup of tea, "I stopped the remarks myself. Maybe not as a lady would have, but—"

To her surprise, a giggle escaped her friend's mouth. "But you know," Lucinda confided, "I think they learned something. At least, Sophronia did. Over tea last Thursday, she apologized for her behavior. I do wish you could have been there!"

Jonna smiled. "You should be glad that I was *not* there, Lucinda. I would not have behaved like a lady."

At that, they both burst into laughter. "Jonna, I must make a confession. You are much more fun to visit with than Dolly or Nell or Sophronia! For certain sure, they will make a great fuss over my baby when it comes, but now that Sidney is gone, I will wager not one of them will actually come to help me."

"Oh, of course they will!"

Lucinda shook her head. "We will see."

Jonna could think of nothing to say, so she changed the subject. "Lucinda, now that Lieutenant Markley has been posted to another fort, will you be joining him?"

A long silence fell. Lucinda concentrated on refilling their teacups, and when she finally looked up, her eyes were wet. "I truly do not know. I do love Sidney—or I did when we were first married—but..." Her voice trailed off. "A woman out here is so *dependent* on a man! Unless she has some way to support herself, a woman needs a husband."

"I think a *lady* might need a husband," Jonna ventured, "but just an ordinary woman, like the laundresses who work here at the post, those women are *not* dependent on a husband."

Lucinda's pale eyebrows rose. "But the laundresses are not ladies! I could never invite one of them to tea."

"You mean they are women, but not ladies? Lucinda, I think that is upside down," Jonna said quietly. "They are human beings, like the rest of us, are they not?"

Lucinda looked thoughtful, and they sipped their

tea in silence. "I will have to think about that," she said at last. "Now, tell me about that nice-looking corporal Lance Singleton from Fort McHenry."

Jonna blinked. "What *about* Lance Singleton?"

"Why, it's plain as pancakes he is interested in you in a very particular way."

"Oh? *What* particular way?"

Lucinda studied her face. "You mean you haven't noticed? You like him, don't you?"

"Of course, I do. He is my brother's friend."

"And yours, as well?"

Jonna hesitated. "Yes, I suppose so. I have not thought much about it."

"But you *do* hope to get married one of these days, don't you?"

She sipped her tea in silence. Did she hope to be married? The only man she had ever felt close to was Jack Corder, probably because of the unspoken bond they'd formed when they escaped from the Sioux together. She replaced her teacup on its saucer. "I do not know what I want, Lucinda. I am still trying to fit in at this army post."

"You mean you do not feel at home here?"

Jonna smiled at her friend. It was obvious that before becoming an officer's wife here at Fort Kearney, Lucinda had never known anything but her comfortable, protected life in the South. "It is a simple matter to change from wearing buckskin to wearing gingham," she said. "Learning those things is easy. Changing what is on the *inside* is more difficult."

"Why, I never thought of it that way," Lucinda said slowly. "Never in my entire life have I had so many weighty things to think about!" She reached over and squeezed her hand. "I am so very glad we are friends, Jonna!"

"I am glad also, Lucinda. You are the only person who invites me for tea!"

****

When she returned to the house, she found Martha rocking back and forth in the porch swing and fanning herself. "Been to visit Lucinda Markley?"

"Yes. We had tea and talked about what makes a 'lady.' "

"Did you tell her you're thinking of going off to Oregon with Sam?"

"No."

"How come?"

Jonna was quiet so long Martha stopped the motion of the swing and peered up at her. "How come?" she repeated.

"Martha, do you *want* me to go to Oregon with Sam?"

"Lord no, child, I do not. I'd like it fine if you stayed here with Martin and me for a good long time. Both of us have grown fond of you, and we want you to stay. Unless you decide to get married, of course." She pushed the swing into motion.

"Married! I do not want to get married!"

Again, the motion of the swing stopped. "Not get married? But every young woman, especially a girl as pretty as you, wants to get married!"

Jonna sank onto the swing beside her. "Are all girls expected to marry? I left the Sioux because the young braves were starting to ask the chief how many horses he would accept for me. I did not want that."

"Well, of course, you didn't. You wouldn't want to

live as an Indian for the rest of your life, would you?"

Jonna said nothing for a long minute. "I never dreamed that living as a woman here at an army fort could be so…complicated. And every day I wonder why it is not more satisfying."

Martha smiled and patted her arm. "You are plenty smart, my girl. It won't take you long to figure it out."

Chapter Twenty-Seven

For the next two weeks, Jonna spent so many hours at the infirmary the patients began calling her Doctor Jonna. She didn't mind. The infirmary was the coolest spot at the fort, so she was reasonably comfortable during the scorching late summer days. Besides, if she kept busy changing bandages and administering medicine, she had less time to worry about Drew.

Each day felt hotter than the last. The sun rose each morning in a clear blue sky, withering every green growing thing its rays touched, and every afternoon, she took a batch of lemonade over to the infirmary patients. Later, she took a Mason jar of lemonade to Lucinda Markley and stayed for tea.

While Jonna was walking across the parade ground one scorching afternoon, Jack came riding through the post gate, dismounted, and fell into step beside her. "What are you doing out here on such a hot day?"

"Taking some lemonade to Lucinda Markley."

He squinted against the sun. "I've been out on patrol with a bunch of new recruits. Half of them are so green they drank all the water in their canteens before noon."

"Is there any news about Drew and Lance?"

He shook his head. "Not a word. Listen, Jonna, when you don't hear anything, that's usually good news."

"Usually?"

"Well, yeah. Unless everybody gets—" He caught himself. "Look, Lance is pretty savvy about troublesome Indians. He'll be—"

"Lance!" She halted and spun to face him. "I am not worried about Lance. I am worried about Drew!"

Jack gave her an odd look. "Yeah, I know you are. I bet you're not sleeping much at night."

She shook her head. "I have bad dreams."

"Maybe you should ask Martha for a cup of her special mint tea."

"No. With Sam leaving for Oregon in two weeks, Martha has other things on her mind."

He nodded. "That's gonna be hard on Martha. Having you there will make it easier."

"It's never easy when someone you care about is gone," Jonna said in a quiet voice.

"Even when they're *not* gone," he said under his breath.

They walked across the parade ground. "Did you know Martha's invited me over for supper tonight?" Jack said suddenly.

"No, I didn't."

"Do you mind?"

"Me! Why should I mind?"

"Just wondered." He looked off to the hazy mountains in the distance. "Sometimes, you don't like the things I say."

"Well, yes, that is true. But I know Samantha will be pleased to see you."

Samantha! He bit his lip to hide a smile. "Well, that's encouraging. Awful hard to eat supper with someone who's *not* pleased to see me!"

****

That evening when he started up Colonel Hawks' porch steps, he heard the colonel's laconic voice from the porch swing. "Come on up and sit, Jack. It's too hot to do anything else."

"Colonel, you have any idea how hot it was out on patrol today?"

"Nope. And don't tell me."

Jack grinned. "It about boiled the water in my canteen."

"I said don't—"

"My saddle got pretty warm, too," he continued. "Pressed my trousers in places I didn't need pressed."

The colonel rolled his eyes. "Have some whiskey, Jack. Might keep your tongue quiet."

The two men sat enjoying what breeze there was until Sam stepped through the screen door. "Supper is ready, gentlemen," she announced with a smile. "The cooks are putting their feet up, so you'll be getting your own second helpings."

While Jack downed generous portions of cold chicken and Jonna's potato salad, he couldn't help noticing how animated Sam was. He also noticed how quiet Jonna was. And he could tell she was watching him. Sure wished he knew why.

Sam burbled on and on about her teaching position in Oregon, and all at once, an unnerving thought flashed into his brain. Maybe Jonna was wanting what Sam had—a clearly defined purpose in her life. Well, hell, she could be Lance Singleton's wife without lifting her little finger. But maybe Jonna didn't *want* that. That made him wonder what she *did* want. He rolled that question around in his brain all through

Martha's apple pie and coffee and even an after-supper snifter of brandy on the porch.

When the supper dishes were washed and dried and put away in the tall walnut hutch, Martha and the two girls drifted out onto the porch with their coffee to join the men. The colonel offered them a shot of brandy, but both Martha and Sam refused. Jonna, however, held out her cup.

Jack frowned. Something was definitely on Jonna's mind this evening, and he'd give a month's pay to know what it was. He watched her sip her doctored-up coffee in silence and gaze out into the trees, but she didn't say a word. And when Sam launched into more of her school-teaching plans, Jonna quietly got to her feet, set her coffee cup on the porch railing, and walked off into the dark. Martha sent him a significant look, and after a moment, he rose and went after her.

He caught up with her at the post gate, where she stood with both elbows propped on the top rail. "I hear you," she said without turning. "You don't walk quietly, like an Indian."

"Yeah, I know. Leather boots aren't made for creeping up on someone."

"What are you doing out here?" she asked.

"Wondering what *you're* doing out here."

She took her time in answering. "I am…thinking."

"Yeah?" He stepped up beside her and leaned against the gate facing her. "What about?"

"I am thinking about Lucinda Markley. About what she will do when her baby is born now that her husband has been transferred to another post."

"Guess she doesn't have much choice," Jack said.

"But she should have a choice. Every woman

should have a choice."

He shot her a look. In the dark, her face was just a pale oval, and he sure wished he could see the expression in her eyes. "Lucinda has a choice, Jonna. She can follow her husband. Or she can go back to her home in…South Carolina, is it?"

"Why could she not go to some *other* place? A place like Oregon. That's what Sam is doing."

"It's not that simple, Jonna. Sam is a trained teacher. Lucinda Markley grew up with no expectation of ever having to work for a living. She was raised to be some man's wife."

"But that is like being in a prison, Jack. She has no way to be free. To be on her own."

"Maybe. That bothers you some, does it?"

Jonna nodded. "What do unmarried women do in Oregon? I mean unmarried women who are not teachers?"

He blew out a long breath. "Some open boardinghouses and take in renters. Some work in mercantile stores selling ladies' hats, boys' shirts, and penny candy. If a woman can use a sewing machine, she could start a dressmaking shop. Some women even give dancing lessons."

"Dancing lessons! You mean teach people how to waltz?"

"Yep. And how to dance Virginia reels and polkas and square dances."

"Do you know how to do all those dances?"

He chuckled. "Some better than others. I'm a good square dancer, as long as the caller isn't drunk."

Jonna was silent for a long minute. "I have no idea what a square dance or a Virginia reel is," she said at last. "There is so much in this world I know nothing about!"

"You're not talking about Lucinda Markley, are you, Jonna?"

She didn't answer, and suddenly, he understood. She *wasn't* thinking of Lucinda Markley. She was thinking of herself. God almighty, Jonna was thinking about a life for herself somewhere away from Fort Kearney. He felt like a horse had kicked him in the gut.

"Jonna, what's brought this on? Why are you asking about these things?"

She didn't answer for a long minute. "When I think about Lucinda's choices, I can't help thinking about my own. I think a woman—even an unmarried woman—should be able to survive on her own. Otherwise, she has no alternative but marriage. I wonder how many women, not only Lucinda but other officers' wives—Dolly Brownell and Nell Schwammer and Sophronia Tipton, for instance—how many of them could survive on their own without their husbands?"

"None of them," Jack said flatly. "Lucinda sure as hell has no way to survive without that bastard Sidney Markley. To be honest, I feel real sorry for her. But she wouldn't last a day working in the infirmary or scrubbing clothes as a laundress here at the fort."

"And here at Fort Kearney, there is nothing else for her," Jonna murmured. "She is trapped."

He gave her a sharp look. "Are you feeling trapped?"

"Not trapped exactly. But I am feeling on the brink of something."

"Yeah?" he said with a frown. "On the brink of what?"

She looked past him. "I am wondering what choices are possible for me. Can I choose the kind of life I want? Or will I be forced to take a certain path because it's the only one open to me?"

He nodded, then realized she couldn't see him in the dark. The flowery scent of her hair was sending a funny zing up his spine. "Jonna, I'd like you to be able to choose whatever path you want. But…" He hesitated, then shoved away from the gate.

"But? But what, Jack?"

He touched her shoulder. "I…uh…well, I sure hope you won't leave Fort Kearney." Under his hand, he felt her shoulder jerk.

"What are you saying?"

He bent toward her. "I'm saying I wonder if you're planning to go to Oregon with Sam."

Again, she looked past him. "I would never leave Fort Kearney without telling you."

"Fair enough," he muttered. Then before he could stop himself, he tipped her chin up with his forefinger and settled his mouth over hers. He could feel her trembling, and he half expected her to jerk free. But she didn't. Maybe she didn't want this, but he sure as hell did. For a long, long minute, the earth seemed to stop turning, and he was aware only of her lips under his and an odd ache deep inside his chest. When he lifted his mouth from hers, she didn't say a word.

God help me. I shouldn't have done that. I shouldn't be standing here with my arms around her, but I'm sure as hell not sorry.

"Jonna?" he said quietly.

"Yes?"

"Let's go on back to the house. I need some whiskey."

Chapter Twenty-Eight

The next morning, after an almost sleepless night, Jonna woke up feeling inexplicably happy. She crawled out of bed before the sun rose and went downstairs to the kitchen, stirred up the fire in the stove, and set the coffeepot to boil. Then she got out a mixing bowl, scooped a cup of flour from the flour barrel in the pantry, and added some milk. As she worked, she thought about Lucinda Markley's future and then did some thinking about her own. She saw the limitations of Lucinda Markley's future, but there were no limitations to *her* future, were there? Maybe she really could go to Oregon with Sam.

She stirred some melted butter into her pancake batter, but two questions swirled around in her brain. One was about Drew. If she moved to Oregon, would she still be able to see him? The other question was about Jack. She felt an unspoken bond with the tall, short-spoken major. She was also beginning to feel strongly about him in a different way, and that was because...well, because he was the only man who had ever kissed her.

She thought about that while she set breakfast plates on the dining table. Lucinda said kissing a man you cared for was like having a dish of stars pour down on your head. When Jack kissed her, it felt like stars were spilling all over her. But maybe kissing *any* man would stir up a dish of stars?

Martha bustled into the kitchen and stopped dead. "Jonna! It's five o'clock in the morning! Whatever are you doing up at this hour?"

"I couldn't sleep."

Martha frowned and sent her a penetrating look. "Is something troubling you?"

She didn't know how to answer that. She couldn't begin to describe all the things she was feeling, so she said nothing.

"Jonna?" Martha peered into her face. "Are you feeling all right?"

"Yes. No. Oh, Martha, most of me feels perfectly all right, but underneath, there is a small part—"

Martha's frown deepened. "*Which* part?" she interrupted.

"Something down deep inside of me. It feels like…like a…a hiccup."

For a long moment, the older woman said nothing. "I see," she said slowly.

"See what?" Sam sang from the doorway. She snatched the red gingham apron off the hook by the stove. "Goodness, what are you two doing up so early!"

"We're in for another scorching day," Martha said quickly. "I thought I'd make biscuits before it got too hot." She sent Jonna a long look, then busied herself at the stove.

"I'll go gather the eggs, shall I?" Sam volunteered.

"Martin already did it," Martha said. "The basket's on the back porch."

Sam was back in sixty seconds, half a dozen eggs cradled in her apron. "You will never guess what I'm going to do this morning!"

"Making scrambled eggs we don't need because Jonna's already mixed up some pancake batter?" Martha asked.

"Packing your trunk for Oregon?" Jonna said.

"Washing up all the breakfast dishes?" Martha said dryly.

"No, no, and no," Sam said with a laugh.

"Well, *what*?" Martha asked.

"I am going riding with Jack!"

Martha huffed out a breath. "What's so unusual about that?"

"What's unusual is that up until this very morning, I always had to *beg* Jack to go riding with me. This time, Jack actually asked me first!"

Jonna cracked two eggs into a ceramic bowl and settled the iron griddle on the stovetop. Sam had lived here at Fort Kearney ever since she was born, and Jack had watched her grow up. Why shouldn't she go riding with him? Besides, it was none of her business who Jack went riding with.

By the time the colonel tramped into the dining room, Jonna had a platter of flapjacks ready, Sam had scrambled half a dozen eggs, and Martha was heating a tin of maple syrup on the stove. Sam gobbled half a pancake, gave her mother a quick hug, and flew off to the stable to meet Jack.

"Good lord!" the colonel said. "Ever since our daughter learned to walk, she seems to do everything at top speed. Why is that, Martha?"

Martha stared at her husband. "Land sakes, Martin. After twenty-two years, you're just now noticing Sam never does *anything* at a normal speed? I wonder how her school students will be able to keep up with her."

Jonna smiled. "Maybe Sam will teach them as fast as she does everything else."

"In which case," the colonel said, "the school term will be mighty short! I can imagine—" He broke off as footsteps pounded up the porch steps, and someone began thumping loudly on the front door.

Martha folded her napkin beside her plate and rose. "I'll go. Martin, finish your coffee."

Jonna heard the front door open and then an agitated male voice. "I've come for Miss Lander. It's an emergency!"

She was on her feet before the soldier could catch his breath. "What emergency?" she asked.

"It's Miz Markley. Her baby's comin', and Doc Brownell sent me to fetch you. You gotta come, miss. She's screamin' something awful."

Chapter Twenty-Nine

The bedroom in Lucinda's house was stifling. When Jonna walked in, Doctor Brownell straightened and mopped the perspiration from his angular face. "Thank the saints you're here, Jonna. She's having a pretty hard time of it, which isn't unusual for a first baby, but I've been here all night and I'm about done in. The birth seems normal so far, but I need to grab some sleep, and I don't want to leave her alone."

"I will stay with her." She shot a glance at the bed where a flushed Lucinda lay, compulsively kneading a washcloth. Her eyes were shut tight, and her lips were pressed into a thin line. The doctor bent over and spoke a few words, then patted her hand and turned toward the door. "Don't let her drink too much water, just little sips."

A guttural moan escaped the laboring woman's lips, and she reached one hand toward Jonna. "Thank you for com—" She broke off and gripped her hand so tightly Jonna thought her bones would break. She picked up the towel the doctor had left, dampened it from the pitcher of water sitting on the maple chest of drawers, and bent to sponge off Lucinda's face.

"I have never felt such pain," Lucinda panted. "My back feels like it's splitting in two."

"Indian women walk between contractions," Jonna said.

Lucinda shook her head. "Can't," she muttered.

"Can you sit up? When a pain comes, I can press on your back. Sometimes that helps."

"How on earth would you know that?" Lucinda grated.

"I have watched Sioux women give birth."

"Very well, I will try." She heaved her considerable bulk into a half-sitting position, and Jonna quickly stuffed three pillows behind her back, pulled a chair over close to the head of the bed, and sat down. "When the next pain comes, lean forward."

The next contraction brought a sharp cry from Lucinda, but she managed to bend forward. While she gasped for breath, Jonna pressed both her fists against her lower back as hard as she could.

"I can't stand much more of this," Lucinda said through gritted teeth. Tears sheened her cheeks.

Jonna wiped her sweaty forehead. "I am sure it will be over soon."

"Not soon enough," Lucinda cried. "It started hours and hours ago—yesterday, I think. And it just gets worse and worse."

Jonna dipped the small towel in the basin of water, wrung it out, and had managed to sponge off Lucinda's sweat-sticky face when another contraction hit. Lucinda cried out and arched her back, and Jonna pressed hard against her lower spine. When the contraction eased, Lucinda slumped back against the pillows and sucked in long breaths of air.

"Jonna." Her breath came in gasps. "Jonna, if I die, promise me you will not give my child to Sidney. He drinks to excess, and he becomes violent. I do not trust him."

"You are not going to die, Lucinda. I know this is an ordeal, but Dr. Brownell says you are making normal progress."

Lucinda caught her breath. "I want this to be over!" She grabbed the rope Dr. Brownell had tied to the foot of the bed and bent forward with a cry. Again, Jonna pressed hard against her spine until the contraction eased.

For hours, Lucinda screamed and writhed in agony while Jonna sponged off her sweaty body and talked to her. As the afternoon wore on, the bedroom turned into a sweltering oven of hot, still air, and Jonna's shoulders ached from bending and pushing against Lucinda's increasingly violent contractions.

Just when she thought she couldn't stand it any longer, Dr. Brownell tramped up the porch steps into the house. After listening to Lucinda's heart and taking her pulse, he nodded. "Won't be long now, Mrs. Markley. Jonna, you might boil up some water and find some more clean towels."

She filled the teakettle and set it on the stove, then stirred up the coals and added more wood, trying to shut out the guttural cries coming from the bedroom. Around suppertime, Sam brought her a bacon sandwich and a jar of cold lemonade, but Jonna was so exhausted she couldn't swallow a single bite. After a prolonged scream of agony echoed through the house, Samantha pressed her hand and fled.

The water came to a boil as another hoarse cry sounded. "Jonna!" the doctor shouted. "Bring that hot water!"

She filled the basin with warm water and had started down the hallway when she heard a baby's thin wail. At the sound, tears stung into her eyes.

Dr. Brownell stepped away from the bed and lifted the basin out of her hands. "You look worse than our new mother," he said. "Go home and get some rest."

"Go," Lucinda cried in a weak voice. "It's your suppertime. But promise you'll come tomorrow and help me choose a name for my baby girl."

Jonna dragged herself back to the house to find the colonel and Samantha rocking in the swing and Jack sitting across from them. At the sight of her, Sam sat up bolt upright. "Jonna, you look completely done in!"

"You should see Lucinda," she said in a wobbly voice. "And," she added with as much of a smile as she could muster, "her baby daughter."

"Oooh!" Sam squealed. "A little girl! How lovely!"

"How is Lucinda?" Jack ventured, rising from his chair.

"Exhausted. But she was smiling when I left."

Colonel Hawks swallowed a sip of his whiskey. "I imagine Doc Brownell is pretty tired, too."

Jonna rolled her eyes. "Anyone who feels sorry for a *man* during a birth has never watched a woman struggle and scream for hours and hours. A man wouldn't last ten minutes in pain like that."

"Point taken," the colonel muttered. "Want a shot of whiskey? You've certainly earned it."

Before she could open her mouth, Jack stepped forward, folded her hand around his whiskey glass, and pointed at his vacated chair. "Sit down, Jonna. You look worse than one of my troopers after a hard day in the saddle."

"Your troopers," Jonna said, sinking onto the rocker, "cannot work nearly as hard as a woman bearing a child." She gulped down a big mouthful of his whiskey and spent the next minute coughing and sputtering. "Thank you, Jack," she said hoarsely.

"Want some lemonade instead?" he said quietly.

"No," she rasped. "I want something that will put me to sleep."

"First, you must eat some supper," Sam announced. "Martha's making chicken and dumplings."

Jonna nodded, swallowed another mouthful of Jack's whiskey, and closed her eyes. Their voices went on talking, but she couldn't understand what anyone was saying. She roused herself only when Martha stepped out and announced that supper was served.

She couldn't force her exhausted body out of the chair. Then she looked up to find Jack bending over her, offering his hand. She grasped it, and he pulled her upright and, without a word, slipped his arm around her shoulders and walked her across the porch. Her legs felt wobbly.

"You want me to carry you?" he intoned.

"No." *Oh, but I do. I want to lay my head on his shoulder and blot out the past twelve hours.*

At supper, she could scarcely lift her fork to her mouth. Idly, she wondered if Lucinda was able to lift a fork to *her* mouth. Finally, she managed to cut a small piece of chicken breast, but gradually, her head drooped lower and lower, and she lost all interest in supper.

Jack watched her, then pushed away from the table, gathered her up in his arms, and started for the stairs.

"Second door on the left," Martha called.

Jonna closed her eyes, snuggled her head under Jack's chin, and drifted off. He dipped his knees to open her bedroom door, walked in, and settled her on the narrow bed. Without a word, she curled up on top of the quilt and was instantly asleep.

For a long minute, he stood looking down at her, then bent to untie her shoes and slip them off. He smoothed back the hair that had escaped the bun at her neck and, on impulse, slipped the hairpins free and let the dark waves tumble over her shoulders. Unable to move away, he sat down on the bed beside her and studied her face. Even in exhaustion, Jonna Lander was beautiful. It made his breath catch.

And you have no business here in her bedroom.

Right. He took a long look at her and forced himself to stand up.

When he returned to the dining room, Colonel Hawks glanced up and grinned. "You look like you've just seen a ghost, Jack."

"No ghost, Martin. Just one tired girl."

But, the colonel noted, the major no longer seemed interested in the chicken and dumplings on his plate.

Chapter Thirty

Before breakfast the next morning, Jonna flew across the parade ground and knocked on Lucinda Markley's front door. To her surprise, Dolly Brownell opened the door. "Oh!" the doctor's wife exclaimed. "I didn't expect a visitor so early."

"Is that Jonna?" a voice called. "I have been waiting to see her. Jonna, come see my baby!"

Dolly gave her a curious look and swung the door wide. "I guess you better come in. My husband asked me to bring over a bite of breakfast for Lucinda. She claims she's starving."

"Of course, she is," Jonna replied in an even tone. "For the last day and a half, Lucinda has done the work of three soldiers fighting a war!"

"Soldiers indeed," Dolly sniffed.

"Jonna!" Lucinda called. "Please come visit me!"

Despite Dolly's frown of disapproval, Jonna stepped past her and entered the bedroom.

Lucinda looked radiant. Nestled in her arms was a tiny pink-faced creature placidly gazing up at her with wide blue eyes. Jonna's heart gave an involuntary lurch, and she choked back a sob. "Oh, she is so beautiful!" Tears stung into her eyes.

Lucinda's face glowed. "You must help me choose a name, Jonna. I know you won't suggest anything as silly as..." She lowered her voice. "...Sophronia."

Jonna clapped her hand over her mouth to keep from laughing aloud. "No, not Sophronia. And not Nell or Dolly, either," she whispered. "This child deserves a special name. Lucinda, what is your middle name?"

"Madison," she said heavily. "It's my mother's maiden name. What is *your* middle name, Jonna?"

She hesitated. "My middle name is Kathleen. But surely that is too Irish-sounding for—"

"Kathleen! Kathleen is perfect! I will always think of you when—" She broke off and gazed out the window. "Oh, dear, I wasn't going to tell you so soon."

"Tell me what? Surely you are not thinking of joining your husband!"

"Oh, mercy, no! Jonna, I have decided to return to my home in Charleston. My mama never stops nagging me to come visit, and my sisters will be over the moon about the baby. They will all be doting aunties! And," she added with an irrepressible giggle, "Mama will be a grandmother for the first time."

"What is your mother's middle name?" Jonna murmured.

"Antoinette." Her face lit up. "Yes, Kathleen Antoinette!" she said with a happy sigh.

Jonna gazed at the tiny creature in Lucinda's arms. Kathleen Antoinette Markley. "Lucinda, are you sure you want to return to Charleston? What about—what about Sidney?"

Her friend's arms tightened around her daughter. "I want nothing to do with Sidney," she said slowly. "The farther away from him I am, the happier I will be. And safer. I cannot trust Sidney anywhere near this child."

Jonna nodded. What a sad thing to have to shield one's child from its father. "When will you leave?"

"As soon as Dr. Brownell says I can travel. I can't risk Sidney finding out the baby was born."

"But when he finds you are no longer here at Fort Kearney, won't he guess where you have gone?"

"It won't matter if he does. At home, I will be well protected, and Sidney would never dare to invade my family's estate."

She left Lucinda contentedly nursing her daughter and listlessly plodded back across the parade ground, torn between happiness for Lucinda and sadness that she would be leaving the post. Lucinda had been kind to her from the beginning, and she would be losing a good friend. She climbed the porch steps, plopped herself in the swing, and rocked slowly back and forth, waiting for Samantha to return from a picnic. Probably with Jack.

After an hour, Sam tripped up the steps, settled herself on the swing beside her, and fluffed out her flounced gingham skirt. "Oh, I do love this place," she said cheerily. "But I will also love going to Oregon."

Jonna bit her lip. She would miss Sam almost as much as Lucinda.

"Don't you want to know about my adventure this morning?" Sam asked.

"I can guess," Jonna said. "You went riding again."

"Yes," Sam admitted with a smile.

"With Jack."

"Oh, no, Jonna. Jack has gone…somewhere. I went riding with Corporal Alexander Rigby."

"Where has Jack gone?"

"Alexander said he rode out before dawn, heading for Fort McHenry."

Jonna jerked upright. "Fort McHenry! That's

where my brother is posted. Did Jack say *why* he was riding to Fort McHenry?"

"Well, no, he didn't. Jonna, let me tell you about my picnic. I packed the nicest lunch, and Alexander and I rode—"

"Jack!" Jonna interrupted. "Tell me about Jack!"

Samantha sent her an innocent look. "Oh, yes, Jack," she said with a laugh. "Well, according to Seamus at the stable, at dawn Jack saddled that black mare he's so fond of and—"

"And?"

"And as I said, Jack went to Fort McHenry to ask about Lance Singleton and your brother."

"What did he find out about Drew? And Lance," she added quickly.

"He isn't back yet." Sam leaned forward and peered into her face. "What are you so upset about this morning, Jonna?"

"Lucinda Markley is leaving the post as soon as Dr. Brownell says she is strong enough to travel."

"Surely she's not going back to that sorry excuse of a husband?"

"No. She is going back to her home in South Carolina."

"Good for her," Sam murmured. "But you will miss her, won't you?"

"Yes, I will miss her. She and the baby will be safer away from Lieutenant Markley, and I am glad for that, but...I will miss her a lot."

Sam nodded, and they rocked in silence until Sam patted her hand, rose, and went into the house. After some minutes, she returned and folded Jonna's fingers around a cup of coffee. "I will tell you more about

Corporal Alexander Rigby at supper tonight. He is almost as interesting as Lance Singleton." She touched Jonna's arm and retreated into the house.

Jonna shut her eyes. She didn't want to hear about Corporal Rigby or about Lance Singleton, either. She wanted to hear about Drew. She couldn't wait for Jack to ride through the post gate.

Chapter Thirty-One

Jonna spent the following afternoon pacing back and forth at the post gate, waiting for Jack to return. By suppertime, her eyes ached from straining to see across the expanse of prairie, and she dragged herself back to the house, picked at Martha's potato salad and baked ham, and listened to Samantha describe her afternoon picnic with Corporal Alexander Rigby. After supper, she dried the dishes and stacked them in the china cabinet, then walked back out to the gate. The sun sank behind the mountains, turning the sky peach and then purple, and still, she waited. Finally, it grew so dark she could scarcely see.

Maybe Jack wouldn't return this evening. Maybe there was no news. Or…She closed her eyes. Maybe it was bad news. She had turned back toward the house when she heard an approaching horse. As the hoofbeats grew louder, she peered into the shadows, straining to see.

The figure of a man on horseback loomed out of the darkness. "Jack? Is that you?" She unhooked the gate and swung it open.

Jack reined his horse up short. "Goddammit, Jonna, don't ever open that gate until you can identify the rider!" He looked tired and dusty, but she didn't care. She was so glad to see him she had to bite back a sob.

"J-Jack…"

He slid off the mare and folded her into his arms. "Jonna, what in God's name are you doing out here at night? What's wrong?"

"I was w-waiting for you," she said, her words muffled against his shoulder. "I hoped you would have some news."

"There is no news," he said heavily. "Colonel Hardesty has sent out two patrols, but they came back with nothing. No wagon train sighted. No oxen. No Indians. And no sign of either Drew or Lance."

"Oh." She tipped her head up to look at him. "Lucinda Markley is going back to South Carolina," she blurted. "And…and Samantha went on a picnic this afternoon with Corporal Alexander Rigby."

"Yeah, I know Rigby. Kinda dull. Sam can think circles around him."

"Don't you think it's strange that women are attracted to…well, men who aren't worthy of them, like Sidney Markley and Alexander Rigby?"

Jack nodded. "What about Lance Singleton? Do you think he's worthy?"

"I am reserving judgment about Lance Singleton."

He blew out a long breath. "Look, Jonna, I've been in the saddle since sunup, and I'm hot and thirsty and not thinking too clearly right now, so—"

"You must be hungry, too. Come on over to the house, Jack. I will fix you something to eat." She turned away. He shrugged, picked up the mare's reins, and followed her.

The colonel and Martha were sitting together in the porch swing when they arrived. "Jack hasn't had supper," Jonna said as she came up the steps. Martha merely smiled and tipped her head toward the kitchen.

In the pantry cooler, she found a bowl of leftover potato salad and a platter of cold fried chicken. She loaded up a plate for Jack and sat him down at the dining table. "I think Samantha is off somewhere."

Jack didn't say a word. He didn't even look up, just hunched over his plate. Jonna stepped into the kitchen, brewed a fresh pot of coffee, and surreptitiously added a dollop of the colonel's favorite whiskey.

"You're not eating?" he asked between mouthfuls of chicken.

"I had supper earlier with the colonel and Martha. There's caramel cake, too. Sam made it this morning, but she didn't eat supper with us."

He forked a big bite of potato salad into his mouth. "She's off with Corporal Rigby, huh?"

"Yes, she is. Do you mind?"

He looked blank. "Mind? Why should I mind?"

"Well…" She hesitated. "I thought…I mean…"

Jack gave her a long look, then laid his fork across the plate. "*What* did you think? Hell and damn, Jonna, you think I'm sweet on Sam?"

"Um…"

He shook his head. "I'm not sweet on Sam, Jonna. Never have been. And Sam's not sweet on me!"

"How do you know?"

Without looking at her, he picked up his fork and stabbed it into his potato salad. "I know," he said after a long pause, "because I know."

She could not think of one sensible thing to say, so she got up from the table, walked into the kitchen, and poured herself a cup of coffee.

"Want some whiskey in that?" Jack said when she resumed her seat across from him.

"I already added some." Actually, her nerves felt so jangled this evening the thought of adding another soothing gulp of straight whiskey was very appealing, but she couldn't continue to doctor her mixed-up feelings by drinking up all the colonel's whiskey.

Jack sent her an odd look and downed another forkful of potato salad. "You want to tell me what's really bothering you?"

She sucked in her breath. "You mean besides worrying about Drew?"

"Yeah. And Lance," he added with a chuckle.

She swallowed a mouthful of lukewarm coffee. "Well, besides Drew—"

"And Lance," Jack inserted.

"Oh, yes, and Lance. I am also feeling sad because Lucinda Markley is leaving, going back to her home in South Carolina. Lucinda was very kind to me when I arrived here at the post."

"Yeah, I remember the day we rode in. You looked scared and uncertain, and I guess not only Martha and the colonel but Lucinda Markley kinda took you under her wing." He shoveled in another bite of potato salad.

"I will always be grateful to Lucinda. And I want her to find safety for herself and her baby," she confessed. "But I will really miss her, and...and..."

"That hurts."

She looked up at him, her eyes shiny. "Yes, it does. I had not expected that. And...well, it's more than that."

"Yeah? What 'more'?"

She swallowed. "It's Sam, too."

"Sam? What about Sam?"

She swallowed a mouthful of coffee. "Sam is

leaving in two weeks to start teaching school in Oregon."

"And you'll miss her, too, is that it?"

"Well, won't *you* miss her?" she shot.

"Some," he said, picking up a chicken drumstick. "Not as much as you because you're closer to her."

She stared at him. "But you're close to Sam, aren't you?"

"Sure, I guess so. I watched Sam grow up. She's a real special girl, but—" He broke off and studied her face. "What is it you're really worried about, Jonna?"

She studied the gingham tablecloth. "I am worried about me, Jack. I am watching my friends go off to build their own lives, and I am starting to wonder what kind of life I am building for myself here at Fort Kearney."

He stopped chewing and gave her a long look. "What kind of life do you want?"

She didn't know how to answer that. "I don't know. I feel lost and uncertain about everything."

He released a long breath. "What's 'everything,' Jonna?"

She studied his almost-empty plate. "I am not sure where I fit in."

"Yeah, you've mentioned that before." He looked across the table at her. "Are you uncertain about me?"

She blinked. "About *you*? No, I am not uncertain about you, Jack. I have never been uncertain about you."

"Well, that's a mercy." He bit into the drumstick in his hand. "So it's everybody else you're uncertain about, huh? Lance Singleton and Alexander Rigby and all the other men at the fort who are just waiting."

"Waiting? What are they waiting for?"

"Waiting to take you on picnics and waltz you around the room at dances. Waiting for me to get out of the way."

She stared at him. "You are joking." He set his drumstick down and gave her a long look. His eyes were so intense it sent prickles up her spine. "Jack?" she said in an uncertain voice.

"What!" he snapped.

"What are you talking about?"

"Oh, hell, Jonna. You're a beautiful girl here at this post full of men with good eyesight. Any red-blooded male within fifty yards of you is gonna want—" He stopped and gulped a mouthful of his whiskey-laced coffee. "...is gonna want to keep company with you."

"Keep company? What does that mean?"

He sighed. "It means taking you on picnics and maybe to a dance or two and for walks in the moonlight. That is if I'd get out of the way."

Suddenly, she pushed her coffee cup across the table. "Would you add some more whiskey to this? I need to think about what you are saying."

He stood up, snagged the bottle of Old Bailey's from the hutch, and dribbled a couple of tablespoons into her cup. Then he sloshed another hefty slug of whiskey into his own.

"Do you want some more coff—?"

"No," he said shortly.

"There's some of Sam's caramel cake in the pantry. Would you like—?"

"No."

"My goodness, Jack, what *do* you want?"

He sent her the most puzzling look she had ever

seen on his face. "Don't ask me that, Jonna."

"But—" She frowned at him. "Why shouldn't I ask?"

"Just don't."

"Why?" she repeated.

"Because," he snapped. "Because if you push me far enough, I might tell you exactly what I want, and that would be the most foolhardy thing I've ever done in my life."

"Wh-what? Whatever does that mean?"

He made no answer, just sipped his whiskey.

"Jack? Tell m—"

"Jonna?"

"Yes?"

"Jonna, shut the hell up!"

Tears flooded into her eyes. She blinked them away and studied her coffee cup until her eyes burned.

Jack didn't say another word.

Chapter Thirty-Two

Two weeks later, Dr. Brownell pronounced Lucinda and her baby able to travel. Nell Schwammer and Sophronia Tipton helped her pack up her trunk with her china and the silver tea set and doilies and photographs and embroidered cushions. When Jonna visited, her eyes widened at the mountain of belongings. The small valise Lucinda planned to take with her on the train would carry only a change of underclothes, along with baby blankets and diapers.

On Lucinda's last afternoon at Fort Kearney, Jonna walked over for a visit. With an aching heart, she sipped the tea Lucinda offered and listened to her friend chatter about her trip to South Carolina.

"Just imagine, Jonna, practically my whole life is goin' home with me! Everything I own is crammed into that little wooden trunk over there in the corner."

Unable to think of one sensible thing to say, Jonna nodded and sipped her tea in silence.

"Never again will a man seduce me with flowers and pretty words!" Lucinda declared. "How foolish it seems now, me and my dreams of bliss. I truly think we women delude ourselves, Jonna. We imagine that a few tingles up your spine means true love forever."

Jonna shifted uneasily in the rocking chair and wondered about tingles up one's spine. She felt tingles when Jack kissed her, but she had nothing to compare it to, so there was no way of knowing what they meant. Perhaps kissing *any* man would produce tingles.

"Where will you catch the train, Lucinda?"

Lucinda smiled. "Colonel Hawks asked that gallant Major Corder to escort me to the railhead at Sand Point. Of course, baby Kathleen and I will be snug in the stagecoach until we reach the station. And then—oh, Jonna, just think of it!—then it will be a mere four days until I am home in Charleston. Oh, I do hope it won't be too hot inside the passenger cars."

Jonna said nothing.

"I am so excited about goin' home!" Suddenly, she peered into Jonna's face. "Why, my goodness, you look positively gloomy. Whatever is wrong?"

Jonna swallowed. "I am happy you are going back to your home, Lucinda. But...but I will miss you so much!"

Lucinda sniffled into a lace-edged handkerchief. "I haven't wanted to admit how much I will miss you, Jonna. You have become my closest friend!"

"What time will you leave tomorrow?"

"Soon after sunup, when Major Corder tells me the stagecoach has arrived and my trunk is loaded. And," she added with a laugh, "as soon as baby Kathleen has been fed. I cannot have her wailing all the way to the train station, now can I?"

Jonna bit her lip and tried to smile.

After a long, sleepless night, she rose at the first pale light of dawn, donned her blue denim work skirt and a gingham shirtwaist, and went downstairs. She didn't feel the least bit hungry, so she decided to skip breakfast, and when the colonel finished his toast and coffee and left for his office, Jonna walked with him as far as the post gate. Jack and the burly stagecoach driver were now loading Lucinda's wooden trunk onto the luggage frame, and Lucinda was pacing impatiently up and down with baby Kathleen in her arms.

"All set now, ma'am," the stage driver called. "Best climb aboard."

Lucinda handed the baby to Jack, turned to Jonna, and threw her arms around her. "Don't say anything, dear one. Otherwise, I will cry, and Doctor Brownell says crying is not good for my milk."

Jonna tried to smile, but her mouth felt all wobbly. She hugged Lucinda hard and stepped back. One more minute and her heart would crack wide open.

Jack opened the coach door, helped Lucinda climb in, and handed the baby to her. The instant he slammed the door shut, something broke inside Jonna's chest. Tears rolled down her cheeks, and her jaw ached from clamping her teeth together.

Lucinda waved all the way through the gate. Jonna watched numbly until the stagecoach vanished in a cloud of dust, then finally turned away, moved listlessly back to the porch swing at the house, and let the tears roll unchecked down her cheeks. *It is awful to say goodbye to someone you care about, someone you will never see again. Truly awful.*

****

Long after darkness fell, Jack tramped up onto the porch where Jonna sat rocking in the swing. "She's on the train," he said quietly. "Got her there just in time." He settled his rangy frame beside her. "You eat any supper?"

Jonna shook her head.

"Lunch?"

"No."

"How about breakfast?

Again, she shook her head.

"Hot damn, Jonna, don't you know that food helps an aching heart?"

She made no answer.

"Come on." He stood up and pulled her out of the swing. "Martha?" he called through the screen door. "Got any supper left over?"

"In the pantry, Jack," came Martha's voice. "Help yourself."

He walked Jonna inside, sat her down at the dining room table, and disappeared into the kitchen. In a few minutes, he stepped out with Sam's red-checked apron tied around his waist. A glass of whiskey appeared in front of her, followed by a steaming cup of coffee and then a plate of warmed-up rice and beans. She stared at it until he bent over her and wrapped her fingers around a fork.

"Eat!" he ordered. "Or drink, if you prefer." He pushed the glass of Old Bailey's toward her.

"I can't," she murmured.

"Yes, you can. Listen, Jonna, drunk or sober, you're gonna get through this. Do you hear me?"

She nodded mechanically.

"Now, eat!"

She cried through half the rice and beans, then gulped down her glass of whiskey in three big swallows.

"Whoa!" Jack said, lifting the glass out of her hand. "Can't get tipsy before dessert. There's half a chocolate cake on the sideboard. Why don't you invite me to have a piece with you?"

She laughed in spite of the ache in her chest. "W-why don't you have a piece of chocolate c-cake, Jack?"

He grinned at her. "Thought you'd never ask."

Later, he splashed the plates through a pan of soapy water, then walked her back out to the porch and settled her in the swing. While they rocked back and forth, he recounted every detail about Lucinda's stagecoach journey.

"The baby cried all the way to the station. And Lucinda did, too, but she forgot her handkerchief so I gave her mine so she could mop up her tears. Right before she climbed on the train, she hugged me and said she'd write to you as soon as she arrived in Charleston."

Jonna alternately laughed and cried until the moon rose, and finally Jack stood up and let out a long breath. "I've been in the saddle since dawn and then here with you half the night. Gotta go get some sleep." He leaned over, pressed his lips against her forehead, and clumped down the porch steps.

"Jack!" she called suddenly.

"Yeah?"

"Thank you!"

He turned away, raised one hand, and disappeared in the dark.

****

The next morning at the breakfast table, Samantha slipped into the chair beside her and patted her hand. While Martha began clearing away the dishes, Sam leaned over and whispered, "Jonna, I have had the most brilliant thought! Would you like to hear what it is?"

"Of course," Jonna replied dully. Sam's "brilliant thoughts" were always surprising and usually impractical.

"Well," she began. "You know that I will be leaving for Oregon next week."

Jonna sighed. "Yes, I know."

"The head of the school board sent me a brochure, and I've been reading it. It says Maple Falls is a small town. It has one school, two churches, a Ladies Aid Society, three boardinghouses, a doctor's office, and a library."

"It sounds like a very nice town, Sam."

"And you'll never guess what else!" Samantha said with a smile. "The town doctor is looking for an assistant! Someone to change dressings and help deliver babies and—"

"No!" Jonna said.

Sam went on without pausing. "…and nurse people suffering from measles and pneumonia and—"

"No!" Jonna repeated.

"…broken bones," Sam finished. "Think, Jonna! You could come with me."

"No, I could not."

"Why not?"

"Because…because I do not want to be far away from where my brother is."

"Or from where Jack is?" Sam murmured.

"No," she said quickly. "Jack has nothing to do with it."

Sam nodded, but the smile on her face lingered. "We could travel to Oregon together. We could even rent a room together in one of those boardinghouses. Think about it, Jonna. Something tells me you're starting to wonder about your future."

Chapter Thirty-Three

She did think about it. On her way back from the infirmary the next day, she met Jack coming from the stables. "Haven't seen you smile since Lucinda Markley left," he said as he fell in beside her.

"I haven't felt like smiling."

He gave her a quick look. "Sam tells me she wants you to come to Oregon with her."

"Yes, she does," Jonna said slowly. "She keeps reading me things from the brochure someone sent her about the town about boardinghouses and Ladies Aid Societies."

"Are you tempted?"

"No. I want to be close to where Drew is posted."

He stopped dead. "Jonna, there's no guarantee Drew will stay at Fort McHenry. Army agents get transferred all over the West. Maybe you shouldn't make a decision based on where your brother is posted."

She stared at him. "Oh. *Oh.* I didn't realize…"

"Does that mean you're going to Oregon?" He held his breath.

"I don't know. I have to think about it."

He nodded. "Well, there's some other things you might want to consider, Jonna. For one thing, next year Sam might take a teaching position in a different town. She might even get married."

"Married! You mean to that Corporal Rigby?"

He chuckled. "Probably not. Sam's lots smarter than Corporal Rigby. Three days after the honeymoon, she'd be bored to blazes."

Jonna laughed. "Well, what about your friend Lance Singleton?"

"Nope. Lance isn't interested in Sam."

"How do you know?"

"Trust me, Jonna. I just know." He sucked in a long breath. "Listen, do you want my opinion?"

"Your opinion about what? About Sam?"

He shook his head. "No, not about Sam. About you. About you maybe going off to Maple Falls."

"Maybe." She sent him a wobbly smile. "I know you're going to tell me anyway."

His dark eyebrows rose. "Do I really do that? Tell you something whether you want to hear it or not?"

She looked up into his eyes. "You know you do, Jack. Usually, I appreciate it."

He blew out a long breath. "Okay, here it is. I think maybe you shouldn't go to Maple Falls."

"Do you know anything about Maple Falls? What sort of town it is?"

"Nope."

"Then why—?"

He stopped and pulled her around to face him. "Because, Jonna, you're only sixteen years old. You don't know anything about life outside Fort Kearney."

"I am almost seventeen, Jack. Some girls are married and mothers already at seventeen."

"But not you," he said shortly.

"Why *not* me? I might meet a man and fall—"

He shook his head. "Not you, Jonna. You won't

'fall' for a man. You'll take a good hard look at him, and you'll study his character, and—"

She propped her hands on her hips. "Jack, you don't know that!"

"I sure as hell do," he snapped.

She propped both hands on her hips. "You are the most exasperating, close-minded, over-protective—You're just like my father was!"

He couldn't help the chuckle that burbled out. "But I'm *not* your father. Thank God," he muttered.

"What?" She took a step closer to him. "Why 'thank God,' Jack? Am I so difficult?"

"Yep." He ambled away from her, leaned against the trunk of a pine tree, and studied her for a long minute. "I'll tell you what's difficult about you, Jonna. And why you won't just 'fall for' a man. You're smart. You question everything. You look beneath the surface of every damn issue that comes up. And," he added in a tired voice, "you are really beautiful, which means men are going to try hard to get close to you."

She stared at him. "Do-do you really think I'm—?"

"Yep." He shut his eyes. "I sure do. Wish I didn't, but there it is."

She bit her lip in frustration. He sent her a smile, stepped away from the tree, and took her elbow. "Come on, Jonna. Let's go stir up some trouble in Martha's kitchen. Martin tells me she's knocked out by the heat and she's lying down, so she won't mind if we make a couple of sandwiches."

"Sandwiches! I'm trying to decide about my future and all you can think about is sandwiches?"

He shrugged. "You want some lunch, don't you?"

She spun away from him and started up the porch

steps. By the time he caught up with her, she was in the kitchen, holding out a ruffly red apron and impatiently tapping her foot.

"Nah." He shook his head. "I don't want your frilly apron. I'm leading a patrol this afternoon. I'd look silly wearing an apron."

"You can take the apron off before your patrol."

He chuckled and watched her tie a blue gingham apron around her waist. "Can't for the life of me understand why cobbling together a couple of sandwiches requires *two* people and *two* aprons."

She didn't answer, just disappeared into the pantry, and emerged with a block of cheese and a plate of fried bacon strips left over from breakfast. "There's bread in the bread safe." She tipped her head at the latched metal container on the wooden counter. "Knives are in the drawer next to the stove."

"Hold on a minute," he said. "Tell me why the heck *I'm* wearing an apron when *you're* the one making the sandwiches?"

"Because," she said in a patient tone, "*you* are making the sandwiches, and you won't want crumbs on your trousers when you lead that patrol."

He laughed, shook his head, pared off four slices of bread, and laid them on the sideboard.

"Butter the bread," she instructed, laying a ripe tomato next to the cheese. "Then slice up this tomato."

He stopped suddenly, the tomato in his hand. "Hey, how come I'm doing all the work here?"

She sent him an amused look. "Because I'm smart, Jack."

He rolled his eyes. "Oh, yeah. I keep forgetting."

She pushed the block of cheese toward him. "Lay

the bacon on top, and don't forget the cheese."

"You give orders like an army sergeant, you know that?"

"Yes, I know that."

He shook his head and cut three slices of cheese, then assembled the sandwiches while Jonna poured two glasses of milk and set them on a painted metal tray. Jack cut each sandwich in half and loaded them onto a china plate, balanced the tray in one hand, and pushed the screen door open. He waited until Jonna followed him out onto the porch, then let it whap shut.

"It's godawful hot out here, Jonna."

"Sandwiches don't melt, Jack." She plopped down in the swing and patted the space beside her.

They ate their lunch without saying a word, and when he thought he couldn't stand Jonna's silence one more minute, Sam tripped up the porch steps.

"Oh, Jack, don't you look adorable wearing that apron!"

"It's Jonna's fault," he muttered.

Sam's mouth quirked. "Oh?"

"Yeah, I'm wearing this apron because—"

"Because Jonna is smart!" Jonna finished. "You said so yourself!"

Sam laughed, shook her head, and disappeared into the house. Jack polished off his sandwich, ate half of Jonna's, and got to his feet. "Gotta go whip some recruits into shape. Thanks for lunch."

He untied his apron and walked off across the grounds while Jonna took the empty sandwich plate and the glasses into the kitchen. She had started to mix up a batch of sugar cookies when Sam wandered in. "How can you stand baking anything on a day this hot!" she said, pouring herself a glass of lemonade.

"I am used to hot days. The Sioux often camped where the afternoon sun hit the teepees."

"I bet they didn't bake cookies in a hot wood stove."

Jonna laughed. "Indians don't eat cook—" She broke off when a voice from the front porch suddenly shouted her name.

"Miss Lander! Major Corder says to come quick!"

Jonna dropped her mixing spoon and flew out the screen door. "What has happened?"

The soldier motioned for her to follow him. "It's yer brother and Corporal Singleton, miss. They're just now ridin' in, and Major Corder sent me to—"

She didn't wait to hear the rest. She raced down the steps and sped across the parade ground. Jack was already at the gate.

"Where is he?" she said.

He pointed across the plain. "Somewhere in the middle of that dust cloud."

"How do you know it's Drew?"

"I recognize the horse he's riding."

Shielding her eyes against the sun, she looked in the direction he pointed. Two figures on horseback were slowly emerging from the haze, and Jack unhooked the gate and swung it open. Jonna took a tentative step forward, then began to run.

The two riders trotted toward her, then split up and rode past. One circled back to her, and she sucked in her breath. "Drew!"

His face was dust-streaked and sunburned, but he was grinning. He dropped to the ground and loped toward her.

Jonna threw her arms around him. "Are you all right? Oh, Drew, you're filthy!"

"I'm fine, Sis. And after eight hours in the saddle, you'd be filthy, too."

"Oh!" She started to laugh, but it ended up in a sob. "Eight h-hours! Where—?"

He looped an arm around her shoulders. "We started out early this morning and only stopped to water the horses. We're both starving!"

Lance dismounted and started toward her. He looked almost as dust-streaked as Drew. All at once, he scooped Jonna into a bone-crunching embrace and smacked a sloppy kiss on her cheek. Over his shoulder, she saw Jack grin and send her an "I told you so" look.

Jack shook hands with Lance and clapped Drew on the back. "The colonel's invited us all to supper after I get back from my patrol and you two have sponged off some of that dust."

"Oh!" Jonna suddenly exclaimed. "My cookies! They'll be burnt to cinders!" She darted away toward the house. "They're your favorite, Drew," she called over her shoulder.

Lance watched her skim over the ground and shook his head. "Sure wish she'd race off like that to bake *me* a cookie."

Jack shot him a look and opened his mouth to reply, then thought better of it and pressed his lips together. *Can't help wondering if Jonna cares a plug nickel whether Lance is interested in her or her damn cookies.*

Chapter Thirty-Four

Supper that evening in the colonel's spacious dining room was interesting. Jack watched Lance hitch his chair close to Jonna's, but when she got up to bring a bowl of biscuits, she quietly scooted her chair farther away. He hid a smile and listened to Drew describe their adventures rescuing the wagon train stuck in the mountains.

"Golly, Sis, I've never been so cold! Hard to remember it was the middle of summer!"

"Then," Lance interrupted, "we had one heck of a problem getting the Indians to release the settlers. If it hadn't been for your brother, all of us might still be stuck up there."

Martha set a platter of fried chicken on the table, followed by Sam with a pan of scalloped potatoes and a bowl of snow peas. "Gentlemen," Martha announced, "you both look half starved, so please help yourselves."

"What happened to the wagon train leader?" Colonel Hawks queried.

Lance chortled. "You mean *leaders,* Colonel. That was part of the problem. The two wagon train leaders couldn't agree on how to get themselves out of the mess they'd stumbled into, and as a result, they didn't do anything. They just sat there and argued until one of the Indian guides—Crow, wasn't he, Drew? Anyway, he gave the wagon leaders an ultimatum, and that probably saved all our lives."

"Sounds like it could have gone either way," the colonel observed. "Glad you're both back safe."

"Oh, man," Lance said in an undertone. "I don't ever want to go through that again." He leaned toward Jonna. "Are you glad I'm back safe?" he murmured.

"I am happy Drew has returned safely," she replied in a neutral tone. "And you, too, of course."

Samantha caught Jack's eye and sent him a knowing smile, and he swallowed a spurt of laughter. *If Lance thinks Jonna is going to fall for such obvious overtures, he's got a surprise coming.*

"I rode over to Fort McHenry a week ago, Jack said. "Wanted to know if Colonel Hardesty had heard any news about you."

Lance groaned. "Why'd you go to the trouble, Jack? Hardesty doesn't know what's happening on his own post, let alone in the mountains!"

"Are you going to transfer to another post?" Sam asked innocently.

"Not right now," Drew answered. "My sister's here at Fort Kearney, and that's only a day's ride."

"Yes," Lance added. "We—I mean Drew—want to stay close to Jonna."

Jack bit his lip to keep from laughing out loud.

"What if Jonna moves away?" Sam asked.

"Moves away?" Lance said in a puzzled voice. "Moves away to where?"

"Well, maybe to Oregon."

Lance blinked. "Oregon! Why would she do that? What's in Oregon?"

"Think about it, my boy," Colonel Hawks interjected. "What's here for Jonna at Fort Kearney?"

Drew set his fork on his dinner plate. "Colonel, besides me, you and Mrs. Hawks are the only family my sister's got."

Lance leaned forward. "You wouldn't really move to Oregon, would you, Jonna?"

"I might," she said, her voice quiet. Jack bit his lip again. Martha raised one eyebrow and looked from Jack to Jonna to Lance and back to Jack.

A frown wrinkled Lance's tanned forehead. "Aw, Jonna, you wouldn't leave Fort Kearney, would you?"

"I might," she repeated.

"Then again," Jack said, his voice quiet, "she might not."

Jonna pressed her lips together. "My future plans seem to be under discussion this evening. I wish you would all choose another topic."

Lance jerked. "Oh, sure, Jonna. We won't discuss it."

Drew sucked in his breath. "Wait a minute. Who is 'we'? Beggin' your pardon, Lance, but seems to me *I* might want to discuss where my sister is gonna live. I don't see how it makes any difference to anybody but me and her. And maybe just her," he added.

Jonna reached over and squeezed his hand. "Thank you, Drew."

Drew picked up his fork, but before he attacked his scalloped potatoes, he exchanged a long look with Jack.

****

Summer began to ease into fall. The air grew crisp, and as the days grew longer, Samantha began packing up her trunk for the move to Oregon. Jonna volunteered to help, and the two girls spent one afternoon in Sam's bedroom amid the tangle of skirts and muslin dresses and flowered shirtwaists that covered every available surface.

"You don't have a trunk, do you?" Sam asked.

Jonna laughed. "I don't even have a valise! Jack and I escaped with nothing but the clothes we were wearing."

"There's another trunk up in the attic, in case you—"

"Sam..." She paused to steady her voice. "Is there really a doctor in Maple Falls who needs an assistant?"

Samantha plopped down on her bed amid a pile of ruffled petticoats and camisoles. "Yes, there most certainly is. His name is Rufus Charles Baldwin— *Doctor* Rufus Baldwin. He took his training in New York City."

Jonna frowned. "How could you possibly know all that?"

Sam smiled. "It's in that brochure about Maple Falls, the one the president of the school board sent. I know the landlady's name at all three of the boardinghouses and who the proprietor of the mercantile is. Benjamin Collinwood is the sheriff. Oh, and the dressmaker's name is Mardith Jefferson."

"*Mardith*? Really? What an unusual name."

Sam laughed. "It's no more unusual than Jonna, is it? Maybe she was named after her father, as you were."

Jonna lifted aside the armload of silky nightrobes draped over Sam's rocking chair and sat down. With one foot, she tipped the rocker into motion and watched Samantha sort through a collection of knitted shawls.

"I wish you would come with me, Jonna. I know how frightening it is to leave what is familiar, but it can't be more frightening than stealing away from that

261

Sioux camp with Jack."

When Jonna said nothing, Sam tossed aside a blue wool shawl and planted herself in front of her. "We can come home to Fort Kearney at Christmas. And," she said with a sly look, "for all you know, Lance might be transferred to a post in Oregon."

"Lance! What makes you think—?"

"Since he's so mooney-eyed over you, I assumed you were smitten as well."

"I am not 'smitten.' "

Sam's grin widened. "Has he kissed you yet?"

Jonna blinked. "Well, no, he hasn't. But kissing someone doesn't make a person smitten, does it?"

Sam flopped on her camisole-strewn bed. "Um, no, a kiss doesn't do that. But a man's kiss can tell you whether you *could* be smitten."

All at once, Jonna found herself thinking about Jack. Jack's mouth on hers made her feel all swirly inside, like Lucinda's dish of stars. Would it be the same if Lance kissed her? She chased that thought out of her mind and tried to focus on folding dresses and nightrobes and laying them in Sam's trunk. Suddenly, she paused with a folded skirt in her hand and turned to Sam.

"Sam, do you ever wonder about the future?"

"Jonna, I want to tell you something. No one knows what the future will bring for either one of us. When I was feeling really scared about traveling all the way across the country to my teachers college in Boston, Papa sat me down after supper one night and said something I've never forgotten."

Jonna stopped the motion of the rocking chair. "Oh? What did he say?"

"He said that if I was careful enough, if I never took a risk, for sure nothing bad would ever happen to me. But nothing *good* would happen to me, either. I think we have to take risks in life, Jonna. We have to reach for things."

Jonna shut her eyes. Sam was right. She was frightened. Not frightened like she was the night she and Jack escaped from the Sioux. Then, she knew what she had to do, and she knew how to do it. This was different. She had no idea how to survive in a town, with mercantile stores, boardinghouses, dressmakers, and a sheriff. The thought of leaving here, of leaving Martha and the colonel and everything she had learned since the day she and Jack rode through the post gates, sent her stomach tumbling to her toes.

Deep down inside, she knew she had to make a life for herself. No one on this earth could do it for her; she had to do it herself. She tamped down a bolt of pure terror. This time, she did *not* know how to do it, and that made her pulse race and her knees feel wobbly.

Tears trembled on her eyelashes. "Sam," she said in a shaky voice.

"Yes?"

"Sam, w-where does one catch the train to Maple Falls?"

"Sand Point." Sam dropped an armload of ruffled dresses on the floor and threw her arms about Jonna's shoulders. "*Sand Point!*"

Chapter Thirty-Five

On Sunday morning, Lance Singleton rode into the fort, climbed up the colonel's front porch steps, and invited Jonna to go on a picnic.

"A picnic? Will Drew be coming, too?" she asked.

Lance studied his boots. "Uh, no. Drew had…something else he had to do."

"In that case, perhaps another—"

"But I already stopped at the mess hall on the way over here and picked up a picnic hamper for us."

"Oh." She wasn't thrilled at the prospect of a picnic with Lance Singleton, but maybe it would be a chance to do some…well, personal exploring. She grabbed a sunhat, followed the corporal to the stables, and saddled up the roan mare she liked to ride.

They rode north, following a meandering stream through cottonwoods and vine maples, and after an hour, they came to a shady creek bank. Lance dismounted and spread a blanket over the sparse grass. Then he began to describe once more how he and Drew had negotiated the rescue of the covered wagons stranded in the mountains. Jonna had heard it all before, but she listened politely.

"It was really cold, especially at night," Lance again explained. "Fortunately, I had my heavy mackinaw, and Drew was practically covered in wool neck scarves."

"I see," she said. "Where did you sleep?"

"Inside one of the wagons. After the food stores ran out, there was plenty of room."

"You must have been hungry, with no food."

"Sure was. But that Crow Indian guide trapped two rabbits and a fat squirrel, so—"

"What does squirrel taste like?"

"It tasted like—Look, Jonna, I don't want to talk about squirrels or Indians or wagon trains. I want to talk about us."

She stiffened. "Us? What do you mean 'us'?"

"About, uh, well, about how much I like you and— Well, I was wondering if maybe the feeling might be mutual."

"Mutual? It might be too soon to know such a thing," Jonna said quickly. What she did *not* say was how disinterested she was in Lance Singleton.

He edged closer. "See, I figure we have a lot in common, and—"

"Oh? What do we have in common, Lance?"

"Well, there's your brother, Andrew, and…" He frowned, searching for words. "Well, we both live at army posts and, um, well, I'm partial to cookies. Sugar cookies," he added quickly.

Jonna almost laughed aloud. She could see the man was floundering, so she took pity on him. "This sandwich is very good," she said.

"Oh, sure. I got the mess hall cook to make them. He brewed the coffee, too."

She waited.

"Like I was saying, I'm partial to—"

"Yes, you said that before."

"Um, what I really mean is I'm partial to…to *you*."

He hitched himself closer. "I mean…" He slid one arm around her shoulders, bent his head, and pressed his lips to hers.

Jonna closed her eyes and waited to feel some spark…or warmth…or…*something.* She felt nothing. Absolutely nothing. Lance's kiss left her as cold as leftover coffee. Maybe she should try it again. She leaned forward, closed her eyes, and kissed him back.

Again nothing.

"Jonna," he said. "Jonna, would you do me the honor of becoming my wife?"

Her lids flew open. "What?"

"I'm, uh, asking if you would marry me."

"Oh. *Oh!*"

"I know it's kind of sudden, but I've been thinking about it for a while, especially when I was stuck on that mountain, and—"

"Lance, stop. It *is* sudden. Too sudden. I scarcely know you." *And the dish of stars that might have jostled me closer to you just isn't there. When Lance kisses me, there is not one single star.*

"Lots of folks get married without knowing each other real well," he said quickly. "It seems to work out okay."

She drew in a long breath. "No, it does not work out okay, as you put it. My friend Lucinda Markley at Fort Kearney found herself married to a man who drank to excess and became violent. She has left him."

"But I don't drink at all, Jonna! Honest, I don't."

She shook her head. *He hasn't the remotest idea what I'm talking about. Even worse, something important is missing. Shouldn't he should be telling me what his feelings are toward me?*

A prolonged silence fell. It lasted through two more cheese and bacon sandwiches and the Mason jar of lukewarm coffee until finally Jonna sighed and got to her feet. "I am expected at the infirmary later today." She picked up the picnic hamper and moved to untie her horse. Lance scrambled to his feet, hurriedly folded the blanket into a sloppy square, and followed her.

They rode back to Fort Kearney in silence. As they passed through the post gate, he caught her bridle and brought her roan to a halt. "I hope you'll think about my offer to marry you, Jonna. I'm an officer, so we would always live in officers' quarters."

She stifled a groan of exasperation. For a man proposing marriage, asking her to spend the rest of her life with him, surely the last thing of importance was living in officers' quarters. The very last thing. But the most important thing, the thing she could not avoid acknowledging, was what kissing Lance Singleton made her feel. *Nothing.*

When he rode away, she breathed a sigh of relief, turned her back on the tall figure on horseback, and walked across the parade ground to the infirmary.

****

Jack accepted another shot of Old Bailey's and settled on the chair across from the colonel, who sat rocking slowly back and forth in the porch swing.

"Kind of surprising, isn't it, Jack?"

"What is? Didn't think much ever surprised you, Martin."

"I'm surprised that Sam's all grown up and leaving home. And Jonna's planning to go off to Oregon with her. That kinda kicked me in the gut."

Jack looked out across the plains, rotated the glass

of whiskey in his hands, and said nothing. He didn't often feel at a complete loss for words, but he sure felt it now. Jonna was going to Oregon with Sam. Tonight, she would celebrate her seventeenth birthday and tomorrow…

He closed his eyes. He didn't want to think about tomorrow.

"Gonna be real quiet around here with both girls gone. Don't know how Martha will stand it 'til Christmas."

Christmas! Jack didn't know how he was going to stand it *tomorrow* when Jonna would climb on the train to Oregon.

"Oh, hell," the colonel said. "Whiskey doesn't help, does it?"

"Nope. Any idea what *does* help?"

Colonel Hawks topped up both glasses. "Huh! If I knew that, Major, I'd be a wealthy man!"

Neither man cracked a smile.

"Got any idea why she didn't want to marry your friend Lance Singleton?" the colonel asked.

"Nope. No idea." He had his suspicions, but he wouldn't share them with Colonel Hawks.

"You know, sometimes I wonder why the good lord made Eve so smart and Adam so pigheaded."

Jack bit back a smile. "Most men are pigheaded at some time in their life, especially around women. I've always thought if Eve was *really* smart, she would have straightened old Adam out!"

"Think so, do you?"

Jack chuckled. "Actually, I don't. Where'd be the fun in that?"

The colonel lifted his glass. "Major Corder, I toast

your sense of humor."

Jack touched his glass to the colonel's. "Not much else to do but laugh when life kicks you in the gut."

Colonel Hawks narrowed his eyes. "Say that again?"

"A man's got to laugh when his heart gets broken. Otherwise, he dies."

The colonel shot him a keen look, then nodded and settled back in the swing. "Broken," he murmured under his breath. "Interesting."

Jack said nothing, just turned his whiskey glass around and around in his hand. Finally, the colonel leaned forward. "You try to talk her out of it?"

Jack sighed. "I talked as much sense as I could to her. Finally, I gave up. When Jonna makes up her mind about something, she's like a mule on a mountain trail."

Colonel Hawks chuckled. "A mule, huh? I see Jonna more like a butterfly than a mule. She's just emerging from her cocoon, and her wings are still wet. You ever catch butterflies when you were a boy?"

Jack frowned. "Hell's bells, Martin, when I was a boy, I was too damn busy mucking out the barn and shucking corn to pay any attention to butterflies."

"Well, then." The colonel sipped his whiskey and rocked back and forth in the swing for some minutes.

"Well, then *what,* Martin?"

"Well, then, you're smarter than most men when it comes to matters of the heart. See, the way I figure it, that butterfly just emerging from her cocoon is busy drying off her wings and stretching them. She's getting ready to fly."

Jack sat without moving.

"Now the *young* boy," the colonel continued, "will

wave the butterfly net around, and when a butterfly blunders into it, he grabs it and holds it tight. That usually kills the butterfly." He cleared his throat. "But the grown man is smarter," he continued. "He lets the butterfly sit there on his palm. He doesn't try to capture it. He just enjoys its company." He shot a look at Jack. "You want some more whiskey?"

Sam stepped out the screen door. "Gentlemen," she announced, "Jonna's birthday supper is served."

Jack purposely took the dining chair across from Jonna because he didn't think he could stand sitting next to her, smelling her rose-scented perfume and watching her hands flutter when she spoke. But once he settled into his chair, he discovered that sitting across from her was worse. Much worse. Sitting across from her, he could watch her face, see her eyes. At least, he couldn't smell that spicy-sweet scent she sometimes wore. Even so, he found himself taking extra-deep breaths to maybe catch a whiff.

She looked so beautiful tonight it made him ache. Maybe it was because tomorrow she would be leaving on her first big step into life outside the post. Maybe it was because that flounced yellow dress outlined the soft curves of her body. Or maybe it was because she was turning seventeen tonight. But goddam, she was so beautiful she made him ache.

After a supper of roast beef, mashed potatoes, and green beans, Martha presented a double-layer fudge cake, and Sam moved around the dining table pouring dark red port into tiny glasses. Jack drank his in two swallows, and without a murmur, Sam refilled his glass. He could almost hear her thinking. Even when she was growing up, Sam could always see through him.

He tried to shut his mind off.

Didn't work.

Martin was quiet as a ghost, letting Sam's chatter fill the room. In fact, the colonel hadn't uttered a single word, just kept looking at Sam and Jonna with an odd half-smile on his lips. And, Jack noted, since they'd all sat down to supper, Martin hadn't once looked at him.

Martha was acting funny, too. She kept slipping into the kitchen, and he could see her bent over the sink, mopping at her eyes.

Jonna's low, quiet voice was sending shivers up his spine, and tonight, it was a kind of shiver he'd never felt before. Every so often her eyes met his with some unspoken message. Sure was unnerving. *If she keeps looking at me like that, I'm not going to make it through the next ten minutes.*

Jonna felt more like crying tonight than she could ever remember. Martha was surreptitiously blotting tears off her cheeks when she thought no one was looking. The colonel was silent as a statue. Sam was lit up as if she'd just swallowed a candle. And Jack…She couldn't begin to puzzle out the expression in Jack's eyes.

She'd said her goodbyes to everyone this afternoon—the infirmary patients, Dr. Brownell and Dr. Solman, even Nell and Sophronia and Dolly Brownell. Seamus, the stable hand, had taken both her hands in his and wished her luck, his eyes suspiciously shiny. Saying goodbye to Martha and the colonel tomorrow would tear her heart in two. And Jack…well, she couldn't bear to think about Jack.

She couldn't think about tomorrow, either. She should be feeling happy. She should be brimming with

271

joy. She knew she wouldn't sleep much tonight, but she prayed that in the morning, she would have the strength to climb out of bed, button up her travel dress, and walk to the post gate to meet the stagecoach.

Jack would ride along on that black mare he'd grown attached to, the one she'd sneaked away from that Indian camp. She pressed her lips together. She couldn't think about Jack now. Maybe tomorrow, when she boarded the train.

This is what I want, she reminded herself. *This is what I know I must do.*

"And finally," Sam was saying, "we will always remember this evening when Momma baked her special fudge cake to celebrate Jonna's seventeenth birthday."

Jonna's breath caught on an unexpected sob. *Yes, I will always remember this evening and the people that I care about. I will remember this for the rest of my life.*

Chapter Thirty-Six

At sunrise the following morning, Jack tramped over to the post gate to help the stagecoach driver load Sam's trunk and Jonna's small valise onto the luggage rack. When the driver climbed back into his seat, Jack turned to the girls. "Time to load up." Suddenly, he found his voice was hoarse.

Sam and Jonna climbed into the coach, and Jack swung the door shut, signaled the driver, and mounted his black mare. It was a five-hour ride to the train station, and he dreaded every mile.

The sun climbed higher, and the morning grew suffocatingly hot. Inside the stage, Sam chattered nonstop about Mrs. Donovan's boardinghouse in Maple Falls and the plans she'd made for her first day of school. Jonna scarcely listened. She felt numb with fear as if she was swimming underwater and couldn't breathe. She concentrated on the sound of Jack's black mare trotting beside the stage and tried not to think.

When the coach finally rattled into the Sand Point train station, Sam climbed down and stood on the platform, practically dancing with excitement. Jonna followed and stood quietly at her side. The station looked deserted. "Have we missed the train?" she asked.

"Oh, no, miss," the stage driver assured her. "We're right on time. It'll be along in ten minutes or so."

Ten minutes. Ten minutes felt like an eternity. She had never been on a train, and never, ever, had she imagined that one day she would be boarding one to travel hundreds of miles away from everything she loved.

Jack wrestled Sam's trunk and her small valise onto the platform, then strode into the stationhouse to purchase their tickets. As he emerged, the locomotive's sharp whistle pierced the quiet, and the shiny black engine puffed into the station. It rolled forward until the passenger car came to a stop, and a blue-uniformed conductor stepped out and clanked down an iron loading step. While the baggage cart attendant trundled the trunk to the rear, Sam gave Jack a quick, hard hug, then scampered onto the train and disappeared.

He steeled his nerves and turned to Jonna. When she looked up at him, a choking sensation stopped his breathing.

"Jack?" Her voice was unsteady.

"Yeah?"

She moved to within an arm's length of where he stood. Her eyes looked wet. "Jack, I am frightened!"

"You're frightened, huh? You think I'm not?"

"But you have nothing to be frightened of," she whispered.

"Not true, Jonna. I'm afraid you're going to climb on that train and never come back."

"Oh, Jack, I—" Her voice broke.

He bent toward her and cupped his hands around her shoulders. "Jonna, before you go, there's something I want to say. Something I should have said before today."

"Y-yes? What is it?"

He looked away for a long moment. "Well," he said, his throat tight. "It's just this. I don't want you to leave Fort Kearney. I don't want you to go to Oregon."

She stared at him so long he thought she hadn't heard him, and then tears began to roll down her cheeks. "W-why tell me this now when I'm going away?"

"Maybe it's too soon to go off to a town where you don't know anybody. Hell, you just turned seventeen last night!"

"It is not too soon, Jack. Some women are already married at seventeen. But not me. You know me better than that. I want to see what life is like outside of Fort Kearney. I want see where I fit in."

He bit his lip. "Yeah, I thought you'd say that."

"I have to go, Jack. You know I do."

"Yeah," he said again. "I guess you do."

He stepped forward, tipped her chin up, and kissed her. When he released her, his own eyes were wet. "Don't forget Fort Kearney, Jonna. And me." He brushed his thumbs across her wet cheeks, bent forward, and kissed her again. Then he stepped back, turned her toward the train, and gave her a little push.

"Don't forget what I said," he murmured.

She turned back to look at him. "I never forget *anything* you say to me, Jack." She walked back to him, stretched up, and pressed her lips against his cheek. "I will miss you," she whispered.

He thought his knees would buckle.

Then she was gone. Her green skirt vanished into the passenger car, and he lost sight of her. The train gave two short, sharp toots and puffed on down the track. He watched it until his eyes burned, then paced around and around the passenger platform for a good half hour before he felt calm enough to untie his horse and haul himself into the saddle.

****

After an hour of listening to Jonna's sobbing, Samantha leaned forward and peered into her friend's tear-streaked face. "Jonna, for heaven's sake, tell me why you are still crying."

"B-because," she said.

"Because why? Because you're frightened? Because of Jack?"

Jonna drew in an uneven breath. "Yes," she breathed. "And j-just…just because."

Chapter Thirty-Seven

Jonna liked Maple Falls with its shady, tree-lined streets and pretty churches. And she liked the townspeople who welcomed her and Sam into their midst. She had been frightened at first, afraid she wouldn't know what to do or say around the boardinghouse dinner table or how to go about purchasing thread or galoshes or carrot seeds at Johnson's Mercantile. Afraid she would not fit in. But now...

Now, she felt she belonged. She had joined the Ladies Aid Society. She served refreshments and helped out at Sam's school pageants. She sang in the church choir on Sundays. As the weeks went by, she had become part of life in Maple Falls.

She loved working for Dr. Baldwin. He told her she added a great deal to his medical practice and even took time to teach her about new developments in anesthesia and explain how schoolchildren spread measles among their classmates.

She made friends with the church ladies and the store owners along the main street, and yesterday, dressmaker Mardith Jefferson asked if she would model one of her creations at the next ladies' tea. Some of the young unmarried men in town and on nearby ranches asked her out to ice cream socials and barn dances; she was becoming an expert square dancer as long as the caller didn't speak too fast.

Best of all, Drew visited whenever an army assignment took him anywhere within a hundred miles of Maple Falls. Sometimes, he rode into town with Lance, but usually, he came on his own and ate supper with her at the boardinghouse.

This Sunday afternoon, she and Sam were hosting a tea at Mrs. Donovan's boardinghouse. Gathered around them were eight Methodist church ladies enjoying Jonna's sugar cookies and a peach tart Sam had made.

Her life here in Maple Falls was satisfying. Only occasionally did she feel unsettled. She couldn't put it into words, but deep down underneath, something niggled at her, a vague feeling that something was missing.

But she had everything she wanted here in Maple Falls, didn't she? She even had an account at the Maple Falls Bank! What more could she want?

****

October melted into November and then a crisp, cold December, and Jack began to count the days until Jonna and Sam would be coming home for Christmas. He kept himself busy. Over-busy, Colonel Hawks observed. Guess he was trying to ease an ache inside. Every day and during many sleepless nights, he thought about the brave, determined girl he'd kissed goodbye and put on the train in Sand Point. He still only half understood why moving to Oregon was so important to her, but he'd said his piece and held her close before she climbed on the train. Now all he could do was wait.

During suppers at the colonel's house, Martha read aloud every single letter Jonna wrote. He knew Sam also wrote to her parents, but for some reason, Jonna's letters were the only ones Martha shared at the supper table.

"Sam and I have a very comfortable room in Mrs. Donovan's boardinghouse. Every morning, Sam trudges off to her school, and every evening, she tells me all about the antics of her students. Sam loves teaching school, even though most nights she sits up until past midnight correcting homework papers, and at supper, her fingers are often ink-stained. I am working for Dr. Rufus Baldwin and learning a great deal. Tell Jack I am now an expert at setting broken bones.

And every evening, the doctor lets me study some of his medical books."

"Medical books!" Jack exclaimed. "Why medical books?"

"Maybe she's thinking about becoming a doctor," Martha suggested.

He groaned aloud. Jupiter, that would be just like her! Hell's bells, he thought. She might be the smartest, prettiest doctor in the entire state of Oregon, but she wouldn't be here at Fort Kearney.

"Or," the colonel suggested calmly, "maybe she wants to be good at assisting that doctor—what was his name again?"

"Baldwin," Jack supplied. "Rufus Baldwin."

"Oh, listen to this!" Martha exclaimed.

"Sam and I are singing in the Methodist church choir! I have an alto voice, and the director is teaching me to read music. Tell Jack I can now sing 'Streets of Laredo' better than he can!"

"Church choir," the colonel echoed with a frown. "That seems kinda odd. Sam never was much of a church-goer."

"And there's more," Martha said.

"Every Sunday afternoon, Sam and I host a tea party at the boardinghouse for some of the ladies of Maple Falls. We hear all the news and gossip, which is quite a lot in a small town."

Jack choked on his coffee. Tea party! He couldn't picture Jonna pouring tea for anyone other than Martha, but he kept his mouth shut. "When are they coming home for Christmas?" he ventured.

"At Christmastime," Martha said with a laugh. "That's a whole week away."

"Maybe I could meet the train?"

"No need, Jack," Colonel Hawks said. "The stagecoach will bring them from the station. Besides," he added, "that's a long ride on horseback, and it's the middle of winter."

Yeah, it was a long ride, he acknowledged. So what? If he met the train, he'd get to see Jonna five hours sooner.

He sweated all week, waiting for her arrival. By Thursday, he'd had enough of pacing up and down in his quarters half the night, and that morning he cornered the colonel in his office. "Martin, I'm going to meet that train on Sunday."

The colonel hid a smile. "Take a heavy overcoat. Gonna be colder than a—"

"Yeah," Jack said.

Chapter Thirty-Eight

The night before they were to catch the train to Sand Point, Jonna and Sam found themselves propped up in their beds, wide awake at midnight. Sam was correcting student essays piled haphazardly on the quilt beside her. Jonna was concentrating on crochet stitches for the lacy wool shawl she was making for Martha and idly humming under her breath.

"What is that song?" Sam asked suddenly.

"'Streets of Laredo.' I sing it whenever I feel homesick for Fort Kearney."

Sam twiddled a pencil in her hand, laid one paper on the finished pile, and picked up another. "When I'm homesick, I sing 'Barbara Allen.' It's an old folk song Momma used to sing to me at night."

Jonna crocheted five stitches and looped the chain through the next stitch. "My mother sang 'I Know My Love.' That's an old Irish song. Sometimes, Papa would sing harmony, and then Mama would cry. Mama always missed Ireland. I think she would rather have gone back to Donegal than set off for Oregon."

"Don't you sometimes wonder what makes a woman follow a man halfway across the globe?"

"I certainly wondered why Lucinda Markley would come all the way from South Carolina to marry that drunkard of a lieutenant," Jonna said.

Sam chewed on one end of her pencil. "I guess

love just bonks a girl over the head, and that's that." She scribbled a comment on the paper she was correcting and set it aside.

"Have you ever fallen in love, Sam?"

"Oh, yes," she said after a slight hesitation. "Back in Boston, I fell madly in love with my mathematics professor. It only lasted two weeks until I found out he was married."

"Were you heartbroken?"

Sam grinned. "I was heartbroken for exactly two days. But I passed the math examination with the highest grade in the class!"

Jonna again began humming "Streets of Laredo."

"What about Jack?" Jonna ventured. "Were you in love with him, Sam?"

"Jack! Good gracious, yes. I was head-over-teakettle about Jack when I was eleven years old, and I was over it by the time I was twelve. And Jack..." Her voice trailed off.

"And Jack, what?" Jonna prompted.

Samantha laughed aloud. "Jack keeps himself to himself. He holds his feelings close to his chest. I know women moon over him all the time, but I don't think he's ever cared for any of them."

Jonna looped another chain through the next stitch and said nothing.

"What about Lance Singleton, Jonna? He's interested in you, isn't he?"

"He is interested, yes."

Sam set her pencil aside. "And? Are you interested in him? You could marry him and set up housekeeping at Fort McKinley. It's something to think about."

Jonna nodded. "Yes, I could. And I have thought

about it. But I'm also thinking about what I want for the rest of my life. What I *really* want." Sam went back to her pile of student essays, and she picked up her crochet hook. She tried to concentrate on her stitches, but she couldn't stop thinking about her life, about the choices she was making.

"Sam, you like teaching, don't you?"

"Yes, I do. It's the most satisfying thing I've ever done."

"Do you ever feel...I don't know...that you're missing something? That the life you're living is somehow not enough?"

Samantha laid her pencil aside and studied her. "No," she said slowly, "I never feel that way. But *you* must feel that way, or you wouldn't be asking me about it." She waited until Jonna's eyes met hers. "What is it you feel you're missing, Jonna?"

Tears suddenly flooded into Jonna's eyes and spilled down her cheeks. She swiped them away with one hand, but they kept coming. Deep down inside, she was beginning to suspect what it was she was missing. She hadn't wanted to acknowledge it, but it was always there, a small, nagging ache. She laid Martha's half finished shawl to one side and fished under her pillow for a handkerchief.

The last time she cried like this was the day Jack kissed her goodbye and put her on the train to Maple Falls. She blinked hard to stop her tears, then noticed Sam was looking at her with an odd expression on her face. While Jonna snuffled and mopped at her wet cheeks, Sam just sat there and smiled.

****

On Sunday, Jack rode half a day in a blizzard to

meet the train from Maple Falls, only to have a cannonball drop into the pit of his stomach when it pulled into the station. Samantha emerged from the passenger car, threw her arms around his snow-frosted coat, and smacked a kiss on his cheek.

"Welcome home, Sam. Where's Jonna?"

"She's staying an extra two days to help Dr. Baldwin with an outbreak of scarlet fever. And…"

"And? And what?"

"And Drew and Lance are stopping in Maple Falls to see her before they start their next mission. She won't leave until they get there."

Jack bit back a groan. Hell and damn!

Sam persuaded him to tie his horse onto the stagecoach and ride inside with her, but after an hour, he wished he hadn't. She talked nonstop all the way to Fort Kearney, and none of it was about Jonna.

Martha and the colonel were overjoyed to see their daughter, but their faces betrayed their disappointment that Jonna had not returned with her. That night, Martha invited Jack to supper, but he felt so glum he begged off. He didn't feel like being around people. He wanted to be around Jonna.

Chapter Thirty-Nine

The day after Samantha caught the train to Sand Point, Jonna settled in the porch swing on Mrs. Donovan's wide veranda to wait for Drew. As she rocked back and forth, she smoothed out her blue wool skirt and tried to sort out her thoughts. She was building a satisfying life for herself here in Maple Falls, was she not? She enjoyed her work for Dr. Baldwin and the Sunday afternoon teas and ice cream socials. Surely that was enough? *Why do I have the nagging feeling that something is missing?*

She leaned back and closed her eyes to help her think when someone tramped up the front steps. "Drew!"

"Yeah, it's me, Sis. Lance is off picking some roses for you."

She flung both arms around him. "Oh, I am so glad to see you!"

"D'you think me and Lance could stay to supper? Been in the saddle since sunup, and I'm starving."

"Of course, you can stay for supper. The minute I got your letter, I spoke to Mrs. Donovan."

A moment later, Lance appeared, a sprangly bunch of pink roses in one hand. He gave her a broad grin and thrust the bouquet at her. "Jonna, you get prettier every time I see you."

Drew groaned melodramatically, and Jonna tried

not to laugh.

After a supper of roast chicken and scalloped potatoes, followed by cinnamon cake and coffee, Drew settled himself in the porch swing, and Lance asked Jonna to go for a walk. They hadn't gone more than two blocks when Lance suddenly stopped and took her hand.

"Jonna, have you given any more thought about getting married? I mean, getting married to me?"

She looked up into his lean, suntanned face and tried to smile. "I have thought about it, Lance. I—"

"Wait!" He dug into his vest pocket and pulled out a tiny black leather box. "What did you decide?" He flipped the box open, took her hand, and laid a gold wedding ring on her palm. "Would you marry me, Jonna?"

She studied the man standing before her. Lance was a good man, an honorable man. But she knew instinctively that wasn't enough. It would never be enough because...

She closed her eyes as a sudden realization poked at her. It had been staring her in the face for months, but she was so intent on proving something to herself, she had brushed it aside.

Well, she had proved it. She had proved that she could fit into town life, but in the process of proving it, she had almost lost something far more valuable than having ladies to tea and accepting invitations to barn dances.

"Lance, I am very sorry, but I cannot marry you."

His broad forehead wrinkled in a frown. "Oh, gosh, Jonna, why can't you?"

She stared at him. "Why can't I? Lance, I can't

marry you because I do not love you."

The minute she uttered those words, everything snapped into focus. Suddenly, she felt she was looking at her life through a pair of Jack's field glasses, and everything became clear. All at once, she wanted nothing more than to pack her valise and climb on the train that would take her back to Fort Kearney.

Chapter Forty

Three days after Sam arrived, Jack made another trip on horseback to the railroad station at Sand Point. The train was late. He gritted his teeth and paced up and down the platform for an hour, wondering if he would live through waiting to see Jonna. Finally, hungry and half-frozen, he heard the faint wail of a locomotive. By the time the train chuffed into the station, he needed a big slug of the colonel's bourbon to calm his nerves.

Then Jonna flew off the train straight into his arms. "Jack! Oh, Jack!"

He didn't waste time asking about Drew or the outbreak of scarlet fever in Maple Falls or singing in the church choir; he just kissed her thoroughly while she clung to his snow-dusted mackinaw, and then he kissed again. When he finally lifted his lips from hers, he found he couldn't utter a word.

It didn't seem to matter because she didn't say anything, either. When he recovered his equilibrium, he set her apart from him and looked into her tear-streaked face. "Jonna…"

"Oh, Jack, I am so awfully glad to see you!"

"I sure missed you, Jonna."

"And I—" Her voice broke. "Every s-single night, I thought about that day we stood under the waterfall on Coyote Creek, remember?"

"Yeah, I remember." Hell, he'd never forget the sight of Jonna grinning at him from under that waterfall. "Somebody might say that's a funny thing to remember."

"It's not a funny thing at all! It meant a lot to me, you helping me gather those herbs for Lucinda Markley."

Jack said nothing, just raised his eyebrows.

"And I remember d-dancing with you on the Fourth of July," she went on. She swiped her gloved hand across her tear-streaked cheeks. "And…"

"And?" he prompted.

"And I thought about when we were waiting for Drew at the post gate, and you kissed me. But mostly…oh, Jack, mostly I thought about the night we rode away from the Sioux camp. I thought about how much what you did changed my life."

"Yeah?" He didn't risk saying more because his voice was unsteady.

"Yeah," she echoed with a grin. "My life has changed in ways I didn't expect. Ways that surprised me. Wonderful ways."

Oh, God, it felt good to hear her voice. Suddenly, he realized he still had his arms around her. But since she didn't seem to mind, he kept them there. Holding her in his arms made him feel kinda shaky inside.

"Jonna, are you happy living in Maple Falls?"

She hesitated. "Oh, yes. Yes, I am happy living in Maple Falls. But…"

His heart did a somersault straight into his belly. "But?"

"But I am not going back to Maple Falls."

"What? I thought you liked working for Dr. Baldwin and singing in the church choir and having Sunday tea parties."

"Yes, I do like all those things," she said, her voice

quiet. "But I am still not going back to Maple Falls."

He shook his head. Maybe he never would understand Jonna. Maybe he hadn't heard right. Maybe... He walked her to the stagecoach and helped her climb in, then tied his horse on behind, and climbed into the coach with her.

She gave him an odd smile. "Jack, don't you want to know *why* I am not going back to Maple Falls?"

He shook his head. "I was afraid to ask."

"Ask," she prompted. "Please, ask!"

He took a deep breath. "You didn't find the town as nice as you thought it would be?"

She shook her head. "No. Maple Falls is a charming town, full of friendly people."

"You don't really like singing in the church choir?"

"No. I do like singing in the church choir. The choir director says I have a fine singing voice."

He huffed out a breath. "Dr. Baldwin is eighty years old and drinks too much bourbon?"

"No," she said with a laugh. "Dr. Baldwin is thirty-seven, and he drinks very limited amounts of scotch whiskey."

A shadow fell across his mind. "You're going to marry Lance Singleton, is that it?"

She laughed again and shook her head. "Of course I'm not going to marry Lance Singleton! I could never marry Lance Singleton!"

"Thank God," he muttered under his breath.

She leaned toward him. "There is a much more important reason why I am not returning to Maple Falls."

He studied her face. "Care to tell me about it?"

"I'm not going back because everything I want is

right here at Fort Kearney. I left something here that I can't live without."

"Yeah?" he asked in a disbelieving tone. "What?"

"You," she said simply.

He stared at her. "Say that again?"

"All the church choirs and medical books and boardinghouse tea parties don't fill the big empty space in my heart when I'm not near you. I have discovered," she added in a quiet voice, "that I do not want to be away from you."

He blinked. "Jonna, are you serious?"

"Of course, I'm serious. I am very serious. At this moment, I am the most serious I have ever been in my life."

He looked at her for a full minute without saying a word. "You don't want to—?"

"Be away from you," she finished. "So unless we want to bring scandal down on Colonel and Mrs. Hawks, I think we should get married."

He gaped at her. "Married! *Married*? Did you say married?"

She smiled at him. "That is exactly what I said, Jack. Unless you have other plans, of course. Do you?"

He was still staring at her. "Do I what?"

"Have other plans."

"Other plans…" he murmured. "Yeah, I've got other plans, Jonna. Lots of them."

"Spring?" she asked.

"Christmas. Next week, in fact. Christmas Eve."

She laughed and planted a resounding kiss on his cheek. "Oh, good. Drew is coming. And Sam said she wants to bake a wedding cake for us." She kissed his other cheek. "And…"

He was almost afraid to ask. "And what?"

"And Martha has been remaking her wedding dress for me. She started last summer!"

"Last summer? Last summer, you went on a picnic with Lance Singleton!"

Yes, I did."

"And he wanted you to—"

"Yes, he did. But I don't want Lance Singleton, Jack. I want you."

Jack laughed, folded her in his arms, and kissed her. Jonna wound her arms around his neck and kissed him back. Twice.

Epilogue

Jonna Kathleen Lander and Major Jackson Corder were married on Christmas Eve in the front parlor of Martha and Colonel Hawks' house at Fort Kearney. Drew Lander gave his sister away, and Lance Singleton stood up with Jack. While Jonna and Jack exchanged their vows, Martha and Samantha blotted away tears, and Colonel Hawks honked into his handkerchief.

During the reception that followed, Sam ladled out whiskey-laced cranberry punch, and Martha cut generous slices of her double-fudge cake. Then, at the end of the evening, Sam handed Jonna a gift wrapped in shiny blue paper and tied with a blue ribbon.

"Goodness, Sam, where did this come from?

"Lucinda Markley sent it from South Carolina. It arrived a week ago."

Jonna pawed through layers of tissue paper and suddenly burst into tears. "Oh, my," she said with a sob. "How did she know?" She swallowed over a lump in her throat and looked up at her husband.

"Jack, look!" She held up the small box.

Nestled in layers of pink tissue paper lay a small white Tiffany candy dish filled with tiny silver stars.

A word about the author…

Lynna Banning combines a lifelong love of history and literature into a satisfying career as a writer. Born in Oregon, she graduated from Scripps College and embarked on a career as an editor and technical writer and, after graduate work at UC Irvine, as a high school English teacher. She enjoys hearing from her readers. You may write to her directly at P.O. Box 324, Felton, CA 95018 USA. Email her at carowoolston@att.net or visit Lynna's website at lynnabanning.net. lynnabanning.net

www.ingramcontent.com/pod-product-compliance
Lightning Source LLC
Chambersburg PA
CBHW052007020726
47501CB00004B/1042